EXILED

Exiled

SHIREEN JILLA

QUARTET

First published in 2011 by
Quartet Books Limited
A member of the Namara Group
27 Goodge Street, London W1T 2LD

A catalogue record for this book
is available from the British Library

ISBN   978 0 7043 7220 7

Typeset by Antony Gray
Printed and bound in Great Britain by
T J International Ltd, Padstow, Cornwall

For Guto, Cal and Ben.
And our time together
in New York.

Foreword

Anyone who has exchanged a handful of pounds for fistfuls of dollars and blown them away on a stash of Apple gadgets, Marc Jacobs scarves and $300 sushi meals has dreamed of living in Manhattan. It is one of those material fantasies. When Jessie got his posting to New York, I stood on our west London balcony and screamed. Postings didn't come cooler. I was so lucky. The only downside which I could possibly imagine was the predictability of going to live in another Western city not unlike London. How adventurous could it possibly be to live in New York? Jessie waved away my worry that it might not be exciting enough. We would have a great adventure together in New York, he insisted. He was my emotional metronome. He supported me.

It is so easy to forget that now.

I saw Jessie as one of life's believers. He believed he would get into the Foreign Office; he believed he would get one of the best postings – at the UK Mission to the UN in New York. He was going to work inside the lungs of international politics. Many people argued diplomacy wasn't where the power was any more. There was always some cocksure City type who pounded Jessie at a party. Why not the Bill Gates Foundation? Why not Google? The most global power was business, not an arcane institution. Was he, perhaps, a spy?

Jessie would argue his case with a relaxed smile and an unshakable conviction. It was all part of the plan: the Jessie Wietzman Plan, which wasn't aggressive or dogmatic, but actually rather assured.

He also believed in me. At an age when most man-boys weren't keen to show a flicker of emotion or commitment, Jessie stood touching me at a friend from the Royal College of Art's party. The evening was like one of those revolving tables in a Chinese restaurant. Only here, it was the grungy guests who circled the flat's minute kitchen.

Jessie was classically handsome, made more interesting by his delicate features. He had grey-blue eyes with feathery lashes as dark as his hair. He was lean enough to give him an edge. He was neat and shiny compared with us flamboyantly dressed art students from the Royal College. His jeans were a pristine navy, his stripy shirt ironed, his black loafers a mirror. I was immediately attracted to his difference. But I also wondered what was wrong with him.

'I'm Jessie Wietzman.' His gaze was the most direct I had ever encountered. I found myself staring at his white even teeth, only slightly apart.

'Oh, Hi! Anna.'

I moved away, nearer to the sink. He was definitely invading my space.

'I'm going to marry you.'

I cringed but still laughed nervously. I was self-consciously in the middle of my twenties. A time when man-boys lurched, and tried to avoid answering questions later. Anyone declaring love must be an idiot.

'Are you? Thanks for letting me know. I'll bear that mind,' I said lightly. I turned to brush him away, but my elbows collided with the modern mixer tap jolting out from the sink.

He smiled, as if amused by a private joke. 'Well, since we are going to get married, you've got to tell me everything.'

I laughed again, less sure. 'Shouldn't you already know everything? I mean . . . if you are going to marry me.'

'Well, you're an artist. You studied at the Ruskin in Oxford, before going to do a post grad at the Royal College of Art, where you are now. You grew up in the countryside. You have wonderful parents. You're the kindest friend. You laugh a lot. You're an over-adventurous backpacker. And importantly, I want to kiss you because you are incredibly beautiful.'

I was silenced. He had targeted me. And I wasn't confident enough to be flattered.

His gorgeous eyes played with me. And those teeth widened into a grin.

'Well – about me. I'm a diplomat. Yes I know, you think I'd be far too conservative a boyfriend. You'd prefer a tattooed looser who drenches dead rats in formaldehyde before getting coked up on a Monday night and takes the night bus home. But I have a car. And I am going to change your mind.'

It took him six months. But he did.

Jessie always looked defiantly traditional. He walked out of Westminster Underground in his Gieves & Hawkes pin-stripe, a conservative pale blue shirt off set by a muted patterned tie. Tall and refined, he had an outdoor complexion, a peppery humour and an energetic innocence – the features of privilege. He fitted right in with the Oxbridge grads in Whitehall.

But what impressed me was he didn't actually belong to their set. He was a grammar school boy who had gone to a redbrick university, before diving into the fast stream of the Foreign Office. This start always set him apart. He had lots of friends there, but no close ones.

I was an art student in my own charity shop fashion, who had a tattoo of the Tantric Buddhist symbol Vajra, representing indestructibility, scratched above my ankle. I prided myself on my difference. Discovering Jessie's swayed me.

It's difficult to analyse the impulse to kiss someone. Jessie was good-looking, confident and reliable, which my previous hippy man hadn't been. What drove me to press my face up against his in the intimacy of a kiss was more about this playful flicker of unpredictability. I thought Jessie saw life as an elaborate game not to be taken too seriously. He made up jokes about politicians and diplomats, actually practically everyone. He was spontaneous – we would walk towards a cinema only to end up spending the evening eating honey rolls in a Chinese bakery, after getting our hair cut.

And we had great sex. Once we discovered our physical hunger for each other, I don't remember re-analysing who Jessie was.

But I do know when I fell in love with him.

It was also, coincidentally, the moment he realised he loved me.

We were standing, choked by the bar in a Whitehall watering hole. I had squeezed in only to be hit by a blanket of nicotine with an after taste of cigars. The bar was shabby, but the customers were eager professionals, diplomats in the making with their Jermyn Street shirts and sharp grey wool suits flanking the bar itself. The only other customers were their doppelgangers, aged by three decades. Their suits were made to measure, but older, their shirts in a wider array of colours. Jessie was beside the bar with his gang. Superficially, he was identical to the rest.

I squirmed through narrow gaps between shoulders to stand only a few feet away, but still not visible. From there, I saw his difference.

The others slouched on to the thickly glazed mahogany bar shelf. They had a carelessness about them. They didn't glance down to see if their pristine suits were resting in a puddle of beer. Their gestures were broad and thoughtless. They scratched their noses and their hair as happily as they would have scratched their balls.

Jessie stood deliberately upright, arms off the bar, unscratching, carving space for himself. I saw an independent strong man surrounded by floppy boys.

'Anna,' Jessie said gratefully. He pulled me towards him.

The slouchers all turned. The opposite sex changed their dynamic. They lifted themselves up to reveal shirts untucked, ties flopping out of breast pockets and damp hops spreading over their forearms.

'Charlie, Matt, Dan and Sam . . . this is my girlfriend Anna.'

Their hellos were casual. A flick of the hand, a deep growl and a scrunch of the hair.

'We couldn't imagine what babe would be with our man, Jess,' said one of them.

Jessie imitated the way this spokesman had dropped his jaw. And they both soundlessly laughed. The others laughed louder.

Something about Jessie's impersonation irritated the thick-haired blond. Or maybe Jessie had always irritated him.

'I don't quite get you,' he jabbed him in the chest with an obvious attempt at playfulness. 'Jessie Wietzman. What kind of name is that?'

'It's American. Well, to be precise. It's Jewish.'

'Jewish American?' added another voice. 'You've been very secretive, you old dog. We've got a Yank in the FCO.'

'No. I'm not technically American,' Jessie said calmly before licking his lips. 'I've got a British mother and British passport.'

Did he deliberately avoid saying he also had an American passport? I didn't even know he had dual nationality. Until it was too late.

He tried to match their aggressive playfulness, but the lines in the corners of his eyes tightened.

'I can't believe you've been let in.'

They all laughed.

'Who let you in, Jess?' screamed another voice through the collective howl. 'You don't belong here. Go home.'

Jessie tried to smile even more. His mouth widened but he couldn't part his lips. Finally, they sensed his discomfort.

'Only joking, mate,' someone said, squeezing his arm.

'So were you brought up here?' added another, still keen to place him.

'Yeah, near Bristol,' Jessie sounded confident again.

'But where did you go to school?'

We walked silently away from the pub after 'last orders'. He was hurt by the conversation but I didn't know him well enough to bring it up. I had never before seen what his difference actually meant.

Finally I said, 'It must be odd, people calling you American when you don't feel foreign.'

I expected him to gratefully agree.

But he didn't. 'Do you know what, Anna? I've spent my whole life being an outsider. I don't belong anywhere.'

I squeezed into his chest in silent sympathy. But as we walked up Whitehall to our favourite Chinese on Lisle Street, behind Leicester Square, I had my own awakening. I had met someone who was my mirror image. My younger sister, Sophie, was the rightful heir in my family. She had done extremely well at university but there had been no doubt she would return home to marry her school love, bride to farmer's son, a close friend of my parents, move to a cottage up the road, extend the family at same age as my mother did. Predictable, 'sorted' and steady. Whereas I had dropped out of university, reapplied to art college, smoked too much dope, dated a couple of phony artists and still didn't know what my future held.

I turned surreptitiously to look at Jessie. He had a relaxed air of determination. I admired that. He knew what he wanted and would fight prejudice to get it. I looked at him again. He was staring at me. We felt our bond. We reached for each other, limbs moulding. Our relationship was deepening. We recognised each other.

We hadn't even kissed when I discovered Jessie's background. His father was a New Yorker, who had divorced his English wife when Jessie was only eighteen months old. He immediately returned to his hometown, married and moved from his Upper West Side roots to 740 Park Avenue, inside the ten narrow blocks that make up the most exclusive zip code in New York, 10021. Howard traded European antiques, but it wasn't a job that seemed to take up much of his time. He had long lunches, debating Republican politics with his tennis buddies. He was a mate of the Mayor. His wife, Nancy, was a WASP of inexhaustible wealth apparently. In photos, she was impossibly fragile, but was unbelievably strong, Jessie insisted. She devoted her entire day after her run round the reservoir in Central Park to a busy 'career' as a philanthropist. One of her many contributions was to the Metropolitan Opera. I imagined her like a Chelsea charity worker; doing good to give one non-narcissist purpose to her day.

However, Jessie said, almost reverentially, she was an incredibly powerful woman. She even had her own full-time lawyer, he added. I laughed. What a conceit to retain legal advice. What on earth did she need it for? But Nancy didn't dominate my thoughts. Why should she?

Jessie's English mother was left to bring up her only son alone. When Howard's lawyer successfully won a bid to stop his maintenance payments, claiming he was unemployed, she stoically worked for the local council as a secretary. She never remarried. It was a moving story, which made me want to quickly absorb Jessie into my large extended family.

Before the age of air miles, Jessie only visited his father in the summer holidays. Their emotional and cultural distance was obvious, understandable. Even after I digested this extraordinary information about someone as down to earth as Jessie, he never struck me as 'American'. A cultural fact my younger pre-New York head formulated as not 'English'. He was self-deprecating and easy going. He had spent his entire childhood living in Bath and all his friends were English. So I didn't dwell.

We were in a Lebanese restaurant in Shepherd's Market when Jessie decided to tell me about his American background. He spoke proudly. He had got into the Foreign Office despite being brought up by a single mother on a tight budget, which didn't extend to tutors or any other extras. I was proud of him. A big part of me longed for his life experience.

When a great job came up at the UN, Jessie moved in on it. It was the perfect career move. I was excited. I had spent my whole life in England, too many years of it in Kent. It was a great big adventure. I couldn't wait.

The glimmer of real estate was the city's early flirtation with us. It was such a sexy feeling. We hugged and squeezed each other's hands as we debated in bars the relative merits of down-town versus up, Brooklyn Heights versus Manhattan. It was an ecstatic privilege. In the end, we spotted our brownstone on the Internet. A beautiful original bare brick apartment that spelt the New York that we imagined from the narrow confines of our hotel. And so we ended up on Upper West Side, by default, seeing it as any other neighbourhood, only nearer Central Park.

We had a busy social life in London. Our young marriage unconsciously supported by friends. Suddenly we were alone on the Upper West Side. We were drawn tighter. For the first six weeks, we sat together at a makeshift table Jessie had created out of an old door he found in the fire escape leading to the roof. I remember his words as we were eating rice out of elegant white cardboard boxes.

'I'm so proud of us for doing this.' His eyes danced and his hands moved towards me. 'Thank you.'

He grinned. Jessie smiled a lot, but he wasn't an eager wide-mouthed type. I realised he had surprised himself, perhaps for the first time. He had done something adventurous. He was actually a cautious, controlling person who calculated risk and then usually tried to reduce it. Not this time. And it made me love him even more. He was courageous. We were having a life experience together.

I lurched forward to kiss him, my hands buried in his thick brown hair.

Our life in New York became coloured in reality – we ordered take out from our local Thai, drank Cuban cocktails in our local bar with our four-year-old son Joshua asleep under the table, shouted over the jazz music in the hardware store on Amsterdam and found furniture on the sidewalk. Our new spot on Google Earth quickly became our home. But it wasn't smothering – a stark contrast to the heavy tog of a suburban duvet. It was a constant adventure and misadventure, tipping overboard into another culture. Every evening we sat with a bottle of wine roaring through our maddest Manhattan story of the day. As the thermometer angrily reddened early summer, the stories became crazier.

We believed it was all part of the fun of living abroad. We were merely willing spectators. That's where we were both naïve. I couldn't imagine that my romantic dream would turn into a dark battle for everything I loved.

How did I allow myself to get caught up in all this? Why didn't I stop it from happening? I still can't say. My only defence is you get submerged in a new culture. The experience is so intense you can't see beyond it. I literally lost my mind. I'll never quite be the same person again.

I can't help wondering now whether it might have worked out differently. Strangely, after all the shocking things that happened there, I still dream of New York.

One

The doorman, Darren, stood under the awning of the pre-war apartment block near our brownstone on West 82nd Street. His legs wide in an upside down V.

'How's tricks?' he mouthed.

He had stood exactly there and said exactly that every day since we moved in five months ago.

Eliot's white wavy bob glistened from the neighbouring stoop. He was always out at this time of night to escape the heat trapped in his aircon-less studio. He closed his Dostoevsky and stepped slowly down to open our cab door with his bookless hand.

'Hey, Anna. Hey, Josh. You're back!'

My personality coloured to his welcome. 'Eliot,' I grinned, 'Hi there. Great to see you.'

And I kept grinning. Not constrained by the little Kent world I grew up in. Free to roam, explore, befriend, fit in and have fun with anyone and everyone.

Josh felt it too. He eagerly turned to the driver – 'Sir, we live here on 82nd between Columbus and Amsterdam. I live in America.'

The driver ignored him.

Eliot had cranked open the door. Yet it still felt closed. After five days holiday in London, the intense August heat jostled, smothered us. Mini tributaries coursed down my legs as if I were incontinent. My pale skin blotched as I unpeeled myself from the black plastic seat and glided out. Or tried to. Any movement accelerated my body's condensation. Josh, always ebullient and energetic, was made indecisive by the heat. He was excited to be home, but he hovered on the street, reluctant to exert the energy required to climb the six or so steps leading up to our front door.

I asked our morbidly immobile cab driver if he could open the 'trunk', which he did remotely without any intention of helping me with my bags.

When I first moved to New York, I clung to my vocabulary. I pronounced 'boot' not 'trunk', 'bill' not 'check', 'cash point' not 'ATM', 'pavement' not 'sidewalk', 'rubbish' not 'garbage' defiantly, as if they were a badge of honour. Gradually, I had to relent. Joshua gleefully imitated people's words and accents. And I reluctantly followed him.

Fitting in was a question of words. Right, you guys?

But I'm fast-forwarding the story.

Back to the street. Overnight, a wall had built up along the sidewalk. Dozens of blue recycling bags, a two-seater sofa, a Queen-size mattress, two dining chairs and a baby walker stood between our stoop and us. Eliot was forced to heave our bags round in a torturous diversion down the street, through the sandwiched cars and then back up the sidewalk. This may sound trivial. But by the time he'd reached the top of our steps, he was sweating from his white roots to the waistband of his shorts.

I turned to the cab driver, automatically thanking and handing him a wedge of dollars.

'Hey!' He rose from slumped to erect in a single movement. 'Hey. Where's my tip? I wait all this time.'

Usually I couldn't resist commenting on the symbiotic relationship between tip and help and, God dammit, politeness. But it was that surreal, confusing time between night and day. So I gave the cab driver five more dollars. I did it wordlessly, a sort of silent protest, which would have mortified a London cabbie. But this man snatched it and accelerated away before I could step back from his window.

I turned back round to Eliot, who warmly dismissed my repeated thanks, even though he was pressing a handkerchief to his forehead to stop his sweat from stinging his eyes.

On the stairs leading up to our second-floor apartment, we were immediately encased by stale heavy air. I moved from one air conditioning unit to another. They were the old-fashioned type, wedged between the open sash window and the window ledge with their vast weight hanging suicidal over the street. They juddered out as much noise as air.

Arriving back home, Josh had a second wind. He raced up to his playroom and I could hear him tipping his box of Lego out on to the floor. Then he was off again. His feet clattered down the stairs and into the kitchen, where he opened the fridge, slammed it shut and raced up the stairs again.

'Can we go to the park?' he yelled from the playroom.

'Josh, it's the middle of the night!'

'So,' Josh stated, leaning precariously over the banisters.

I sweated our suitcases up to our third-floor bedroom, banging them unceremoniously against the exposed brick walls. I craved water. I gulped the whole bottle left beside our double bed, which was inches from the wall on either side. All that was left of the room was a jigsaw-sized rectangle of wooden floor on which I tipped out both our suitcases. I couldn't sort out the mound of dirty clothes now.

Joshua's room was the antechamber to our bedroom, or alternatively, you could view it as the corridor leading to our terrace. Once he was in bed with water, a cup of milk and Pooh bear, I had this stumbling desperate desire to sleep.

'I'm not tired.' Josh sat up in bed, intending to get up.

'Yes you are.'

It was a predictable exchange. He had slept on the plane, so he was bouncing with energy. Actually, he always had boundless

19

energy. He was a four-year-old after all. I finally left him talking to himself. I stripped and crashed under my sheet. My body was greedy for horizontal sleep. Gluttonous as it turned out.

I was having an uncontrollable dream. The kind you have when you're stretched spaciously in your own bed.

'Hey, lady, your kid's out there.'

I sat up. I wasn't actively awake. My head was empty. A spinning lightness oozed from my brain to my toes.

'Josh? What's happened? Where's Josh?' I panicked.

I would have screamed, imagining Josh had broken out of the house and run into the street in front of a cab. But his pale, blonder image of me was grinning round the doorway.

There they were. Three armed NYPD policemen in flack jackets with their boots pressed against the end of our bed. Or I thought they were. At that moment, I couldn't have sworn whether they were real or not.

The shouting started again.

'What, are you crazy? Endangering the welfare of a child. That's what it is, you know. It's a crime.'

'They're policemen. Real policemen mummy! They jumped off the roof on to the terrace. Can you believe it?'

I couldn't. I couldn't begin to work out what was happening, what had happened. I should have been scared, shocked. Three policemen had climbed down on to our terrace, letting them-selves in, right into our bedroom. But I felt this overpowering jet lag, which made me detached from what was happening. I can't say definitely, which man was shouting. Probably the large tightly packed one with the red hair and anaemic skin. Even jet-lagged, I tried to regain three or four inches of lost dignity. I pulled the sheet up over my visible breasts – but not much more.

The redhead squatted uncomfortably. His trousers tightened to bursting. 'Hey bud, are you OK? Gimme five.'

Joshua wasn't interested. 'Is that a real gun? Do you kill people?'

The redhead ignored him. He was interested in Josh's health and safety. He was up, leaning towards me again. As he moved, his feet shunted my dirty underwear towards the bed. 'You locked him out there. What kinda punishment is that? What kinda person does that? I have kids of my own you know. I couldn't imagine treatin' my kids like that.'

I struggled to pull myself together. 'I didn't lock him anywhere. We've just flown back from England. I was asleep. Josh was probably jet-lagged.' My voice sounded pitiful.

'Listen, lady, are you trying to say I didn't see what I saw?' He made it sound so ridiculous, so unbelievable an excuse.

As my nerves kicked in, I realised I was beyond my experience. Obviously, few New Yorkers would be smiling if the NYPD forced their way into their apartment. But I'm not talking about that. What I didn't know was who these pumped-up men were. What made them tick? They were probably Irish, probably from the Bronx. But what did that mean? I had absolutely no idea. And how could I persuade them to leave?

I leant slightly towards the redhead, planning to get out my bag to show him our boarding passes, but my move made him madder.

'I mean the worst things happen in the nicest places. I'm like, I'm like . . . '

'I'm so sorry. Sir, I'm so sorry, sir,' I repeated, thinking it couldn't hurt.

'Huh, that's a little late coming.'

Was he relenting?

As if he read my mind, he raised his voice again, 'And I mean, where is your husband?'

A man! He wanted to deal with a man, not a woman in lacy knickers from the bargain tub in Victoria's Secret. I coughed to try and round my vowels. 'He's at a meeting in Washington.

I flew back from London on my own with my son. He'll be here early tomorrow. My husband, that is.'

'Does he know his son coulda died?'

'I fell asleep, jet lag. Josh was in bed.' I was aware I was pleading. Pathetic. But I couldn't see any other way.

That incensed the dark man on his right. 'No he wasn't. He was out on a terrace at FOUR A.M.'

Joshua never went on to the terrace at night. During the day, he went out to over-water his flowers. So confused by being wide-awake, he must have gone out to check on them and then couldn't get back inside. He couldn't fall off the terrace – it was bricked up too high. He would have to catapult himself up and over. But I sensed that wasn't the point.

'It sounds strange. But it's not four in the morning for him. He's on British time. It's his day time.'

Neither of the three seemed to be able to hear me.

'We were alerted by the neighbours. That there was an endangered child. Locked out on a terrace.'

One of my neighbours had called the police rather than ring the doorbell until they woke me up. Too much effort for 'an endangered child'. I was angry. I needed to get up and out of bed, assert my grown-up self. But I was semi-naked.

I thought of our 'get out of jail free' card – our immunity from prosecution in the States. It wasn't a vague British Embassy promise, but a laminated gym membership-like card. It was frowned upon to use it for a trivial reason. But I was desperate.

'My husband's err . . . ' I coughed nervously, not knowing how they would react. 'Actually he's a . . . British diplomat.' That felt good. A British diplomat. That special relationship, which meant you have to get out of my home. You mother-fuckers.

I had had enough. 'Listen, sorry, you totally misunderstand the situation. There isn't a problem.'

The redhead seemed to have been waiting for this moment. 'Are you giving me lip, lady? I mean after all this.'

The others said nothing. But they abruptly turned and started leaving. Joshua was with them, eager with his questions. 'How did you get down off the roof? Do you have ropes? Or did you use a ladder?'

I wondered myself how they had abseiled down on to our terrace. What was wrong with the front door?

The redhead turned with one last bite of bile. 'When I get abuse, I act . . . '

I didn't catch the rest. As they started down the stairs, I hurtled out of bed, grabbed a pair of shorts and a glittery tee shirt from the floor. I was as mal-coordinated as Josh. Finally I strode two stairs at a time after them. I wondered what the etiquette was in these situations. Should I thank them for their concern and their time? Or did New Yorkers tip them?

They were by our double front door. They needed to be let out as it was locked manually from the inside. I shuffled round our hall table searching for the keys, eager, desperate to get them out. Already joyful that this was nearly over. Already imagining regaling my friends in London with this colourful story. This was the life experience I craved.

As I opened one of the doors, they squeezed out making the glass shake in the wooden frame.

The redhead left last. 'As I said, we gonna remove the child to get him checked out at the hospital.'

He picked up Josh. It happened so fast. He was on our stoop. He was leaving with Josh. With my son. I hadn't even seen their badges. I didn't even have their names. I lurched from the hallway down the stoop after him. I think I screamed, 'No!' But I don't remember. As I landed at the bottom of the steps, I heard a crack in my shoulder. I didn't feel any pain. I crumpled, collapsed.

I had this sensation that my whole life, all of our plans, our dreams, my craving for adventure, for a bigger riskier journey, everything that had happened to get us here to New York had all been leading up to this moment. I had traded my nationality in for this void.

It was the men of the street who rescued me. Dirk, a homeless man, who lived on the church steps further up the block, was there first. I was vaguely aware of him only because he was wearing Jessie's old trainers. Darren the doorman and Eliot weren't far behind.

'They've taken Josh. They've taken Josh.' I gulped for air, sounding unreal even to myself.

But Darren, Dirk and Eliot had a plan. They were going to help. They would walk me to the 20th Precinct, which was further up our block. The NYPD must have come from there. Then they'd call a cab to take me to the hospital. I was held up by my waist, my keys, purse and cell phone were found, the door was locked, and I was manoeuvred slowly up the street. They talked calm, concerned words, which I couldn't hear.

How could I have been so naive to think fitting in abroad was just a question of words?

* * *

I could feel the hot stillness and see the sallow dawn light as we moved slowly towards the 20th Precinct. It was a grey concrete and brick three-storey rectangle that wouldn't look out of place on the South Bank. Except it had the obligatory flagpole on the roof, with the American banner hanging down limp and airless. A vast yard hugged one side of it, though all the police cars and vans were irregularly parked on the street. The cars advertised their 'Courtesy, Professionalism, Respect' in large letters across the passenger door.

'Hah!' I snorted, aware I was clenching my molars.

Eliot was hurt. 'This is not typical, right? I am sorry this is

24

happening to you right now. You've got to know, these are New York's finest – they fight danger like nobody else.'

I had joked with Jessie about how New Yorkers worshipped anyone in a uniform. OK. Firemen, post 9/11, were understandable. But the uniformed in general were heroes, whereas we Brits vilified them. Maybe this was because the NYPD would rescue a child locked in an illegally parked car, whereas their London equivalent would slap a parking ticket on the windscreen and order a tow truck. At this moment, I would have done anything for a couple of pedantic ticket issuers.

If it wasn't for this hapless trio, I'd have been lost. My friends were in London. They would be up, but calling them was ridiculous because they couldn't possibly begin to understand the situation I was in.

Darren, Dirk and Eliot could. They circled and collectively lowered me on to one of the metal chairs in the large reception room. Inside the police station was bare, almost makeshift. The chairs had an unceremonious hardness, even by British police station standards. Once, I had been into one in London when my bicycle was stolen. I only remember the extensive paperwork that constituted a 'report', though the conclusion even before it was written was it would never be found. London wasn't operating under zero tolerance.

New York was. There were two people in front of me, who clearly expected the police to help them. Before dawn. The pale blonde hid her weather battered New York skin behind big black glasses. She didn't take them off, but she was happy enough to loudly announce her problem. 'I wanna report an identity fraud.'

Her dramatic jargon made me smile. Her words were that big, that global.

She had the NYPD officer's full attention. 'They have created an internet site under my name,' she breathed in shortly. ' . . . Under my name!' She hurriedly unbuckled her

Coach tote bag. 'Jessica Levine. That's me,' she insisted, thrusting forward her ID card. 'They're saying they are me.'

Meanwhile, the man, who had been waiting, was on the pay phone with an officer beside him. 'Careful, don't let him get wise,' he advised, holding a credit card in his hand. 'We wanna get him.'

I clearly lacked the dramatic flourish necessary for this next operation. And I was the one who had lost my son. I wanted to lurch forward, demand to see Josh, but I wouldn't make it without fainting. My shoulder had a violent pulse that thumped to a different rhythm to my head. I gave a desperate sob, a cocktail of shock, fear and pain.

The officer babysitting the credit card fraud phone call wandered towards us.

Eliot's face was tight with sympathy. He squeezed my hand. 'I'm gonna talk to them. Please, Anna, it's gonna be OK. Sit there.'

As feeble as it sounds, his words were a huge relief. A New Yorker was taking over, who wasn't intimidated, who knew what to say, how loudly to say it and understood what they were saying back. His gentle intonation rose with singsong insistence. It seemed to be working.

Eliot stood talking to the officer a few paces in front of my seat. He turned to me with a grin. 'Hey, nothing to worry about, Anna. It's all good. Standard stuff. They've taken Josh to get checked out by a paediatrician in the emergency room. He could be suffering from heat exhaustion. And then he'll be back in no time. They'll call you on your cell the minute the doctors give him the all OK.'

They had taken my one hundred per cent healthy son to hospital. 'How dare they? He was boisterously well. They are hysterical, ridiculous. Paranoid.'

Or was I the woman with the black glasses? New York was getting to me. 'I'm going straight there. Which hospital is he in?'

'New York Presbyterian. You know, the one right far down on the East Side.'

Eliot made it sound a long way away.

'Where exactly?' I tried, not very successfully, to control my anger.

'East 68,' he sighed, as if the distance made it hard to contemplate. He cheered up. 'It's one of the best hospitals in the United States. I mean Number One in the whole state. The best. You should get yourself checked out there too. You've done some real damage to that shoulder of yours.'

'Yes you're right, thank you, Eliot. I'm going there now.'

I stood up and felt the pain race from my shoulder to my neck and down again to my back. I was going to be sick. I breathed in hard. The dry air conditioning made me gulp.

Eliot, Darren and Dirk were keen to get me into a cab. There was no suggestion they would come with me. How could I expect them to? Despite our brief intimacy, the fact was I hardly knew them. We said hello, had the occasional chat. But they weren't friends, let alone best friends. I was lonely, alone. I thanked them and attempted a wave, but I couldn't smile.

Seeing them through the cab window, standing in a line along the corner with Columbus Avenue, they appeared welded to the block. They could help anyone with anything on West 82nd Street, between Columbus and Amsterdam. But I had to step out away from them across the Park, down the East Side. I was beyond their reach. They had literally done all they could.

The East River was calm and inky, a meditation. My cab moved down the FDR Drive smoothly, without the usual jerky daytime tailgating.

I leaned forward, absentmindedly but instinctively saying, 'You know we shouldn't be on FDR Drive.'

The driver was silent as they always were when they were taking a roundabout route.

'You should have taken 72nd Street and then Third Avenue.'

I sat back. I wasn't in the mood for a fight over the cab route. I wanted to sit back and think. I wished I had Jessie with me. For seven years, nothing big had ever happened to me without Jessie being immediately involved.

Jessie's mobile rang and rang. There was his voice quietly assured.

'You're through to Jessie Wietzman. I'm sorry I am un-available to take your call. Please leave me a message.'

It was so disappointing. I wanted to tell him everything. The NYPD broke into our apartment. Can you believe it? The police! And they've taken Josh. Jessie would listen to the whole story without interrupting. Then he would make it better. I physically missed him.

But I couldn't explain it all in a message.

In the end I said, 'Jessie darling, could you call me? It's important. We're OK though.'

I called him again. It still went to the answering machine.

If I couldn't share it with Jessie, I wanted to speak to some-one else. I wondered if I should call his father, Howard. And then I wondered whether I wanted to. No doubt he could help. But what would his reaction be?

I took in the water again. I didn't have any real memories of New York yet. So it made me think of the Thames, which always reminded me of Jessie seeing my final piece for the Summer Show.

Jessie leant his bicycle against the wall of the studio where I was working on my final post grad piece at the Royal College of Art. He had forgotten his padlock and had carried his bike up four floors. We had both been working late. Outside the windows was shadowy, a grey black. My painting was at the end of a studio – a vast canvas stretching twenty foot wide and twelve foot high.

Jessie had been hugely supportive and enthusiastic to see it

28

in the early stages. But I had resisted and purposefully not told him anything about it. I wanted to see his reaction without diplomacy or self-censorship getting in the way.

Once he had let go of his bike, I insisted he close his eyes. I gently pulled his left hand towards the centre of the room. He smiled, sliding his feet dramatically until I stopped him an optimum distance away. We were still holding hands.

'Open your eyes.' My stomach lurched. It was like hunger. I was so nervous that he might laugh. Or even worse, be shocked.

He looked intensely at the painting. I did too, trying to see it through his eyes. The River Thames I had painted was apocalyptical. The angry black swirl of water met a raging vermillion sky. I had layered the oils, thickening the canvas to a three-dimensional effect. Out of this post-biblical age emerged a naked girl. She appeared to be striding out of the canvas. She was literally larger than life. She was fit and strong. Her eyes were blacked out. But her fingers were stuck forward in a V sign.

I was suddenly embarrassed, shy of the bold rebel I could only create with oils.

'It's brilliant,' he said, more forcefully than he could possibly mean. He looked straight at me with admiration and love. It was heartfelt. And I chose to take it at face value.

He paused. 'Whom is she swearing at?'

'Well, I don't know. I just painted it.' I paused. ' . . . My tutor says she's a symbol of the strength of humanity rising up from a crumbling planet.'

'Really?' He raised an eyebrow.

We both laughed.

'I know, crazy isn't it? I want to shock people. Which I know is childish . . . ' I petered out.

'Well, you might want to prime your parents, especially as she looks like you.'

'God, you're right.'

We stood silently.

Finally he said, kindly, 'It's great. You can afford to rebel.'

I blushed with over-privileged guilt. I was the only artist in our vast extended family. When I think about it now, it was one of the reasons I wanted to paint. I needed to shake off the conservative comfort of my parents, aunts, uncles and cousins. They could never imagine me as anything other than the skinny tomboy, tree-climbing Anna. Niece Anna, cousin Anna, daughter Anna, sister Anna. I had spent my whole childhood liberally encased. I was unable to grow up if I stayed in Kent, like Sophie, and spent every weekend with the inevitable houseful of my relatives. I would always be that gawky country girl.

Unable to make eye contact with Jessie, I realised that I was playing at being Tracey Emin without the excuse of the screwy past. Why was I doing it? I could take a far easier path. I didn't need to be complicated. My life had always been simple. But I craved the depth that went with more chaos.

I turned to kiss Jessie.

The cab turned right off the FDR Drive on to East 71st and then left on to York Avenue, an anomaly on the East Side. It was parallel to Lexington and Madison Avenues, but cultural and economic continents away from them. York Avenue was a grubby trail of cheap nail bars, pseudo Italian restaurants and Celtic pubs backed by grey tower blocks and the odd old red brick building.

I was determined that the cab would drop me right outside the emergency room. After several misunderstandings, a loop round the one way and repeated negotiations, I was left on the sweeping cobbled drive in front of the main awning marking the entrance.

New York Presbyterian didn't resemble a British hospital. It was a gigantic Hyatt hotel complete with five-star guests. They were in matching monochrome ensembles: thin cotton twin sets and knee length shorts. I half wished I wasn't in my thigh high shorts. Whatever. I could see the emergency room. I carefully negotiated the swing door into the reception, where three or four well looking people were watching a vast TV screen. A security guard hovered in front of his low table.

What a relief private medical care was. Theoretically, I was a righteous Brit, against the principle of it. But here and now it looked and smelled delicious. The air was perfectly cool and fresh. There was no one waiting at the reception window, and the nurse immediately emerged to bring me round into a small room behind her glass counter. She nodded with a calm understatement only seen in New York amongst Hispanics. I guessed she was Puerto Rican.

I told her about Josh. 'I am desperate to see him now.'

'We need to fix your shoulder first.'

I protested. It was weird to be cut off from Josh. Since I stopped working in an art gallery two years after he was born, we had hardly ever been apart.

'Sorry, you are too sick. We need to get you better.'

I had dislocated my shoulder she sagely explained. She took my temperature – high; my blood pressure – unbelievably normal. I started to relax.

I smiled gratefully. 'Thank you so much. I appreciate your help.'

She led me back out of her room to a line of cashiers sitting beneath a sign: 'Billing Department'.

'Am I going to see a doctor?' I started to feel anxious again.

My nurse nodded calmly. 'You have to do your insurance first.'

A man in a wheelchair was in front of the line of chairs opposite the bank clerks. He seemed half asleep.

Two seats down, a girl was chatting gaily on her cell phone. 'Yeah, I'm down at the emergency room. I wanna get checked before my insurance runs out.'

I was stressed. What if my insurance didn't cover this hospital? I hadn't even thought about that. What if I was given a bill for thousands of dollars?

I walked up to the friendliest looking cashier and produced my health insurance card. I was savvy enough about New York to always carry it in my purse.

'Hello, I've got comprehensive insurance . . . ' I hesitated, because the woman on the other side gave me an empty stare. 'Aetna? Do you take that insurance?'

She didn't say anything, but jerked her head in the direction of my card. I pushed it through the metal chute.

She pushed back two forms.

'I'm in quite a lot of pain. Could I do them after I have seen the doctor?'

She shook her head. 'Over there.'

I scribbled, crossing bits out and cursing the fact I needed to put my address on both sheets. I returned to the counter. 'OK. I've done them.'

She took them without comment. 'Wait there.'

The electric doors leading into the heart of the emergency room stayed ominously closed. And I lost the control I had managed to keep. Tears dripped down my face, the pain was unbearable.

Nothing happened. She didn't call me back to the counter.

I felt despair. I checked my mobile. No missed calls.

Where was Josh? I felt nervous and agitated without him. My shoulder pounded. I strode to the counter. 'I'm sorry but I'm going to be sick.'

This was private medical care. I was going to be whisked through.

'Everyone here is sick, mam. You need to wait your turn.'

'No, physically sick.'

'What?'

'Sick,' I gesticulated, putting my finger into my open mouth.

I threw up half missing the shelf in front of her window, half missing the floor. Snot and humiliation made me throw up gratefully.

'Throw up. You mean, throw up,' she said.

She shoved a metal tray and a few paper towels through the chute.

Finally I stopped. I moved slowly back to the chair and bent forward, my eyes closed, both hands clutching the metal tray, pathetically wishing more than anything else that I was back in London, or even better, back at my parents' house in Kent.

'Anna Wietzman?'

I looked up. The doors had swung open. A bright whiteness shone from beyond them. I was blinded by the light. And in the glow, I saw not one doctor, but two. They were smiling and coming to get me. I had arrived. The first person in the white coat led me in. I half turned to look at the man in the wheelchair; I would have given him Josh's card if it might have worked. So he too could go to heaven. But I couldn't bring him with me. And he was left there in purgatory.

Seemingly minutes later, I was lying in my own room gazing at the brightly coloured NY 1 News, strong after a morphine injection straight into my bottom. I had had my shoulder manipulated back into place. A smiley Mexican man had been sent to get me breakfast.

Then the redhead policeman appeared. He was gentler now. Or maybe it was the effects of the morphine. 'Hiya. OK. Josh is OK.'

'Great. Thank you. I am sorry about all this,' I said, keen to placate him.

'But I gotta warn ya. Any more situations and ya could lose Josh. Ya understand me?'

'Yes. Of course.' But I didn't take him seriously. Morphine and diplomatic immunity now morphed into one happy picture of us all together.

Josh raced in clutching a DVD of *The Little Mermaid*, which he had been watching in the paediatric wing and was intent on finishing it in my room. I gave him an emotional hug, which he shook off in his eagerness to find someone to load his DVD. His energy had returned in the even, cool air of the hospital. Minutes later, he had commanded a nurse to find the spot when Aerial lost her voice. He lay beside me eating half my cream cheese bagel.

I stroked the back of his neck, which he loved. My Josh. My little boy.

As I sipped a takeaway café latte, I already imagined us both back home. Back to our normal life in New York.

Two

I lay on our dark brown sofa with three pots of face creams my mother had given me. Their benefit was superficial, but they were a comforting reminder of home. My head was barely lifted by a thin cushion. Jessie was perched perpendicular with my legs arcing over his thighs. He was stroking them with the balls of his soft hands.

I had recovered enough to colour the last twenty-four hours with vivid impersonations. Jessie's face rewarded me with its concern and then, quickly, humour. We giggled about Josh eying up NYPD weaponry, the ridiculous victim of credit card fraud, and the irony-challenged hospital insurance receptionist. Our mouths were wide with laughter over the DVD machine above my hospital bed and the male maid getting me takeaway breakfast.

'I wished you'd been there,' I sighed.

'I should have been.'

We were still and silent in mutual appreciation, eventually broken by the sound of Josh thumping on his playroom ceiling with the stick end of his hobbyhorse, a new ploy for getting our attention. The thump became more insistent.

Jessie swung my legs up and strode towards the stairs. The phone rang. He picked it up from where it was lying on the built-in bookshelf.

'Hello, Sharon.' He raised his eyebrows.

Jessie had practically no family: only his father, mother and stepmother. Sharon was Jessie's only American family friend – the daughter of his father's oldest school crony. The one person of his age Jessie had seen regularly every summer. The only friend he already had in New York, when we moved here. This fact made Sharon precious. Jessie was loyal and affectionate towards her. And so was I. Though she could be a little crazy and in many ways we had nothing in common with her.

I listened to his restrained version of last night. I could hear Sharon's strong voice punctuated by exclamations.

The conversation was thankfully short.

'She insisted on coming over to see you.'

I closed my eyes. 'No, no,' I said dramatically, only half meaning it.

Jessie giggled. He had the most high-pitched giggle for such a grown up man. It always made me smile, especially as it emphasised the narrow spaces between his teeth, which I adored.

'I'm getting out of here,' he pronounced dramatically. 'I'll get us all something to eat.'

Even with the air-conditioning on high behind me, I was exhausted by the prospect of Sharon. Her hair was in long chin curving layers that always blow-dried. She had a tiny face with bright small green eyes that hid behind her dark waves. But it was her voice that was at the heart of her personality. The hair, the cute lilac halter neck over her toned, tanned shoulders and her weekly manicured nails were all 'maintenance'. Superficial to who she was – a professional mother who gave up her job as a colourist (an adviser to numerous top companies: she was ahead of the game on Wasabi green) to concentrate her considerable brains on bringing up her two children, well, more specifically her four-year-old son Nathan who had 'issues'.

When I think of Sharon, I smile sadly because I will never see her again. I even miss the energy of her madness. Then again, her insanity doesn't touch me now.

Back then the force of Sharon's voice was bulldozing me from where she was sitting upright on a chair beside the sofa, where I was slumped. The pain returned to my shoulder like a subconscious dream.

'You see. Anna; it's a question of choices. Teaching them to make better choices.'

'I understand what you're saying, if they were thirteen-year-old boys. But Nathan and Josh are only four.'

'It's important to get it right early on. Look, I'll give you a good example. We're on the school trip to the zoo. The other kids are looking at the monkeys, laughing at the seals. But not Nathan,' she pauses, for extra emphasis. 'Not Nathan,' she repeated, 'Nathan was playing around with the water fountain.'

She raised her waxed brows as if no greater point could be made in a court of law.

'Maybe he's going to be an architect.' I ventured, trying not to smile.

'No. NO!' She was frustrated as she always was by me. She confused my humour with a lack of commitment to life. Sharon was a hundred and ten per cent committed to life as she saw it.

I wondered how much longer Jessie would be.

'He has a Social Attention Deficiency Disorder. He finds the fountain more enjoyable than the company of other kids.'

'I don't blame him.' I did giggle.

'Why do you find it so funny, Anna?' Her chin jutted out from the corners of her layered hair. 'What is funny about that? It's sad. I don't want him to be an adult who is not a communicator, a social being.'

I had to sit up.

'You can't dictate how Nathan will be as an adult. I was incredibly shy at his age. Is anything wrong with me? Don't answer that. Anyway, some people are always shy.'

Sharon was triumphant. 'No. Every successful adult American can communicate with his peers.'

I was going to point out being loud and chatty didn't necessarily equate with being socially adept. But I resisted.

'I want him to be socially sophisticated.'

She leant forward in her chair, gulping at her water, her long tanned legs touching each other but not the chair, and barely her short black shorts.

'But he's only four.'

At this point, a Brit would change the subject. There would be this tacit understanding that we were never going to agree. But Sharon was oblivious to this social code. She had to prove her point.

'I want to make my children better, more intelligent, more rounded people. Why should I not want them to be the best they can possibly be?'

Unlike Nathan, her two-and-a-half-year-old daughter, Rachel, was proving to be a docile, conforming child. Lucky, Rachel was only subjected to tri-weekly physical therapy to strengthen her work on the monkey bars, which she couldn't master, and improve her pencil grip.

Anticipating her triumph, Sharon added eagerly. 'OK, OK, I have another story for you. After a therapy session downtown, we walked together into Central Park.'

Nathan rarely went to the playground. Sharon believed it was too cold for four months of the year, and currently too hot, to be outside. Also he didn't have time, even now in the summer holidays. He had at least three hours therapy a day with analysts up and down the West Side. She had laminated his therapy timetable, which she carried in her bag at all times. Sharon defended her need for a Caribbean sitter, because she couldn't get to all these sessions without help.

She was now dreamy. 'Nathan spotted this rock. He started talking to it. Eventually he lay down and put his head on it.'

This had to be an exaggeration because Sharon would never let him lie in the Park. He would get filthy or get strep throat.

'He's like one of the early members of the Dada movement. He can see art in the most abstract objects. He can raise that object to something of beauty. And you know what I thought?'

'How cute,' I smiled, trying to empathise.

'Oh please! No. I thought I wish he had the ability to communicate his love of art to others. Instead of only being able to share it with himself.'

A nod was all I could manage.

'That is the single reason why I'm working so hard to make him into a better person. And there are so many parents out there who are in denial. I am not one of those.'

I was getting uncomfortable. It was a relief to hear Jessie and Josh noisily climbing the stairs.

'If you don't mind me saying, Josh needs to learn a sense of responsibility. He needs to learn boundaries. You need to get help.'

'Sharon, hello! Great to see you.' Jessie rounded on her with his warmest smile.

I wondered if he had heard what she said.

'Bagel and coffee?'

'Hi, Jessie. You poor thing. You must be so stressed.'

Sharon didn't even look or speak to Josh.

'I was telling Anna that she should see a therapist. There's a great lady at the end of your street.'

I flinched. Because Jessie didn't flinch. His reaction was inexplicable. Well, to me at the time. This didn't dawn on him, or me, during his short conversation with Sharon. Or even after that. Not until the end.

Jessie nodded back affirmatively to Sharon. 'Funnily enough, the NYPD suggested a little counselling. I know it's the way people deal with things here.'

'What's counselling?' Josh interjected.

'Help,' I answered Josh swiftly. 'Did you go to the police station?'

'To apologise – I thought it was the right thing to do.'

'You so did the right thing, Jessie,' Sharon insisted. 'If Social Services had been called in, they would have insisted on counselling.'

39

'Would they?' said Jessie looking at me to see if I'd appreciated the point.

This memory pushed forward. I was six years old, playing in my parents' garden. I climbed high up into a Horse Chestnut tree. I kept climbing. There were more and more branches. I sat embedded in them, looking down through a hammock of fanning leaves. After a while, my father appeared below, smaller than I had ever seen him. His head stretched up as he chatted to me, the distance between us now huge. So I leaned down to answer him. Down I fell. Scraping, scratching, breaking through the branches that had held me on the way up and then a convincing thud as my arm took the weight of my body and I hit the ground. I broke my left wrist and forearm in several places. Mum was out and my father's car had broken down. He set my arm with a large stick and a crêpe bandage. Then he put me on the seat of his bicycle and with him standing up over the cross bar, cycled to the local hospital.

I never considered this to be a sign of neglect. They were laid-back liberal parents. As I hoped we were. Or was I wrong?

Still, I said, 'I survived plenty of knocks. It's part of childhood. Anyway, Josh wasn't even hurt or in danger. This is all ridiculous.'

As I sat up furiously, I felt a dull ache in my shoulder.

Jessie paused before speaking. 'Nancy and Howard would freak out if they ever found out you had clashed with the NYPD'

I persisted in spite of myself. 'Why? It wasn't my fault?'

He was keen to conclude the conversation. 'It will be seen like that.'

I made a throaty sound to signify my impatience, not with Jessie because this couldn't possibly be his viewpoint.

As if to placate me, Sharon leaned forward as she stood up to go. 'Honey, I'll lend you my copy of Mel Levine.'

'Who, sorry?' I sounded grumpy and guarded.

'You don't know about him? He is the leading child psychologist. *A Mind at a Time* is absolutely brilliant.'

I managed a grimace.

Jessie smiled breezily as he disappeared to fetch plates and mugs. Somehow I managed to steer Sharon away from therapy with a promise to read the book. We finally settled into an in-depth discussion of restaurants. The subject passed.

We excused ourselves. Josh needed to get out for a run in the Park.

Sharon reluctantly left us to have a family afternoon. 'Listen, remember, we love you guys.'

Jessie's lean legs were awkwardly folded around Josh's. They clamped into position at the top of the steep slide in the shaded Diana Ross playground. Josh was excited. They both gave me a vast wave, which I returned as they moved, squeaking and slowed by Jessie's gripping trainers and his adult weight. They were both up and running off. It was difficult to see which was boy and which, man. Josh loved being chased up and down the rope ladders, along the wooden walkways. And Jessie always obliged. He was always close behind him, but never quite catching him, making scary noises and raising his hands.

I loved being with Josh in the Park. We went there every day, even if it was broiling outside. There was something about a little boy outside in the bright sunshine that was the complete essence of childhood. Watching my grown man, his dad, chase round after Josh, made the scene complete. Even with my painful shoulder, I registered the moment, appreciating it all the more after last night. We were a family again.

When we finally extracted Josh off from the swinging lorry tyre with promises to bring him back early the next day, he raced ahead of us up 82nd Street, circling his arms like a windmill. And we walked behind him, laughing with parental pride at his ecstasy for life.

As we got to our stoop, our limp long-haired neighbour was climbing up her steps with her vast hairy dog. 'Everything all right?' she said, with a dry smile. 'That kid is *always* getting into trouble.'

I realised she was my snitch.

'You called the NYPD?'

'Yeah,' she said, without any embarrassment or guilt. 'He was locked out there.' She smiled, proud of herself. 'And he's so accident prone.'

She had witnessed Josh falling down the step of our stoop. Once. I tried to work out what to say, snide but subtle, but she was through her door with her gargantuan Afghan. I imagined what life must be like for that large animal in her small apartment.

Before she slammed the door closed, she added, 'Stay safe, Anna.'

*   *   *

Jessie didn't mention child therapy again. A week later, I had forgotten about his reaction to Sharon. Maybe all happily married couples wiped out the little contradictions to the overall narrative of their marriage. We were happy. I am not saying that defensively. It was the truth. But the truth is always shady, as I discovered when we were sitting with his parents in Bemelmans Bar at the Carlyle.

Everything about Bemelmans summed up Jessie's parents. Bemelmans was the half-French, half-German artist who wrote the iconic *Madeline* children's books set in a convent school in Paris. He was commissioned to paint the bar, and covered the walls with animals celebrating in Central Park, including an ice-skating elephant. This story, undoubtedly, added to the appeal. Nancy was a devoted Europhile.

The paintings were over-awed by the bar's lavish Art Deco design – back-lit glass columns, nickel trimmed black glass topped tables, brown leather banquettes, all glittering under a 24-carat gold ceiling. The bar was windowless, giving it a romantic prohibition frisson.

As a London couple might pop to the pub for a couple of pints, Howard and Nancy reserved a table at Bemelmans (where there was a twenty-dollar service charge a head) for cocktails every Friday night. We started joining them as their 'regular date'. They had a favourite long summer cocktail which they drank religiously until Labor Day, when they switched to their favourite short winter one. We were BC – before that ordained date, which marked the official end of New York summer, whatever the weather. So Nancy had an Old Cuban – a mojito with aged rum and bitters topped with champagne – and Howard had a gin-gin mule – gin, ginger beer, fresh mint and lime juice.

When we arrived, Nancy and Howard were already in the corner of an S-shaped banquette with their drinks on the table, bang in front of their knees.

Howard could have been a well-to-do golfing accountant living in Guildford. He was a large man with the kind of toned bulk that comes from exercise and over-eating. He played tennis every morning and spent much of the rest of the day debating whether to play indoors or outside the next morning. Apart from that, he ate up and down the East Side, particularly in the ornate salon, *La Grenouille*. He dressed as such an obvious Brooks Brothers advert – sports jacket or blazer, slacks, loafers – that he was faintly unreal, especially beside the glittery angularity of Nancy.

Nancy was the thinnest person I had seen who didn't have cancer. Her empty flesh had fallen long ago. Her nose and cheekbones were exaggerated while her eyes sunk deep into her skull. Her hair, dyed a deep blond, descended into a long

43

Sixties-style fringe. Tonight she was wearing a suede band, which sat between her fringe and her smooth and sleek bob. The band matched her taupe suede trousers. I don't mean to imply that Nancy was tacky looking. The thousands of noughts at the end of her purchases, her personal shopper in Bergdorf's, the heavy chunky carat gold bracelets and the white cashmere sleeveless tee shirt she had teemed with the suede trousers, all helped to guarantee an overall result that was expensively magnetic.

The *Guardian*-reading Kent girl embedded in me was snobby about her spending. Of course, the reality was I was in awe of her money and her visible consumption of a corner of it. I comforted myself, wondering how much plastic surgery she had had. On the Upper East Side, surgery was merely an extension of good grooming. If you didn't have it, people would think you couldn't afford it. Close inspection suggested she might have had cheek implants, eyelid work and subtle lip enhancement – no swollen baboon features on Nancy. But whatever tucks and tightening she had had, they hadn't been able to hold up skin that had no calories underneath.

OK. This whole description is venomous. So I have to explain that I am biased. She wasn't any skinny Upper East Sider I might admire, envy and bitch about from the wrong other side of Madison Avenue. She was about to play a crucial and destructive part in what happened to me. And that would taint anyone's view. She was an elegant woman I admit. She looked perfect. She looked like a woman in control.

I envied how immaculate she was. There was this obvious appeal to Nancy, however superficial. She made me feel inadequate in a certain way. It wasn't just the clothes. She was overtly physical and that was intimidating.

Nancy was giggling and girly, peeping out from under her deep fringe. When she did, her face softened into striking beauty. You could see the babe she had undoubtedly once been.

Only she was Snow White's stepmother, who refused to believe what the mirror now stated. There was something about seeing right up into the armpits of a woman in her sixties that made her seem strangely naked. Even in this furnace heat.

Nancy was positioned with Howard on one side and Jessie on the other. She was leaning into him as if for warmth. Jessie moved closer to her. He could sense her need.

I smiled weakly. I was weakened by the fact I was technically under-dressed. This was a permanent problem when I went out anywhere with Howard and Nancy. I was actually wearing my most glam of outfits – black, five-inch Steve Madden shoes with wooden wedges, a flowery silk bodice and black skinny jeans. I had put my hair up and had a large choker dangling with a green stone round my neck. But somehow, my pale skin, small features, grey eyes and straight light brown bob were insubstantial beside Nancy's exuberant closet and prominent tan-tone skin.

I had been staring at her a lot this evening. To cover it up, I blurted into the Howard and Nancy jocular, giggly conversation, 'We've got a great story to tell you.'

It sounds stupid after Jessie's warning, but I did it without thinking. I wasn't a particularly calculating person back then.

Nancy gave her coyest smile. Howard mirrored her. His teeth super white.

'Jessie, you haven't told me. Let's have it. Not another sporting accident. Things always happen to you two.'

All smiling, all happy. Two Old Cubans and two gin-gin mules, clinking together.

I caught Jessie's eye. I was intending to change the subject, pretend I had forgotten what I was going to say. Act stupid. For the sake of peace, harmony and cocktails in Bemelmans on a Friday night.

Maybe it was the two gin-gin mules he had already drunk. Or maybe he cared too much about their reaction. Jessie waved his arm with an exaggerated worried look, which stated: 'Don't tell them about NYPD.'

I thought Jessie was wrong. Nancy and Howard would giggle about roof-hopping policemen. I couldn't resist. 'Well, the NYPD climbed down on to our terrace . . . Stormed into our apartment . . . Into our bedroom. They were armed.'

I imagined their gasps, horrified laughter. But they were both silent.

'It was terrifying at the time,' I continued, 'but it's quite funny now.'

Jessie grinned slightly foolishly. He was definitely drunk. 'Yes, Nancy, it's official. Anna's been having run-ins with the NYPD. Her Majesty's Service would not approve.'

Jessie has . . . had . . . indisputably good judgment, except when he was drunk, when he got purposefully careless. It was probably a reaction to trying so hard to be careful the rest of the time.

He grinned again to himself.

Howard coughed nervously. 'What the hell did you do?'

I was sensitive to the obvious aggression in his tone, but he was my father-in-law. 'Josh was jet-lagged. The NYPD don't run into jet-lagged children.'

Even my slight mockery of the police went down badly.

'The NYPD do a terrific job for the city of New York. They have busted the crime in Manhattan. Why did they need to burst into your apartment? That's what I wanna know.' Howard sounded less and less genteel.

'Because Josh was jet-lagged, and on the terrace at night. But he was safe,' I protested.

Jessie might fall asleep. He had had a tough week, but I couldn't help feeling annoyed he wasn't giving me more support.

'Anyway. No harm done, as my mother would say.' I thought this platitude might rein Howard back.

46

'That is totally dangerous.'

Nancy had left Howard to tick me off. She had waited. Almost as if she wanted me to be worn down first, before she piled in. Or were two Martinis making me paranoid?

'In my experience, it's always women who are at fault. I sometimes hate my own sex,' she almost boasted. 'Of course, I am an absolute A1 fan of men.'

Jessie giggled. Howard smiled.

'Sorry,' I stressed. That would be enough to silence her.

She could be coming on to me. She gave me a sexual pout that clearly worked on men.

'Anna dear, I would have thought after your little . . . you know . . . difficulties, you would have taken greater care of Josh.'

We had struggled for three years to get pregnant before finally resorting to IVF. We had funded the first time; my parents had paid for the second go. We couldn't ask them again, and we had no more spare cash so Jessie had asked Nancy and Howard to pay for the third attempt, which thankfully worked and brought us Josh. I was sensitive about the fact Josh was scientifically produced and paid for by Jessie's rich stepmother, especially after I had met her.

But Nancy chose to bring up my IVF treatment so casually. She wasn't toying with me the way a woman would. She was assaulting me like a bloke. She chose to take my silence as submission.

'You know, if you'd like a little help,' she leaned forward confidentially, woman to woman. 'I happen to know there's an excellent therapist at the end of your block. She has a fabulous reputation.'

She could have been describing a nail bar. Only I hardly took it that way.

Jessie raised his head, giggled and wiggled a finger at me. 'Ah, there you go, Sharon's right, you need to see a shrink.'

His head dipped down towards the table.

'Don't be ridiculous,' I stated. 'Please can we change the subject.'

'Let's order another round,' Jessie slurred.

The waiter came, the drinks came, but the atmosphere had changed. My only solace was Jessie was laughing about it all again. He was too drunk to talk when we got home. By the next morning, my anger had died down, though I did mention Nancy's therapy dig.

Jessie dismissed it. 'She wasn't trying to be hurtful Anna. They all see therapists here. It's like exercise. Just something they do.'

I wasn't convinced. She was a difficult stepmother-in-law. But what could I do? Just ignore her.

*   *   *

Jessie and I were once fantastic together. We were meant for each other in so many ways. I still maintain that. I can still appreciate our happiness.

We were going to a party. After a day in yoga pants and trainers, I craved a few hours of glamour and forgetfulness. New York was a license to dress up. Champagne, patent triangular heels and a skinny dress. I felt a rebellious lift as I closed our front door, leaving our baby-sitter, a preposterously elegant student at Columbia, behind.

Jessie and I headed on to Amsterdam Avenue, fingers locked, arms swinging lightly in the September air, which indulgently didn't call for a cardigan. The hope, the promise, the sheer excitement of being expats propelled us out for a few drinks before the party. We never went to the same place. It was a waste in a city brimming with bars. Tonight, we walked – people watching, bar and restaurant watching. The sidewalks were active. Even on a Monday night. I felt an energy seeing so many people eating out – singles, couples and families. Every seat outside the glossy black Hi-Life bar restaurant on the corner of 83rd and Amsterdam was full; so were tables across the road outside Fred's, a curiously popular bar and restaurant that could be a Surrey pub with photographs of dogs as a jigsaw on the walls. Despite my unsteady height, we kept moving, block after block. Up around 98th, Amsterdam got less buffed, less chino-ed. Jewish delis, Italian restaurants, the odd fishmonger and garish nail bar. All full and busy. We turned right across 98th to Columbus. Steam was rising out of the funnel in the street and the road was blocked at the end. We walked back downtown, passing a Thai-looking woman delivering a cart of tightly packed laundry bags, a nun on a bicycle and a policeman smoking. Yellow cabs jolted passed us. The steady sound of people on the move. We didn't stop. New York propelled us forward.

Finally we decided on a bar a few blocks from our street. Its airy modernity guaranteed it would have been packed in London or any big city in the UK. But here, in the city of choice, it was not the chosen bar this Monday night. A smiling Chinese girl, swathed in black tee shirt material, immediately sashayed towards us. Jessie and I grinned at each other. We hadn't become complacent about being greeted and not grunted at. This supposed universal truth – all New Yorkers serve you with a smile – has its full-on exceptions. But this balmy night, nothing darkened the New York of our dreams.

We chose the brown leather sofa near enough to the vast glass front to give us a view out on to the sidewalk.

As the waitress handed us the menus, she spoke eagerly. 'Hey, you're from England!' Naive enough to think it was still a good passport to hold.

'Yes, we're living here.' I pressed my leg gently against Jessie's. Not without a certain pride that we had made it.

Jessie echoed my excitement. 'Yeah, my wife's British. But I'm actually American. My father's from New York so I feel like I belong here.'

Jessie was merely responding to her enthusiasm. Or was he?

'Oh you guys. That's awesome.' She smiled through our silence.

It was only in the Pinot Noir *v.* Merlot decision-making silence that followed, I re-played what Jessie had said. It was the first time he had ever described himself as American. It was like a gear change in a fast car. Easily missed. And I was so ready to do it, dismiss it as Jessie's desire to find common ground with everyone he met.

Jessie's casual renunciation of his citizenship was lost in our clinking of glasses. We started the debrief of our days, which happened readily and easily outside home. Everything that happened to us out here was part of our NY experience, which should enrich my art, though I hadn't painted since we arrived. I had no excuse – Josh's playroom was vast and had washable wooden floors. For some reason though, my life was more colourful here, I was less inspired.

'How was your day?' I turned to Jessie.

'Oh packed – Lebanon mostly.'

I was impressed and in awe of the way Jessie spoke of a country's problems as other people spoke of profit margins or delivery dates. It was simply that the map of his day happened to be global. What he did mattered. With the distance a disappearing glass of Pinot Noir gives you, I realised it was a hugely attractive part of Jessie.

Jessie sighed. 'An endless pile of paperwork which is never going to resolve anything.'

That was not his line. 'Diplomacy's the only way. You've always said that.'

'I know.' He turned vaguely away from me. 'But you realise out here, it's only money that gives you power.'

'Rubbish. In England, people are powerful who aren't outlandishly rich.'

'Only if they are born someone. If you become rich, you become powerful.'

I heard his sudden certainty. I was thrown. He had chosen a career in diplomacy, not finance.

'Like Nancy,' I threw in.

He paused, as if profoundly considering Nancy. 'Yes.'

'How's our signature Pinot Noir from the Willamette Valley?'

The giraffe of a waitress leaned back over us. Great wine, but can't you give us some space?

But Jessie was eager to be diverted. 'It is a rich blackberry in tone. What do you think Anna?'

'Yes. Lovely. Thank you.'

The giraffe's head bent towards us.

'We wanted to try it after watching *Sideways*,' Jessie enthusiastically leaned forward.

'Oh, did I love that movie. I was born and raised in Pasadena.'

'Really? What brought you to New York?' Jessie poured another glass for each of us. 'Would you like a glass?'

No, no, no.

'You are too cute. I can't I'm afraid.'

Was this ever going to stop? Come on Anna, stop being a reserved Brit. Enter into the spirit of hey presto Americana. But I couldn't.

'College. I'm a freshman at Columbia.'

'Our sitter's at Columbia. Megan McCloughin?'

I was out for the night only to be discussing our baby-sitter with a student? I'm sorry, but I hated this.

'Jessie, we ought to get to the party.'

The giraffe turned into a parrot.

'You guys going to a party, what fun! Is it uptown?'

'No. Downtown, near the Williamsburg Bridge,' I said shortly, with what I hoped was subtle enough annoyance for a Yank to get. But no.

'I live in Williamsburg. It's like totally arty. Like that's what I love about it.'

If she said 'like' again I was going to pour my drink over her.

'This is such a great bar, let's not go. I don't want to traipse downtown to be with a load of expats,' Jessie stated.

Theoretically I agreed with him. Only the bar had been ruined for me. Three was a crowd, especially when one was a rapacious waitress.

'I've spent all morning talking to Dirk and the Argentine lady in the grocery store. Oh, and the mothers at school. I want to get out.' I heard a childish whine to my voice.

'OK,' he smiled sympathetically, stroking my hand. 'But we should make more effort to get to know Americans.'

Three

I was getting to know a real American. A New Yorker, born and raised. From a distance, she looked highly maintained, perfect. But close up, she had that weather damaged skin seen so often in New York. Whether it's the Siberian winter wind, the August heat or the general pollution, it's clear that no amount of dollars save the rapid ageing of New Yorkers' faces.

The headmistress of Josh's international school was American and so were most of the pupils. International was an aspiration, not a fact. Her outfit suited the Vice President of Any Incorporated, and so did her style of running 'the business' of pre-school education. Which was considerable – the fees for Josh to do five mornings a week until 12 o'clock were $17,800 a year. I hasten to add we weren't paying the fees. I was grateful that Nancy got Josh a last minute place in any nursery. She was on the board of the school.

The headmistress had called me early on Tuesday morning. Or rather her assistant had. 'Paula would love you to stop by.'

I had already learned this casual invite was coded. It didn't mean in the next couple of weeks, but later today. I suggested ten minutes before I picked Josh up at the midday.

'Sure. Why not come over at eleven?'

'Sure,' I had echoed, mirroring her tightness in my tired skin.

I was facing her. There wasn't a clue that this was the room belonging to the headmistress of a nursery school because the only sign of childhood, or childish life, was two neatly framed photos of her own children. It was too tidy and clean. She was too tidy and clean. Where was the paint-stained overall? Where was the pen wedged in her frayed hair?

Paula's nail bar-groomed fingers were currently smoothing

her notes for our chat. She called it, 'our little get together.'

She started, 'Are you a happy Mommy huh?'

That was me. Even though she was Paula, I was Mommy.

I crossed my legs hoping she could see my tattoo. She was watching me intently as I did it. So I scrapped my chair back from the table and uncrossed them.

I took the risk, 'Actually, I'm feeling a bit rough. We had a big night last night.'

This piece of information was greeted without a smile, without a sound.

So I hurried on. 'Josh has settled in so quickly.'

She was resolute and flicked her eyes down to her notes. 'I'm afraid there has been an incident.'

An incident. The words immediately diverted me back to my bed with the NYPD shouting and then I remembered we were only talking about pre-school. I desperately wanted a glass of water, as well as a coffee. And to get out of here.

'Joshua has given us great cause for concern.'

What could he possibly have done? I was waiting for her to break into a smile.

'Joshua deliberately rolled the classroom carpet yesterday,' she spoke quietly, carefully.

She paused, leaving space for me to answer. She really wasn't going to smile.

Finally she added more forcefully, 'When it unrolled, it caused serious injury to one of his classroom associates.'

She paused to let the gravity of the situation register. She was still. I was stiller.

'The child hurt its head on the corner of a desk and had to be taken to the emergency room.'

Paula paused to let that sink in.

'Oh no, I am sorry. I am so sorry. Is he or she OK?'

'She will probably have a scar.'

'Oh no. Who was it? I must call her parents.'

Paula wasn't going to get diverted by my sympathetic murmurings.

'When he was questioned at length by his teachers as to why he rolled the carpet . . . .' She paused, 'He denied any involvement. He said a wata bug did it.'

I laughed. Josh was obsessed with the cockroach-like water bugs that had scuttled round our apartment during the heat of the summer. It was a funny, clever way to try and squeeze out of a tight spot. Wasn't it?

'I do not find that an appropriate response. Absolutely not appropriate.'

Her thin reddened lips tightened so they were barely visible and her hands were as clenched as elegant hands could be. I had walked into this room not having the faintest idea where I stood in the pantheon of early education until I heard Paula's words. What she was saying was ridiculous.

'I mean, Nancy Wietzman herself agreed.'

I was alerted by her name. 'Sorry, what has Nancy got to do with this?'

'Anna, Nancy Wietzman, whom of course you know, is one of our most esteemed board members. And she was reading a story to the class at exact time of the incident.'

'Was she?'

I couldn't imagine Nancy in a tiny chair in front of a classroom of infants. It was strange. It wasn't the kind of grand, global volunteering she usually did.

'Yes, she is extremely committed to our community.'

Paula was aggressive now. I was no longer Mommy. Mommy didn't behave like this.

I tried to rescue the situation.

'I am so sorry. I am. He shouldn't have rolled the carpet.' I hastily held up my hands.

Only I must have said it too lightly.

'Honestly. I am not laughing here, Anna. You know, three

issues like this and we are committed to contacting Social Services. Yes, it's serious.'

What a horrible thought. Though I quickly dismissed it and ploughed on. 'Josh does have an over active imagination. But it is one of his strengths. I'm sure you will agree.'

'It is not appropriate for him to use his imagination outside the "Imagination Station".'

My stomach lurched. I leaned forward, placing my arms firmly flat on the table. The tigress in me reared up, big, strong, ready to lash out.

She leaned back, breathing in with a complacent smile. 'Here at Tower Pre School, we are creating responsible, caring, international human beings. The future of this earth, of our planet is going be in their hands. We want them to explore their own reasons for doing things, and work as a community to resolve their issues.'

What did those words actually mean?

'He was just curious to see what would happen when he rolled the carpet.'

'Oh please, Anna. He needs to learn responsibility . . . ' She paused.

Responsibility? Such an aging word; like 'housekeeping', 'life cover' or 'an enhanced pension scheme'. I hardly felt ready for it. That's why I had escaped abroad. That was why I had married Jessie.

She breathed in to emphasise her words. 'Nancy did mention that there has already been an incident at home.'

Why on earth would Nancy tell Paula about the NYPD? It was tactless. Paula clearly thought it was her trump card in some bizarre kind of way.

'But we don't want this to escalate . . . '

She left that thought hanging between us. The silence increased until it was as large as the emptiness in the room. I realised she was expecting something of me.

She produced a piece of paper and passed it gingerly, as if her nails were drying, over the table. She was going to get me to sign some damage waiver form.

'Over-scheduling or Under-scheduling – the great social challenge facing modern parents today.
A day's workshop by Cynthia Wong, organised by the Mommy and Me Program. $350 including lunch.'

She smiled triumphantly. 'I suspect Josh is under-scheduled. What about our after-school programmes? Computers?'

Why, and how, had I ended up justifying my parenting to this woman?

'Cynthia has worked with Mel Levine. She is excellent at scheduling the under-fives.'

The mention of Mel Levine and I was up. 'You want some psychologist to tell me what I should do with my own child?'

I should have stopped myself. Paula – I found it easier to call her that now – was shocked.

'You seem very hostile.'

I stood behind the meeting table, holding it for support. 'He rolled a carpet because he thought it was funny. God forbid he has a sense of humour. Of course, he shouldn't. Roll the carpet, rather than have a sense of humour . . . '

I was trailing off because as her face closed inwards, her lines seemed to get more pronounced, her eyes a darker black, and her skin whiter.

Then I realised two of the mothers of children in Josh's class were watching me from the other side of the glass. The wealthy in this city hated a showdown. It was a sign of being too close to your roots, to the street.

I took the leaflet and turned to the door, past her assistant's desk and out through the heavy fire door into the outside air. Then I saw one of the most beautiful mothers slide up in a white tee shirt, which must be on its first ever wear, and a pair

of black leather trousers. I lifted my chin and my mouth into a
smile. I turned down the road before she could come with me.
I immediately called my mother. She was so easy going, she
would shrug off the whole scene.

'Mum, hi.'

'Anna.' Mum sounded as if she knew I was about to call.

'How are you?'

'Barnie has a stomach upset. I'm about to take him to the
vet. But Dad's here.'

'I wanted a quick word with you actually,' I said hastily.

Dad had an unpredictable temper, usually fuelled by other
people's supposed follies. His anger could be as harsh as his
florid face. My mother's unearthly calm diffused his rage. She
was utterly reasonable, many would say too reasonable. But it
was why they had such a happy marriage.

I rushed on as I had always done with my mother since I was
a child, telling her the whole story. Then I waited for her to
laugh. She didn't.

'Are they insane? That's appalling.' She was my echo. Was I
turning into my mother?

But I didn't want sympathy. Not from mum anyway. She
was laid back. That was her line. And I wanted her to play her
pre-allocated role.

'I hate to say it, but it's a Jewish thing. They are so uptight
and competitive you know.'

'Mum. How can you say that? You don't even know any Jews
except Jessie.'

She was only reasonable within the tight limits of her own
experience.

'I say it with all due respect. There are obviously some exceptions like Jessie. But he's British isn't he? Not Jewish at all.'

I blushed, angry and embarrassed by my mother's ignorance.
I was so ashamed I defended the school.

I finally made abrupt excuses and ended the conversation. I

walked to one of the small cafés on 72nd Street. I sat at one of the tables outside. I needed to breathe, remind myself how cool it was to be in New York.

'Adopt a dawg!' spat a woman, thrusting a leaflet into my hand. She was wearing a mid green velour tracksuit, which could feasibly look good on the right chic soul in the right chic gym. But she must have been at least seventy. Her face had sagged long ago into loose insignificance. Her white long blonde hair and chipped bright pink nails said she was hanging on in there.

'I love dogs. But I don't have a garden I'm afraid,' I smiled. This was one of the great things about New York. People cared passionately about animals, causes, and community outside their own selfish materialism.

To show I was more than approachable than she would expect a Brit to be, I added, 'But we do have a wonderful terrace here which I love.'

New Yorkers worshipped any outside space. The wrought iron fire escape across from our terrace was crammed with colourful pots.

'I knew it. I knew it.'

Her face was too close to mine, leaning over my latte.

'Beautiful people adapt dawgs. Ugly people don't. Ya ugly. Ya ugly.' She got louder and louder.

I blushed. Humiliated.

'She's ugly,' she was howling from back on the sidewalk. 'She's ugly,' she pointed at me with a candyfloss nail.

I expected the waiter to come out and rescue me. But he observed the scene from the safety of inside. I started waving in his direction, signalling for the check. He looked away from me as if I was too tainted to take money from. I had no choice but to skulk away. I would have called a friend in London, but I was aware it sounded barking to be upset by such insanity.

I called Sharon Rosenbaum because somehow the idea of her was comforting. I wanted to tell her about the pre-school, but instead I blurted out the story about the dog woman.

'You shouldn't talk to the crazies. Absolutely never.'

Then she moved on.

*　　*　　*

Josh was becoming neurotic, despite my best efforts to counter the hyperbole of other children at school with bald facts. He believed he was hypo-allergic – to dogs, dust, nuts, yeast, and milk. The list went on. He was obsessed. Josh became allergic to fish, green vegetables and then all foods he disliked. His most common question was: 'Are ya allergic?'

It was one of the many hopeful New York afternoons at the very beginning of October. The fall was moving in late this year. The leaves were flirting with a little colour, before hotting up into psychedelic reds, yellows and oranges. The sun was cheery. New York was wonderful, just for the light. On these bright afternoons, I loved being in Central Park. We were walking towards the Turtle Pond after school. I leant over to take an enthusiastic bite of Josh's apple.

'Hey, don't do that. You've got germs.'

'Firstly, don't "hey" me. Secondly, I don't. Thirdly, we're family, so we share everything.'

'Oh man. Everyone has germs,' Josh was resolute. His face flashed so that his blond hair glinted metallically in the sun.

'You only have infectious germs if you're ill. But I'm not,' I said patiently.

'Ya gotta keep ya food to yourself.'

I sighed. 'Of course you can share food.'

'No. NO.'

He grabbed the apple and hurtled off up the path in the direction of the quaint wooden deck jutting out into the pond. It was a popular position from which to view the animal life below and stand right beside the lake. Despite the various delights below, it was surreally over-shadowed by a vast mock castle – a Disney-like interpretation of Austro-Hungarian – with the powerful towers of midtown ranged behind it.

Josh thrust the apple through the wooden slats surrounding the deck and into the lake. He turned to a tourist, with an outsized set of cameras, to explain, 'My mom's got germs. Nanna says so.'

The lady with the multiple cameras spoke back in Estuary English. 'How interesting. How did she get those then?'

I was distracted by who 'nanna' was. Josh called my mother, 'grandma', and Jessie's mother, 'Sally', as she disliked being labelled a 'grandma'.

'He's joking. New York sense of humour,' I said hurriedly, with a broken laugh.

The woman appeared genuinely curious. 'They don't have it, do they? Humour I mean.'

'Oh yes. New Yorkers are very sharp and funny actually.' I heard myself defending them, out of instinctive loyalty.

'You live here then,' she persisted, with the kind of curiosity you have when you're on tourist time.

'Yes. Well, we're here for three or four years.'

'Then you'll go back to the UK?'

'Definitely.'

I heard my mother in my answer. Back home, safe and sound. I wasn't sure Jessie would agree with me. Was England still home to him?

Josh distracted me with a whine. 'I've got tummy pains again.'

To distract him and because I was genuinely curious, I asked, 'Whose nanna?'

Josh was wide-eyed. 'You know.'

'I don't. Is she a friend at school?'

'You know, Daddy's second mummy. His American one.'

'Sorry?' I heard myself using the tone I had used with Paula when I discovered Nancy was reading in class. I quickly corrected it. 'Oh right. When did she say to call her that?'

'At school mummy,' he said impatiently.

'Oh yes, she came to read to your class.'

'She reads every day.'

Like every four year old, Josh was prone to exaggeration.

'No? Surely not.'

'Lots,' he said firmly. 'But my tummy really does hurt.'

'Dactor's office,' Jesus didn't betray any trace of enthusiasm. There was nothing obviously divine about my doctor's Puerto Rican receptionist Jesus, or perhaps the thousands of others in NYC who shared his name. He was a chunky short-legged black man, who was made psychologically sedentary by his C-shaped desk encased with paper. Despite Jesus' reluctant tone, I always quickly got to see my old Jewish doctor on the ground floor of a pre-war on Central Park West, which was unusual in New York. And that made me keener to pick up the phone now.

We had to walk up five blocks. Josh moaned all the way, 'I wanna get a cab.' Every time he repeated it, I clenched my teeth.

Finally, he wrenched free of me and strode off the sidewalk into the road and put his arm out. Before I could get to him, he'd stopped a cab. '86th between Columbus and Central Park West please sir.' My son was out of control.

'Josh,' I pulled him back from the door. 'We are not taking a cab.'

The cab waited, assuming the kid was king. Josh lunged for the door again.

'No!' I heard my voice rising angrily. 'No, we are not taking a cab.'

'I wanna a cab.'

I have to admit that I resented Josh at that moment. I dragged him howling up the blocks to the doctor's office. As I pressed the buzzer on the inner door, I was relieved there was no doorman outside.

Jesus didn't react to Josh, despite the fact he was screaming.

My doctor came out into the waiting area and led me up through his wall-to-wall filing cupboards to his office.

He had the air and appearance of a painter rather than a member of New York's medical profession. His wiry white hair was in a civil war with itself. He hand wrote his notes in long loopy ink, always starting by rhetorically asking the patient's age not in years, but months and days.

'So how old are we now?'

'Four.' Josh perked up. He was no longer crying or looking obviously ill. He swung round and round on the revolving stool in front of the doctor's desk.

'Well, no. You're four years, three months and six days. Right?'

'No. Four,' Josh persisted.

'Are you sure?' He raised his bushy eyebrows. 'I was watching your BBC last night. A funny programme. Did you see it?'

The doctor's phone rang, as it always did. 'Halo.' He paused, sounding British. Pen down, absorbed.

'You needa rub them and smell. Yeah. Be well.'

'That was my daughter Elizabeth. She's buying a pineapple in Fairway. She always calls me. "Dad, how can I tell if this is ready to eat?" '

He held Josh's eyes. 'So, how do ya know when a pineapple is ripe?'

'You eat it.'

'Nooo . . . You smell it.'

'You are kidding me.'

My son was a zealous convert to New York slang; and I was

63

having a thoroughly British moment. All those refugee-style waiting rooms I had squashed through to see an NHS doctor, only to get two minutes and thirty seconds to explain your complaint, get a prescription and get out again. But now I got restless going through this obligatory fifteen minutes note taking and general non-sequiturs, which religiously prefaced any conversation about why we were in his office.

'What about avocados? Do you know how you tell an avocado is ripe?'

'What's an avocado?'

'What's an avocado?' His eyebrows shot up again. 'It's actually a fruit. But it's kind of like a vegetable . . . Do you know why it's called an alligator fruit?'

Josh shook his head silently. He was always entranced by our doctor, even though he didn't understand half of what he was saying.

'Because some of them have bumpy skins. Where did avocados originate from?'

Josh twirled his stool back and forth. Not even aware that it was a question.

The doctor turned to me.

'West Indies?' I struggled to think as I was distracted by the fact it was six o'clock and I wanted to get Josh, who was now clearly well, home.

'Wrong. Mexico. The avocados you buy here in Fairway actually come from California or Florida. Or sometimes, Guatemala.'

I was silent. He paused. 'Let's see. You had strep throat on 08/31/2008. No visits since then. OK now. So how are you feeling today?'

'Great,' Josh grinned.

I was annoyed: With Josh for faking it, with me for becoming the sort of person who believed him and with the doctor, because he was an eager witness to it all.

'He's been complaining about stomach pains. He's probably making it up,' I said feebly, crossing my legs.

The eyebrows shot up again. 'Kids don't make up pains. How is your tummy, Joshua?'

'I'm hungry.'

'Let's have a look at you. OK.' On went the stethoscope.

'That's so cute,' Josh slurred.

The wiry head lifted up. 'Feels good.'

'Yes he's fine,' I said limply. 'Sorry for wasting your time.'

He held his hand up. 'What am I gonna say?'

I had no idea. But I was about to be given a little more wisdom for the price of the health insurance.

'He needs a lot of hugs from mommy. Tummy pains are sign of stress. Distress . . . or allergies. Lots of hugs. OK?' He paused but didn't look to me for affirmation. 'In any case, I'm gonna put you in touch with Nathan Pollock. He's a gastroenterologist. You will like him – he's a FON, a friend of Nancy Wietzman's too.'

That reminded me it was Nancy who had recommended my doctor.

He walked us back up the corridor and turned to Jesus. 'Give her Nathan Pollock's number. OK. Be well,' he turned quickly away and then back again. 'What's today? Tuesday? OK. You're gonna call me on Friday and let me know how Josh is gettin' on.'

Josh needed the loo. I went in as I always did. He undid his jeans, pulled them down and then his pants and sat down to pee.

'What are you doing?' I stared at him.

'Peeing.' He stared back at me blankly.

'You're sitting down,' I whispered.

'Yeah, nanna said I should. It's less messy.'

That was weird. Surely?

'When did she take you to the bathroom?'

'I don't remember.'

I breathed. 'OK, well. You're a boy. You stand up and pee. Don't listen to her.'

Josh looked helplessly back at me.

Jessie was laughing over the top of his wine glass. 'Anna, you are mad.'

I shifted my bare feet underneath me. Now I did feel more than a little ridiculous.

The minute Jessie had opened a bottle of wine I had told him what had happened at the doctor's earlier that day.

'You don't think that's weird?'

'Which bit?' He grinned. 'No, I'm joking, you maniac.'

'But she took him to the loo and told him to sit down. That's so emasculating.'

'Anna, it's probably an American thing.'

'You think so?'

'Yes.'

I still wasn't sure.

'What about her mentioning the NYPD at school? That is so disloyal. I'm sorry . . . I know she's your stepmother.'

'Well, you clearly didn't think it was that big a deal at the time. You've only mentioned it now.'

That was true. I relented. We both gulped our wine.

Jessie gave me his earnest look. 'Nancy takes her philanthropy seriously. She gets deeply involved.'

I was doubtful. 'What, reading to the children in school?'

'She's probably doing it to get a feel for what goes on.'

'Well, I suppose, you're right,' I stretched my legs, feeling the ease that comes from the first glass of wine.

As we moved on Nancy was slowly forgotten.

Four

Nancy invited us to a premiere benefit at the opera. She gave me a phone eulogy about the tenor – her favourite of all time – Guatemalan Jose Fuentes. She was only going to hear him because he was doing this aria believed to be unsingable in Rossini's *Il Barbiere di Siviglia*.

I knew nothing about opera. Jessie, who had had enforced opera lessons from Sally, hated it on principle. We had never been to the opera together. I had been with my parents, perhaps, three or four times in my life. They appreciated opera – it was one of many notes in a civilised British life along with a trip to Florence, or a good goose on Christmas Day. This was not how Nancy viewed opera. She was a top sponsor of the Met and on their Council for Artistic Excellence as a Founder, which amounted to no less than a contribution of $500,000 a season. This clearly was a serious passion.

Before she ended the call, she added, 'Dress appropriately.'

'What's appropriate?' I had to ask. I didn't want to get it wrong.

'Any one of your cute little numbers,' Nancy gushed.

'I hear from Josh you read stories to his class,' I couldn't help saying.

'Oh yes, I simply love reading to them. It's so rewarding.'

Jessie was right. I was barking mad. My mind flitted back to opera.

I called Jessie at work. 'Oh fantastic,' he enthused, 'the Met with Nancy will be an incredible experience. She'll know all about it. And everyone there.'

I was overdressed walking down Broadway, past Fairways in

my party number, embroidered with red flowers and held up by the tiniest of straps. I imagined Nancy in one of her minimalist numbers and wished I was wearing trousers – until we entered the lobby of the opera house. The open stairs curled up the levels carpeted in a royal red. They were hardly noticeable under the flamboyant weight of a vast crystal chandelier and two paintings by Marc Chagall. Managing to overwhelm even the chandelier were women dressed in full-length gowns of silk and taffeta, wrapped with fur shrugs and cloaks. Their hair was swept up in chignon, twists and curls; their necks were bejewelled. They didn't lean on the stairwells but stood erect watching the people arriving on the ground floor. We had walked in on a Transylvanian ball circa 1800.

'You are under-dressed,' Jessie said.

I started giggling. 'Well, it's Nancy's fault. She said a cute dress not a nineteenth century ball gown.'

He squeezed my hand, looking worried. 'There's nothing we can do about it now.'

I gaped at all the fabric which flowed down the bodies of the women. Metres mattered more than anything else.

'I'm literally the only one in a short straight dress.'

I had to stop in the centre of the ground floor lobby. I needed a moment to take in the scene.

'You look like an escort compared with this lot,' Jessie said unhappily, as he anxiously scanned the stairs for Nancy and Howard.

I distracted myself with the sights and pointed, 'Look at that woman's necklace. Oh my God, it's humungous.'

'Don't point.'

It was hard not to point at the diamond chocker three inches thick. I tried earnestly to look out for Nancy. But all the women were like her – impossibly thin, impossibly delicate yet older, worn despite their beauty.'

'Oh, thank God, there she is,' Jessie sighed.

Nancy was standing one level above us in a floor-length dark brown strapless silk dress and a full-length fur cloak that sat miraculously on the corners of her shoulder blades, without moving, as she waved back to people trying to get her attention from the floor above and below. Diamonds poured from her ear lobes to her shoulder blades. Her dress was the backdrop for more diamonds, which covered her neck, throat and the visible curves of her breasts, which had clearly been hoisted up for the occasion. Even I admired them. She had a coterie around her in a U-shape. Two of them might still be in school. Smooth milk-faced girls whose jewellery was largely confined to long shiny hair.

Jessie bounded up ahead of me. 'Dad, you look the same. Nancy, you look stunning,' I heard him say.

She did.

Nancy moved to kiss Jessie on both cheeks. She held his shoulders lightly as she did it. 'The charming Jessie.'

'My charmless son.' Howard grinned. He was wearing exactly what he always wore, as if a blazer and chinos could be worn on all occasions. I was amazed he hadn't received strict instructions.

'Nancy, I'm so sorry. But you didn't say full-length.' I was only attracting her to my missing reams.

'Don' worry, you look sexy,' said Howard.

One of the girls giggled. I wasn't quite sure if she was embarrassed by Howard's comment, or by my bare legs. I tried to laugh. The effect was feeble.

'Jessie, I am delighted to introduce you to Pamela Beard and Ashley Mellon. Both these beautiful intelligent girls are coming out this season . . . '

They were beautiful. Pamela was dark, with her line of hair tucked in a schoolgirl way behind her ears. She had bright earnest eyes and an innocence that rested on her naturally pink cheeks. Ashley was a blond carbon copy of Pamela. Ashley was in the palest of creams, a vaguely floating chiffon dress which puddled on the ground; while Pamela was in a pale blue, netted strapless dress that looked vintage but probably was a designer's copy of a vintage style.

Nancy slightly raised her shoulders for extra emphasis, ' . . . at the *Bal Crîllon des Debutantes* in Paris.'

I couldn't help coughing. It came out as a splutter. All three women moved their shoulders slightly back.

Nancy seemed to stiffen, before adding, 'And this is Anna.'

'His wife,' I added. Was I being over-sensitive? Normally I felt aggrieved to be introduced as his wife, as if I was of no interest except as an appendage. Not someone who was a promising artist from the Royal College.

'The one in the short red dress,' Jessie added grinning.

Both girls giggled uncontrollably, as if on cue.

I laughed too.

Nancy turned her gaze and attention back to Ashley and Pamela. 'Who are you wearing? Let me guess. Chanel?'

'Nancy, you would know,' gushed Pamela.

'And Ashley you are in vintage Christian Dior? Both classic and timeless.'

This was Nancy the fairy godmother.

Howard wasn't listening. His eyes were roving round the guests. I tried to catch Jessie's eye. He was also absorbed, looking for an introduction. But Nancy talked on. 'You girls must know all about the building, so you must help me inform Anna.'

I smiled politely.

'The paintings are by Marc Chagall.' Nancy only moved her left forearm in their direction.

I nodded vigorously to show I knew that.

'The building was a conservative statement built in the Sixties out of concrete and travertine.'

She waited for that thought to sink in.

I nodded again.

'Which are the most famous buildings ever made out of travertine . . . Anna you must know?'

'Sorry, I don't even know what travertine is. I'm clearly a philistine.'

'Well, travertine was a material used on the Colosseum in Rome; the Sacré-Coeur basilica in Paris and the Getty Center in Los Angeles,' said Pamela, with a bright smile.

'And you're not even majoring in architecture. Remind me again, you're in your sophomore year at Harvard majoring in . . . '

'International politics.'

Jessie was amazed. He had, like me, wrongly judged her to be beautiful but stupid. The discovery made me feel slightly insecure.

'Clever girl. You two will have a lot to talk about. Jessie read politics in England and he currently works at the United Nations.'

'Do you? How exciting.' Pamela said, clearly impressed and fascinated. Her reaction was like mine when I first met Jessie.

Nancy led us in a procession. She was at the front, her hand resting on Howard's bent elbow. Pamela followed, talking animatedly to Jessie about the UN. They were both absorbed. Jessie was captivated. I saw us in them. Me, a pretty young girl, him, a dashing diplomat. She was in awe.

I forced myself to be distracted by Ashley who was bringing up the rear with me. 'How do you know Nancy?' I murmured.

'She's a great friend of my parents. They are close friends with Pamela's parents. Pamela's father used to be married to Nancy.'

'Goodness. That sounds incestuous.'

I hadn't meant to say it. She seemed shocked.

'Everyone knows everyone. It's a small world.'

We were led to a table in the corner of a private restaurant where two bottles of champagne lay cooling in an ice bucket surrounded by crystal and white linen. A waiter had to be fetched to pull the chairs back so Nancy, Ashley and Pamela could sit down in their gowns.

When glasses had been poured Nancy announced, oblivious of Howard, 'Chin, chin, everyone. Thank you so much for coming. You will not be disappointed I assure you.'

'I can't wait,' gushed Pamela. 'I've only heard him once before.'

'I can't wait either,' Jessie echoed, smiling at her.

I felt the slight itch of jealousy.

Nancy's narrow lips, for once, rested wide open exposing her bleached teeth and a flash of her tongue. 'You are going to die, Jessie.'

Her smile had all the glow of her recalling her honeymoon. In the dimmer light, she looked younger, less thin and intensely glamorous. 'I can't tell you.'

'You enjoy opera obviously?' Jessie turned to Pamela with interest. He seemed taken by her. What man wouldn't be?

'I love it. I heard Jose Fuentes at La Scala, his high Cs have to be the most seductive.'

Was she for real? Or was she trying to impress Nancy? Jessie knotted his eyebrows trying to understand.

She realised. 'Tenors are noted for their high C's. It marks them apart. The way they perform at that extremity.'

I couldn't say anything. I had turned up for a jolly freebie and found myself at a post grad lecture.

Unexpectedly loudly, Nancy chimed, 'You see, how well educated an East coast American woman is. Not a single woman in Europe is as cultured and civilised any more.'

'Yes, I agree, myself included.'

Nancy gave a quick smile and a little laugh. 'Oh, I hear you've been in trouble again, naughty Anna.'

72

I blushed in spite of myself. Was she talking about the rug rolling?

'You have been swearing in front of Joshua,' she wiggled her finger at me.

She was like the snitch in the school playground. The Alpha female. 'Sorry I don't know what you're talking about?'

Jessie shot me a concerned look, which I returned with a bold grimace.

'Joshua loudly said, "fuck" today,' she pronounced with what sounded like a certain relish. Or perhaps it was just her delivery.

'I didn't know that.' Of course I was on the defence. 'Children pick up rude words, Nancy. It's what they do.'

'Anna,' Jessie was worried. 'Is Josh swearing?'

Annoyed by his concern, I fought back. 'It's perfectly normal for a child to experiment with rude words.' I turned to Nancy. 'Though I appreciate it probably does sound shocking to you.'

'Giving birth doesn't give one a sense of right from wrong,' she smiled round at her circle of guests.

Her insult was somehow acceptable dressed in her armour of diamonds. I tugged the hem of my red dress.

'Anyway, no harm done. I spoke to Paula and the teachers in the class. I know how these things work.'

'Thank you, Nancy,' said Jessie earnestly.

Being dragged in front of Paula, at least I had the advantage of being able to defend myself. And I was clearly seen as responsible for Josh. But I had been bypassed by this latest 'incident'.

Howard stood up abruptly. 'We oughta go, Nancy.'

I looked at him gratefully. He smiled back at me.

Howard and Nancy walked away.

'Christ! I can't believe she did that.' I squeezed his arm to remind him of us, our idea of funny.

Jessie frowned. 'Nancy recommended Josh to the school. She's on the board. How do you think this makes her feel?'

'Well, she got her own back. In front of an audience. I'd have thought you might have defended me . . . '

I expected him to apologise.

'How can I when Josh is swearing in school?' He was genuinely annoyed.

'I didn't teach him to say it, did I?'

'Where else did he get it from?'

I sighed. 'He picked it up. Maybe from me but . . . '

I looked down at my red dress.

Thankfully, the opera was spectacular escapism. Cinderella, set in the city of Seville with Victorian costumes. Basically everyone was trying to marry Rosina, including her guardian, Doctor Bartolo. Failing that, in Rossini's world, the Count. He gets the girl in the end. It was easy to follow because I was reading the sub titles on the screen in the back of the seat in front. I noticed Howard and I were the only ones reading them. I was ecstatic, listening as these voices headily flew around. Jose Fuentes (who was Figaro) performed his aria as if he hardly had to breathe in. And he managed to make it seem so light, so playful and so easy. I loved it.

Also, it was funny. It made me laugh out loud. But Nancy and Pamela continually dabbed linen handkerchiefs in the direction of the tears that silently spilt from the corners of their eyes. At one point, they even held hands, so intense was their mutual understanding of the 'unsingable' aria. Which I discovered, as we made our way round to Jose Fuentes' dressing room, was sung with all the obvious poetic beauty a slim handsome Guatemalan offers fossilised Upper East Siders.

Nancy had forgotten about my transgression. She was holding the corners of her dress, sashaying with enthusiasm down the inevitably grubby corridors, which led back stage and to Jose's dressing room door. We followed, with Howard and me taking up the rear. There was already a queue outside his room. Not a huddle of friends or a couple of fellow singers, but a line of women. Were there that many wealthy women donors with the right to wait here?

Pamela was all of a flutter. 'It's Placido and his brother. Oh.'

Once he was pointed out, I saw the neat man on the grey office-looking chair to our left was indeed Placido Domingo. Not that I'd have spotted him in a crowd on Broadway. Nancy launched forward as if she knew him well. Only, as if he anticipated the attack, he turned his back on her and talked to the man and woman beside him.

Nancy moved quickly back in line. 'He's with his family,' she said, as if to assure me, because I was the only one who made eye contact with her.

The door to Jose Fuentes' dressing room was firmly closed.

Jessie was pretending to read the notices on the wall. He was excited. The showbiz element appealed to him whereas I was slightly embarrassed we were queuing up to fawn over this tenor. Pamela was eyeing herself in a Chanel compact mirror, before proceeding to get a lipstick out of her cream satin evening bag and apply it. Jessie turned to watch her.

Finally, the door opened. In its place was a diminutive dark man in a gay-looking cream cashmere jumper. The woman at the front of the line leaped forward, jostling him.

We had four more people before us. Instead of trying to muscle forward, Nancy was determined to edge back. By the time we reached Jose, we were his last fans.

Nancy held one hand to her glistening neckline and touched him with her other hand. 'Jose. Nancy Frelinghuysen Hughes.'

Nancy had dragged out her maiden name.

When his perfect face continued to look blank, she added hastily. 'We last met at La Scala.'

'Oh yeees. Nancie . . . 'ow arrre you?'

They kissed on both cheeks. It was difficult to tell if he kissed her, or she leant forward to be kissed.

'It was . . . I was so moved. What a pleasure. Thank you Jose.' Her praise sounded more like a confession whispered through a dark grille.

Nancy was trying to create a sense of intimacy. Howard broke it, pulling out a minute digital camera and handing it to Jessie. Without consulting Jose, Nancy leapt to his right and Howard moved in on his left. Jose did a pretty good job of smiling through the first two shots. Jessie closed the shutter decisively only to be waved on by Nancy to take more. Jose's smile had lowered into a straight line.

'Con mucho gusto,' she said, with an enthusiastic teenage wave. 'Jose, adios.'

This time Nancy kissed him on both cheeks. It was only as we turned to leave that I realised she hadn't introduced any of us. Not even the lovely perfect girls.

We gave the first cab to the girls. Nancy gave them cheery waves before turning to Jessie. 'I do hope tonight has helped you to understand.'

There was a heavy silence between the four of us. I sensed Howard knew what she was talking about, but he wasn't about to help Jessie out.

'Nancy . . . sorry?' He hid his confusion in politeness. 'Thank you so much for tonight. What an experience. We're hugely grateful.'

She seized both his hands. She managed to look dark and light, manic and normal. 'You can be a part of an important American dynasty.' She paused. 'A dynasty started by the Frelinghuysen's in 1753. Three centuries ago. Do you understand what that means?'

Jessie glanced at Howard, hoping he'd help him out. After all, Jessie wasn't related to Nancy. It wasn't his family dynasty she was talking about. Howard looked away. He knew Nancy was going to give this lecture at this point in the evening. The whole thing was staged.

Nancy focused her gaze on Jessie. 'It could be your dynasty. You could be somebody. That is all I want for you.'

Her steel grey eyes fixed upon him. 'Don't you want to get to the heart of money. You exist in a petty world where it's all about trying to make it, ultimately make money. I am talking about being beyond such trivia. Working out how to give money away. That's where the greatness lies.'

With those words she slipped majestically into her black car, which had just arrived. Howard wordlessly followed her and gave us a silent wave from the door.

'Bloody bitch,' Jessie said, as their car snailed away leaving us in the cabless cold. 'She's so fuckin' manipulative.'

He never swore. His reaction confirmed what I wanted to believe. I didn't analyse Nancy's side of the story. What did it matter what she wanted? We squeezed hands and arms and he pulled me, hobbling across the road, to an Irish bar with a reputation as a hangout for singers, actors and journalists. We made ourselves a haven on the right side of its mahogany corner. Me, perched on the high stool, Jessie standing.

'OK, we need mojitos,' Jessie pronounced, ticking and tapping his fingers against the bar.

'It was an experience,' I insisted. I could show largesse since he was the one who was angry with Nancy.

'Nancy is a bloody experience.' He flicked his hand towards the barman, who studiously ignored it. Jessie finally dropped it, I thought defeated.

'How dare she humiliate you like that?'

'Humiliate me,' he exploded. 'She didn't humiliate me. She was pathetic. I don't feel humiliated at all.'

I nearly laughed because he did look comical. He was angrier than Nancy's dressing down deserved. I nodded and stroked his arm.

'No, I bloody hate her.' He let out a stressed sigh and started jerking a beckoning finger towards the barman. 'Here. Please.

We've been waiting bloody hours.'

Again he turned his outrage to me. 'How the hell does dad put up with her?'

How I smiled. It's so easy to be magnanimous when you feel on top. 'She does have a soft side . . . well, maybe not.'

'Hi, Hi! Yeah, two mojitos.'

In the lively, easy chaos of the bar we viciously assaulted Nancy and the whole opera night. After one particularly large gulp, Jessie did a majestic imitation. 'It's not about making money Jessie. It's about giving it away. Yeah, right!'

'The whole night was a performance,' I could say with a wide smile, sitting on a tall stool faced with a gorgeous mojito and a husband I loved a great deal.

Jessie sounded moody and irritated. 'Those poor girls were cringing as she grovelled for her photo. They had more self-awareness than to run away on an ego trip.'

'Did they? They loved it as much as she did,' I added playfully. 'That Pamela would have been after you if I had so much as lingered in the loo.'

'Anna, don't be ridiculous,' he said, with a weak smile which acknowledged that he thought she fancied him.

'Were you hugely flattered?' I asked half-heartedly, wanting a denial.

Jessie finished his mojito. 'Who wouldn't be,' he laughed. 'I'd love to go on a date with Pammy – obviously in my pre-Anna life.'

We both smiled.

Jessie added, 'Instead, I'm going to content myself with organising an internship for Pamela.'

I started the second mojito Jessie had already ordered. 'She really wants to work at the UN?'

'Desperately. She wants to be a diplomat,' Jessie said earnestly. 'Nancy is so destructive, she reduces everyone to talking about labels.'

Perched on a bar stool, bitching about Nancy, raving about the opera, I was happy in my red short dress.

*   *   *

Paula and Nancy were standing outside Josh's classroom in the tiny corridor between the 'cubbies' and the glass windows. They were both immaculate as always. Paula in a grey wool trouser suit that was too heavy for the early fall weather. She was neat – silver earrings and a silver bracelet, red lipstick and ivory nails. While Nancy was wearing a tailored cream felt jacket, narrow black trousers and a frilly black and cream silk shirt.

There was only one detail about them that was different and extraordinary. It made me quickly aware of the gravity of the situation I had, unwittingly, unleashed. Swept on top of Paula's thickly styled bob was a vast pair of the sort of Perspex glasses I last saw in our school science lab, or actually, come to think of it, when I visited the dental hygienist. Nancy was wearing her Perspex glasses. They were oversized on her narrow face.

Both women had the expression of NASA scientists when faced with a tricky experiment. Both of them ignored me.

Had they managed to buy these glasses the moment the State of Emergency was announced, or did they have them ready in a top drawer for inevitable occasions such as these? I couldn't possibly have asked.

And what on earth was Nancy doing here? It was as if she was now involved with every daily situation in the school. What about all her other projects?

Paula's message on my cell phone was shrill: 'Of course, it happens. We have, unfortunately, had head lice in the school before. But this time, Joshua has brought an *infestation* into our community.'

Every schoolchild regularly got lice in the UK. And even in

New York, they were common. It was hardly Josh's fault, but still I sensed his history and mine was piling up: rugs, fucks and lice. We were not doing well.

Three running mothers formed a *Charlie's Angels'* line-up in wildly different jeans and heels. They arrived simultaneously at the classroom door. Inside, half the children had been removed already.

The blonde one, Jennifer, was going to hug Paula. Hug the un-huggable. Then Paula saw me. She gave me what can only be described as a disgusted look.

Jennifer turned to speak to Paula and Nancy. 'I've got a whole list of lice agencies: Lice FB1, Head Sanitizers and Lice Crusaders. I've just gotta deal.'

Nancy gave a narrow smile, 'You are so brave.'

'I am absolutely going for Lice Eradicators,' insisted the brunette, turning to her for comfort. 'I mean, they send a team to spend a whole day not only cleansing the infected hair but the entire environment.'

The other two were slightly put out they hadn't discovered this company, but still eager for information.

Paula solemnly declared, 'The only way to deal is to throw money at the problem.'

The brunette continued as if she was describing her favourite cookie recipe. 'You know, first they detoxify the polluted hair and body. Then three lice experts look over every follicle with a magnifying glass and tweezers. They send a team to your apartment and car test and spray everything. There's a one hundred per cent guarantee. Quite frankly, it's two thousand dollars. But I would pay triple that for peace of mind.'

The trio of jeaned moms nodded vigorously over their Black-berries as they exchanged lice fighter numbers. Paula, I sensed, wouldn't pay that kind of money to delouse her own daughter but she knew her market – bankers' preciously preserved off-spring – equated money with peace of mind.

Nancy insisted, 'Lice Eradicators are coming in here as soon as the last kids have left. I give my promise that we will leave no book, toy, or carpet hair untouched.'

Paula nodded a silent acknowledgement. Jennifer and her pals were appeased, and passed us in to the classroom and out again with their girls. Paula accosted Jennifer's daughter at the door, peering into her blonde tresses with her glasses tight to her face.

'She don't seem to have them,' she stated.

'Great news,' intoned Nancy.

Their linguistic double act was designed to be reassuring.

'Quite honestly, I would prefer to get her done anyway,' said Jennifer.

Her daughter stood patiently underneath the three women.

'Of course,' Nancy touched her on the arm.

While Paula whispered, 'Lice Eradicators have a confidentiality agreement. They've done kids in all the best private schools in the City.' She put her finger to her lips.

'We are going to have to take a break after all this is over.'

'Absolutely. Don't bring her back until you are ready.' Nancy's expression was of someone comforting the bereaved.

Mother and daughter were gone. Their driver, who had been leaning against a lamp post on the pavement outside school, smoothly rounded their black Lincoln Town Car, opening the door, rounding the vehicle again, before immediately backing out of the cul de sac. The car completed its three-point turn with Paula waving until it was invisible.

Paula frigidly turned on me. It was as if all the goodwill and soothing she had been forced to do focused her fury on me. 'You have created all this stress for my parents, for my whole school community.'

I sensed she meant 'you have created all this trouble for me'. Dealing with these rich bitches is hard enough without feeding their neuroses. And you, Anna, have done that.

Nancy stood behind her like her security. 'This is an awful situation, Anna. I do hope you appreciate. This sort of incident could lead to a run of the parents out of the school.'

There was that word again. 'Incident'. She was my step-mother-in-law. Why wasn't she on my side? What happened to family?

'Paula, Nancy, I am very sorry there are head lice in school. But who knows who gave them to whom in a class of 20. You can't blame Josh.'

Or me, I wanted to say. I was easier to accuse than Jennifer and her long-haired beauty of a daughter.

Paula ignored the obvious truth. 'Buy these kind of glasses.' She pulled them off and held them close to my face.

They had become an emblem of her determination, her strength as a headmistress to come out on top, whatever situation was thrown at her. Head lice weren't bringing her pre-school into disrepute. Tower Pre-School was not going to suffer under her stewardship. I couldn't help admiring her Rottweiler loyalty.

'Yes, I will buy a pair.' I placated, wanting to touch her arm to make her feel better.

But she was already striding towards her office with the glasses back on her nose.

Nancy carefully took her glasses off and placed them in a large black Chanel bag I had just spotted, propped on the floor by the lockers.

She then turned to me. 'Anna, I so want to help you, but you have got to help yourself.'

I had spotted Josh across the courtyard, inside Paula's office, looking miserable. He had a sheet wrapped round his head and another sheet swathing his body. He was in New York purdah. No happier than most covered women were about the arrangement, the enforced covering up.

I turned back to Nancy. 'I'm sorry but every mother knows

you can't stop your child from getting head lice. They get them from other children.'

'Anna, you know what I mean.'

I didn't. I really didn't.

She turned from me, carrying her bag in one hand and waving silently as she walked away towards her black Lincoln car.

I was unnerved. But I turned quickly away because I could see Josh's tears pouring down his face.

'Mummy,' he cried, as soon as I walked into Paula's office.

The humiliation, the shame, the unhappiness of being isolated, of being blamed, etched into his face. 'I've . . . I've I've got lice. Aaaaahaaaahhhh,' he sobbed vast hopeless gulps.

I was angry Paula had put him through all this and made him believe they actually were painful.

'Sweetheart, I am so sorry. Lots of children get head lice. They don't hurt, do they? Just tickle a little bit. And they come out easily. OK? I promise. Let's think of a nice treat. Chocolate.'

Paula stood over him seemingly determined not to make things better for me, and therefore, for him. She silently passed me a leaflet.

Lice Eradicators, the only professional private
salon eradicating head lice in NYC.
100% guaranteed. 100% confidential.
Endorsed by dozens of the most
prestigious private schools in New York.

'They'll spray everything in your apartment.'

I was tired. Even at the thought of it. I wasn't going to do more than wash his bedding.

'Do not bring him back until they say he is one hundred per cent guaranteed.'

Five

Sharon arrived at our apartment in a subdued state of agitation. Her anxiety only showed in deeper, tighter wrinkles round her eyes and two indentations, as dark as henna, in between her eyebrows. Otherwise, she was impeccable. She was in a lime green sweater and jeans, which I swore were black with a slight green tinge. Hair blow-dried, eyes mascara-ed. Something though wasn't quite right.

Her husband, Isaac, was a neutral man. He wore neutral clothes – beige cashmere jumpers, checked shirts in minimal blues. He didn't volunteer his opinion. Jessie and I sensed he preferred Sharon to articulate their viewpoint to the wider world.

Today was no different. Sharon exclaimed, over our terrace yet again, even though it was only large enough to fit a small square table for four. The four of us squashed at the sides of our steel table, while the children perched on stools in a corner of the terrace.

Sharon had asked if her friend Yolanda could come. She hadn't arrived yet. Apparently, she was always late, often by hours. It was strange to imagine Sharon tolerating such slackness. Who was this demi-goddess? I wasn't sure we were going to discover her hidden depths today, as we had eaten our waffles and were on to second lattes.

Jessie and I managed to steer Sharon's conversation away from her concerns about Josh and his 'incidents', which she was happy to discuss even with the children on the terrace. Jessie and I flashed each other surreptitious looks, which made me feel playful and buoyant, when Sharon swerved to her pet subject. Education.

'This tremendous brunch is a good and special time to tell

you,' she paused dramatically, her tone, I sensed, heightened by the second latte which I'd never seen her accept before.

'Tell us what?' I could not help the slight tease in my voice. 'You're not pregnant?'

'Oh no!' she squirmed, seemingly oblivious of her children. 'We've made a far more important decision, probably the most important decision of our entire lives.'

I waited. Jessie was half-grinning – vaguely flirtatious, vaguely amused. Isaac, I noticed, was looking at Josh's flower-pots.

'We have employed Monica Clements.'

'Monica . . . who is?' Jessie asked, helping me out.

'An education consultant. I mean, when I say an education consultant, I mean *the* education consultant in the whole of Manhattan. She is the guru of kindergarten applications.'

Jessie unintentionally diminished the importance of this news when he reached for the plate of waffles. 'Another one, anyone?'

Sharon dismissed his offer with a curt wave. 'Monica is . . . '

She sought Isaac's eye contact for help or words, I wasn't sure.

'She not only helps you choose your list of schools, but actively promotes your applications,' Isaac explained, before adding apologetically, 'well, it was Sharon's idea. I suppose it is important in the current situation.'

I wasn't sure whether the current situation was Nathan's mental state or the state of NY private education, which was believed to be more competitive than getting into the Ivy League. The reason was parents thought kindergarten was crucial and the apparent link between your 'early years' education and whether you ended up at Harvard or Yale.

Jessie wisely chose to stick to education. 'I hear it's impossible getting into kindergarten. God, we haven't even thought about it.'

85

Sharon saw the opportunity wide open. 'I keep telling Anna. Again and again. You cannot drop your application on the doorstep after the holidays. Most lists will be closed by then.'

'Well go on, tell us about Monica.' I touched her lightly on the arm.

'She guarantees you get into one of the best schools. For my mind, and the future of my son Nathan, I can't put too high a price on that.'

She leant back from the table as if concluded. Isaac nodded gently back in a sort of tacit agreement.

Jessie turned to him wonderingly. 'Is it terribly expensive?'

'Terribly,' Isaac said, sounding relieved to say it out loud. 'Twelve thousand dollars.'

'Oh my God!' Jessie blurted.

Sharon frowned.

She raised her shoulders, pushing them back into a yoga neutral position. 'I mean, personally, I don't put a price on Nathan attending one of the greatest schools in this city.'

Jessie and I simultaneously nodded impartially, aware she sounded upset. But Isaac didn't rush to her defence.

Instead, he turned his chair round to Josh and Nathan. 'Hey you guys, shall we go to the Park?'

Sharon frowned.

'Isaac, this is not the time or place.'

Isaac resisted. 'We should go to the Park. Yolanda's not coming.'

'This is not a question about Yolanda. It's about you diverting from the big issues in our lives.'

'Sharon, I am trying not to . . . ' he searched for the word, because unlike Sharon he didn't have them easy or eager. 'Dwell on the colossal expense, but we are so close to . . . '

We all waited, even Sharon.

'The edge,' he said finally.

Jessie and I eyed each other, wondering which edge he was talking about.

Sharon reddened in blotchy patches. 'I do not find this an appropriate moment to discuss our finances.' She was scratching her left palm with her left fingers.

'I'm ready for a bit of a stretch,' Jessie said tentatively.

But Isaac didn't seem to hear him. 'We are with friends. And I personally want to discuss the fact we're broke, especially when I have a wife who chooses to ignore this fact.'

Sharon and Isaac had an apartment near the top of an extremely tall tower across the road from the Lincoln Center. It was minute. The sole contents of the sitting room were a tiny worn sofa, a TV and one glass cabinet. The children's room had a bunk and one cupboard for their clothes and toys. But the apartment had a magnificent view of the tops of the trees of Central Park from the kitchen window. Sharon and Isaac must have rented it for at least $6,000 a month. Isaac ran his own finance business – a mystery to us, we weren't sure what he did. But finance meant money and we'd never been under any impression they were anything other than rich.

So I was sure Isaac was exaggerating. Thankfully we didn't have to probe, as Jessie vaguely heard the doorbell ring and scraped back his chair along the grey painted deck.

As Yolanda opened the sliding doors even wider, she illuminated the glass. She had a wide face with cheekbones that managed to be both big and curvaceous. Her short body was large in that kind of undulating way that suggested sexual openness and a relaxed nature. Her dark hair collapsed into folds around her shoulders. She could be Latin, standing on our terrace step in a bright red plunging tee shirt and black trousers. I later discovered she was Greek. Once the introductions had been made and she was armed with a coffee and a waffle, she started hauling off her white high-heeled rubber boots, pulling out her bare hot-pink pedicured toes and folding them underneath her. Then she pulled a Tupperware box out of her bag. Inside were chocolate fudge biscuits that she had made this morning.

I was instantly attracted to this 'normal' confident, careless person. She was a rare bird in New York. I felt like grabbing her into a huge hug. I have never so wanted to have someone as a friend. I could imagine her reaction to my stories about Nancy and Paula and the school.

'Sharon mentioned you're a fantastic artist?' I leaned towards her, finding myself using my hands more than usual in a desperate bid to mimic her physical largesse.

'God I wish I was,' she flicked her hair aimlessly over her shoulder with a self-deprecation that was disarmingly different to most New Yorkers. 'I love it. It's my passion more than anything else. But my grown-up job is to represent actors in an agency.'

'Well, that's pretty amazing.'

She laughed a deep guttural sound. 'Wow, this is a great apartment.'

She said it with genuine enthusiasm.

'We love it. A brownstone is the cliché of how we imagined New York before we moved here.'

'Me too,' she smiled a thick-cheeked grin that rolled out into her hairline.

'Where are you from?'

'Long Island. It was quite a move into the city.'

She turned to Jessie. 'I cannot believe Anna has had a baby. She's so skinny.'

Flattery gets most people anywhere.

'Yeah, she's still gorgeous,' Jessie smiled.

This normal person was bringing out the best and the normal in both of us. When I reluctantly went to the loo, I found myself smiling into the mirror. I saw the reflection of the

Origins creams – my mother's leaving present – lined up on our white wall shelf.

Yolanda's arrival made no difference to Sharon's behaviour. She retreated into a private conversation with Isaac which was punctuated by her vigorous hair shakes.

Yolanda completely ignored their obviously mounting scene. 'You must come to Williamsburg sometime. We would have to go out as my apartment is so minute compared with this.'

I could hear screams from Nathan upstairs and in a bid to hang on to our new friend, hastily suggested we all go to the Park. We were all ready when Yolanda asked to use the 'bathroom'. Her voluptuous shape and equally voluptuous deep green handbag struggled into our tiny retro tiled bathroom.

I saw Yolanda squeeze in. It was merely one of the many millions of images which filed in front of my brain waiting to be downloaded. What I mean to say is, I didn't process it. It held no importance at the time. I forgot it instantly.

*   *   *

All the pots of cream my mother had given me were gone. I blinked, because the fact they had disappeared was a conjuror's act. But the shelf was bare. Once I was up off the loo, I bent down low to look around the bath, the floor, inside the mirrored cabinet. But they weren't there. I opened the door halfway. Josh and Jessie were rolling puppies on the sofa, both yelping excitedly.

'I've lost my creams,' I murmured. 'Josh, have you been playing with them?'

Josh didn't reply.

'Josh, I asked you if you took mummy's pots of cream from the bathroom.'

He was suitably confused. 'No, what creams?'

'Are you sure, Josh?'

Jessie volunteered that I must have left them somewhere. I

could have agreed. I did leave things in other bags, in other places. I was a loser of things. But I was also stridently honest. This was my particular downfall. That moment in most films when the truth could remain buried, irrelevant somehow. But some goody two-shoes raises their arm. 'No sir, that wasn't what happened. It wasn't.'

I was back in the bathroom scouring the floor and looking at the shelf again, willing it to return the creams. I even searched through my dressing gown hanging behind the door. Maybe, maybe, they had fallen into its pockets?

People living in a cavernous house with a room-sized bathroom perhaps won't believe me when I say that I couldn't have mislaid anything inside that bathroom because it was five foot by four, with one shelf and one cabinet. There was nowhere they could be. And I had seen them on that shelf before we left for the Park. They had been there.

It suddenly came back to me. That missing image . . . one in a million. The voluptuous body . . . the voluptuous bag squeezing into the bathroom.

'Yolanda stole my creams,' I said it aloud to myself because I actually couldn't believe it.

The tremendous insult, the invasion, the meanness of a working girl coming to my apartment and stealing my present. The sheer audacity of her behaviour. The disappointment. How could this wonderful person I had desperately wanted to be my friend have stolen from me? Put a full stop to any chance of friendship. To any chance of me having a real friend in New York.

Jessie was no longer playing with Josh. He was up. 'What are you talking about? You've lost them.'

That was the easy answer. It could so easily have been the answer. But it wasn't. It wasn't the truth.

The truth was in the reflection of my creams in the mirror. 'Modern Friction' – No 1 bestselling scrub in America, 'Modern

Friction for the Body', 'Ginger Rush Body Cream', 'Youthtopia firming cream with Rhodiola', 'Youthtopia firming eye serum with Rhodiola' and, the luxury of all luxuries, 'White Tea Skin Guardian'. All gone.

'I can't believe she would take my creams. I can't believe it.'

I felt totally broken by the discovery. Not so much by her dishonesty, but by how wrong I had been about her. How desperate I had been to be her friend.

Jessie called from the sitting room. 'You're mad. Next you'll be accusing Sharon.'

I didn't look at him. I kept looking at the shelf. 'No, it wasn't Sharon. She'd never want somebody else's used creams.'

Jessie's anger lightly reddened his face.

I considered him, his dark hair, his grey eyes, and his intelligence. 'She wanted my husband and my apartment, so she took my creams.'

I blushed. Maybe it's a female thing. But I knew I was close to the truth. And I had to confirm my hunch. 'I'm going to call Sharon,' I said, more decisively than I felt.

Jessie strode to bathroom door and yanked it fully open. I was taken aback by the aggression of his movements.

He relented, instantly. 'Fine. If you want to embarrass yourself and me. Call her. Tell her you think her close friend is a thief. Oh, and will they come round for brunch again soon?' His words jumped out staccato. 'We're trying to fit in here. Belong. This is our home.'

'Sharon's not the thief.'

There was silence between us – a heavy rage, which pressed us apart.

He snapped coldly, 'You are crazy, honestly Nancy is right. You should see a therapist.'

His mention of Nancy grated. 'Why does everything suddenly come back to her?'

'Don't be ridiculous. You are paranoid.'

91

'I can't believe you've just said that.'

I was shaken by his coolness, his ease at writing me off, so I deliberately called Sharon. And Jessie deliberately went upstairs.

'This is mad,' I was profoundly nervous. 'But I had these creams in the bathroom. They're not there any more.'

I hoped Sharon would take my cue.

'I am sorry. What are you saying? Nathan's not a thief.'

'No. No.'

She was silent.

'By mistake, Yolanda may have dropped them into her bag . . . '

I realised what Jessie and the sensible rest of the world knew – you can't accuse a friend of a friend.

'What exactly are you saying?'

What exactly was I expecting her to say? I hadn't worked through this conversation. I had somehow, naively, imagined that someone who told everyone her child was in therapy would be liberal or understanding of my accusation.

'You want me to give you my friend's number so you can accuse her of stealing?'

I breathed in. The silence between us was awesome.

'You must be joking.'

'I'm sorry, Sharon.' Was I mad? I was terrified Jessie was behind me listening.

'I have to say I am shocked.'

'I am sorry, Sharon,' I repeated.

As if to rid herself of me, Sharon said hastily, 'Her cell's 646 555 6657.'

The phone cut off. I finally called Yolanda and left a message.

*   *   *

Josh bit another child. This other child needed stitches. I needed a large mojito. Instead, I was back in Paula's office.

92

Only this time Paula wasn't waiting for me. I was waiting for her. As I sat in her pristine cube, I felt gloomy looking at the tower block across the courtyard, blocking any proper view. After I waited almost fifteen minutes, Paula came in. She maintained an open door policy. Only today, she closed it behind her.

'Anna, hi.'

She didn't look angry as she was over the last 'incident'. Nor did she have appropriate literature or notes. She didn't glide round behind her desk as she had done before. Instead, she sat in a chair close to mine. She was strangely still and quiet for a few minutes. I had been resigned to a jargon-heavy tick off. Her silence worried me more.

Finally, she sighed almost gently. 'I am a single mom, you know.'

I nodded. I hoped sympathetically.

She squeezed her scarlet fingers into a prayer position. 'I've raised my child alone in this city. And that's tough. Really it is.'

This conversation was leading somewhere. I had no instinct where. I tried to harness it with concrete facts.

'Paula, I am appalled by what Josh has done. I am going to severely punish him.'

I expected her to interrupt me. But she didn't. So I hurried on.

'I am so sorry. He knows it is wrong to hurt another child. I don't know why he did it. He has never done it before.'

Paula waived her hand. Was it in agreement or was she dismissing the incident?

'We don't always know what is best for our kids. Even I don't always know what's best for my child. But I recognise that.'

Christ. She was opaque. I was lost.

'I do know what he did was wrong, Paula.' Did I sound too defensive?

'I know, I know,' she said reassuringly.

93

Where had her arch aggression gone? I was unnerved by this new softly soft Paula.

'There is nothing wrong in needing help, Anna. We all need help in our lives.'

Her hands had returned to the prayer position.

'You know, I see a therapist. My cognisant friends do see a therapist. My ability to deal with so many complex issues is largely due to the fact I'm in great analysis.'

Shit. Was she suggesting I needed therapy?

She gave, what I have to admit, was a genuine smile. 'And you are so blessed to have someone as psychologically and physically connected as Nancy Wietzman on your side.'

The mention of Nancy made my stomach quiver. 'Sorry. Have you been speaking to Nancy about this?' I consciously tried to say it lightly, without sounding worried and defensive. I rubbed my lips against each other before speaking. 'I appreciate your divided loyalties. But as Josh's mother, I do feel his behaviour in class should be confidential.'

Paula frowned, so I could see the hairs above her lip. 'I do not appreciate your hostile and inappropriate attitude. I am loyal to every one of the parents and kids in our community here. It is my first, my only concern.'

My armpits were damp. Something was terribly wrong. But I ploughed on. 'He shouldn't have bitten a child. But he's not the first or last child who does that, aged four. Personally, I think it's because you contain boys here to such an extent they are more likely to be aggressive.'

She didn't answer.

So I tried a last, desperate tack. 'Oh goodness,' I gave an exaggerated look at my watch. 'I ought to go and pick up Josh.'

I stood up. 'Thank you for your time, Paula.'

'I am sorry, Anna, I need you to sit down.'

I barely perched back on the chair to demonstrate my

reluctance to stay. She touched my shoulder, which made me flinch.

'Things are gonna to be OK, Anna. I want you to stay . . . relaxed.'

'What is going on, Paula? Would you be straight with me?'

How I regret those words. Not that they changed anything. My fate was already decided. But that moment of hearing it still rings in my ears when I try to get to sleep.

The suede stroking was over. 'Our school's protocol is that three serious incidents close together leave us with no choice. We must bring them to the attention of Social Services, which we did and discovered there was an outstanding incident at home.'

'Sorry? Are you talking about Josh being on the balcony? He was jet-lagged. It was completely safe. It was a huge misunderstanding. I can explain . . . '

'Please, Anna,' she held up her hand like a policeman stopping traffic. 'As I said, luckily in this case, you have Nancy.'

She stood up. I wasn't sure why. But I stood up too. We walked back together to reception.

Nancy was sitting in the receptionist Cynthia's chair. Her legs were crossed and she was swinging round with one foot perched on the foot support and the other loose in the air. She slowly lifted herself out of the chair and glided towards me.

'Anna. Let's go for a coffee.'

She gave a significant, if indecipherable, nod to Paula and took me by the elbow. She moved in close to me. It reminded me of how she did exactly the same movement with Jessie that time at Bemelman's. It was difficult to tell if she was trying to comfort me, or needed my intimacy. I was too lost to do anything but silently acquiesce.

'Nancy . . . ' I sipped my coffee from the polystyrene cup in the café at the bottom of the apartment block, one corner away from school. 'I'm just a little confused as to why you are so involved. I mean, not just with the school, but Josh's behaviour.'

We were sitting on either side of a wobbly round metal table beside the black shiny bar in the café. Our hands were practically touching, the table was so small. I held my coffee cup with both hands. Nancy took my hand away from the cup and held it. It took all my will not to remove it.

'I care about you, Josh and Jessie. You are my family.'

Her green eyes were direct and insistent.

I sighed, worried. 'What do you think Social Services will do? Just note the case?'

'Probably . . . Don't worry about it. Whatever happens, I can help you.'

She gave me a warm smile.

'Trust me. I can sort it all out.'

'Can you?' I was grateful, 'Thank you, Nancy.'

'Don't even think about it. I will liaise with Social Services and the school.'

I nodded. I didn't have a choice. I couldn't even successfully deal with Paula. Clearly I would have no joy with Social Services.

'A piece of advice from someone who has been married for ever . . . ' she hugged my elbow again, 'I wouldn't tell Jessie about all this. He'll just get worried. Let us sort it out first.'

So I left everything to Nancy. She was powerful; she knew how everything worked. It was the sensible thing to do. I had my deep reservations about her. But I wrote them off.

*　　*　　*

Admitting what I did next is embarrassing. I still don't know what I was thinking. Was I that impressionable? A mere barometer of my environment – tipping this way and the other.

I rushed Josh into bed, because I had to start reading the book Sharon had lent me by Mel Levine. I felt driven to it.

96

Was Josh irresponsible? Was he stressed? Was I being self righteous about the New York school system? Maybe I was prejudiced? Racist even, like my mother. Was I failing Josh in some way? There was a body of authority pointing at me. Jessie was working late as I searched our shelves for *A Mind at a Time*, which was lying horizontally on top of a pile of others.

I still remember opening the book on the Contents page. I scanned the chapter headings. *The Early Detection of Dysfunction*. I closed it quickly again. It was pornography for the mind, terrifying yet compelling. There I was opening it again. *The Intake Controls/ The Output Controls*. I flicked over the page. *Are some kids too successful socially?* I heard every parent's inner insecurity in that question. My insecurity. *When a mind falls behind; Getting a mind realigned (but not redesigned)*. There was something addictive about the definitive in these labels; the promise of answers to the uncontrollability of childhood. I felt the attraction. If I started reading the book, I would get hooked. I would get out my pen and start underlining certain phrases, folding back the corners of pertinent pages, even resort to feathering Post-it notes out of the top of it. I would read and absorb every word. Possibly even re-read, and re-read it again.

It was such a relief when I heard Jessie shake the stoop door open and bang it closed. He was invigorated as he marched towards the sofa where I was lolling. He hugged and kissed me enthusiastically, but immediately moved away, keen to talk.

I craved his distraction. I shifted my bottom to hide the book. 'Good day?'

'Busy. I've just had a quick drink with Howard.'

Jessie called his father Howard. I wondered whether he did it to detach himself from his father and his politics, or whether it was just a habit.

Jessie squeezed lengthways on to the strip of sofa in front

of my right shoulder. 'He brought this friend of his along,' Jessie's face, close to mine, danced with amusement. 'Who makes billions. Literally.'

'God, what does he do?'

'He manufactures sausages.'

'Only in America,' I giggled. 'Poor Mr Walls, why was he born British?'

Jessie hugged me. 'Don't you find it amazing?'

I heard that awe in his voice again.

'No. The way he makes his money is hardly imaginative or interesting.'

Why didn't I want him to admire this obscenely wealthy man? The money made him crass and naff, the human equivalent of exclusive golfing shoes. And yet, there was part of me that was intimidated by unbelievable wealth.

'You're being a snob, Anna,' he said aggressively.

'Sorry.' I didn't want to disagree with him. We both moved to either end of the sofa, our bodies partially turned towards each other.

Jessie checked himself. His voice was back to its calm, even rhythm. 'He came here from Ireland with nothing. And now he belongs.' He shifted towards me, conciliatory. 'Do you know what was so refreshing? He said, "I feel comfortable working with money. I always have." It's like Pamela, she has none of those British hang-ups about wealth.'

'Pamela?'

'I just thought of her as a good example – she started at the UN today. She uses her wealth to get choice and freedom.'

'And she chose the UN, did she?' I could hear the slight sarcasm in my voice.

'Yes she did,' Jessie said earnestly. 'Anyway, Howard thought Connor Flint could be a kind of mentor.'

'What you talking about? He's a sausage producer not a diplomat.'

'The kind of person who could open doors for me.'

The only answer I could hear myself giving was a literal one. Doors are open for you. You are at the beginning of a great career. But I didn't, because Jessie was taken with the idea.

'I mean . . . ' He scratched his hair above his forehead like he did when he was confused. 'It's such a small cliquey place.'

'The UN?'

'Diplomacy.'

'But you travel the world, meet interesting people, make a difference. Manufacturing chipolatas in Idaho is pretty insular.'

'Ohio.'

'What?'

'His factory is in Ohio.' He padded in his socks across our wooden floors towards the kitchen and the other end of the apartment.

I followed him quickly towards kitchen – a space for our vast fridge freezer and a stand-up stove.

'What are you saying?' I said gently.

He poured two more glasses of wine and swigged his rapidly. 'There's a great big world out here. I can be part of it. That's interesting, isn't it?'

I wondered with a flash of insecurity whether Jessie wasn't just bored with his work. He spotted my concern and changed the subject.

'How was your day?'

I thought back briefly to the biting incident, Social Services and my conversation with Nancy. I didn't tell Jessie any of it. Did I act on Nancy's advice? I'm still not sure.

Josh went into the shower. And we were back to daily life – the how's and when's of the next twenty-four hours.

*   *   *

'Social Services have agreed that Josh can be placed with a responsible family member until all this is cleared up.' Paula stated this after only a cursory hello.

My words rattled out. 'They can't do that. He's British. What are you talking about? He's my son. And I'm English. This is outrageous.'

'Anna, he has an American passport. He's a citizen of the United States, on home soil.'

'We have diplomatic immunity. My husband's a British diplomat. Sorry, you can't do this.'

'I am not doing anything, Anna. I'm simply telling you what Social Services have told us. It's OK, Anna.'

'Sorry, we are talking about Social Services taking my son.'

I hoped she would deny it.

Paula paused, 'They have already stated that he can stay with a family member. Nancy is going to help you out.'

'Help? Her? She said she would sort this out.'

I was aggressive. But that didn't stall Paula.

'She has. Nancy has kindly assented to look after Josh.'

'Excuse me? Nancy is taking Josh? Oh my God.'

OK. I shouldn't have said that. But I was upset.

Paula's tone made it clear she saw no reason to soften the blow. 'Excuse me, Nancy has kindly offered to take Josh.'

'There is no way Nancy is going to have Josh. What are you talking about? He's my son. She's a crazy lunatic on the Upper East Side. I am coming to get Josh right now.'

'Listen, Anna, he has already gone home with Nancy.'

Was there relish in her voice?

'It was much easier to sort without you being here.'

'You've let her take Josh? He's mine. My little boy.'

'Let's talk later, Anna.'

The line went empty.

That moment haunts me still.

Six

I was in perpetual motion. My body was moving as fast as my mind. As soon as Paula cut off, I instinctively called Jessie. I raged and rambled on to him, again ransacking the recent school events, the 'incidents' and the conversations with Paula and Nancy. I heard myself make excuses for my part in the whole disaster. I felt angry and upset, of course, but also guilty, though it wasn't as strong as the pain I felt. Jessie didn't interrupt, as he usually did to establish clarity out of my craziness.

Finally, I prompted him. 'God, what are we going to do? You should speak to the Consular General.'

It was his call to action. I was relying on his logic and intelligence to give me the answer.

He sighed, 'Anna, I already know about all this. Nancy called me.'

Nancy had told Jessie what had happened? Even in my state, I noted how perverse her behaviour was.

'She did, did she? She explained how she has taken our child?'

Jessie sounded earnest. 'Anna, she explained to me how she has been helping you with Social Services. Sorry, us, I mean.'

'Sorry? She told me not to tell you. That she would sort out the issue with Social Services. That it would all be OK.'

I felt small at this point. I had allowed Nancy to treat me as if I was underage, unable to deal with the pains of reality. And then, she had gone over my head to my husband.

'Anna,' he said, as if explaining the situation to Josh, or was I being over-sensitive now? 'It isn't Nancy's fault, is it? She was just trying to help. But Social Services are involved. It will take a while to straighten out. In the meantime, Josh isn't in some sort of institution or anything. He's with my family . . . our family.'

I wanted to say I considered Nancy to be more foe than family. But I couldn't. Why had I trusted her to speak to Social Services? I bet she hadn't even made the call to them. But why would she pretend she was going to help me? I couldn't believe that she would have got involved and not managed to fix it. When did Nancy not get what she wanted?

'It's not right Josh is living with Nancy,' I played for time. 'It's not up to Social Services to decide. Who can we speak to at the embassy?'

Jessie snapped. 'We are not involving the consulate.'

'Why not? Social Services have no right to act. He's a British citizen.'

'He is also an American.'

'Hardly,' I whipped back.

'He has an American passport, actually,' he said drily. 'Now listen, Anna. He's staying with Nancy and Howard. It's only for a little while. And they will get to know their only grand-child. And Nancy's been involved with Josh from the beginning. I mean, after all, we wouldn't have Josh if it weren't for her. Would we?'

That hurt deeply. It was a fact I didn't even want to con-template.

'Listen, I'm going to call Social Services and I'll call you back.'

I was going to sort this out myself. Right now . . .

Action. Action. Action. I used it to keep me calm. I googled a central helpline number for Social Services. I explained to the sweet sounding lady at the other end, probably somewhere in Albany, what had happened.

'OK, mam. So which district is he in?'

'Sorry, do you mean zip code?'

'No, mam, which Social Services' district?'

102

I thought. 'If I gave you my zip code, or the zip code of the school, would you be able to work out what Social Services' district it was?'

'No, mam.' She sounded resolute.

'OK. There must be another way of locating the department dealing with my son? If I gave you his full name..?'

'No, mam. Just give me the case number.'

'Case number?'

'The number on the file.'

Stay patient. It isn't this woman's fault. 'Sorry, what file's that? Should I have one?'

'When they filed the information, they will have allocated a case number.'

Her utter belief in the bureaucracy was irritating me.

'All right, all right, I don't seem to have that. But can I speak to someone anyway who might be able to help?'

'Not about this specific case without a case number.'

Her tone never changed.

My voice jarred. 'My son was taken away from me by Social Services. Someone must know about it.'

'Yes, mam.'

'Can't you find who that is?'

'No, mam. Not without a case number.'

'For God's sake, this isn't fucking 1984.' I felt my anger rise. 'You can't ordain that my precious British, yes . . . British son has been taken away from his family. This is not right. This is criminal. It's illegal.'

She didn't react. She didn't say anything.

Her silence made me furious. 'Do you know what? I am going to sue Social Services. And I'm in the right place. The right country. I will not only get Josh back, but millions of dollars. And you will regret this.'

She still didn't hang up, as her British counterpart would have done.

'This is New York in 2008. You can find out anything. Surely you can find details of what's happened?'

'Mam, I need a case number.'

'Is that the only thing you can say? "Mam, I need a case number".'

Calm down, Anna. She'll never help you otherwise.

'OK. I know, sorry, sorry . . . I'm shouting at you and I know it's not your fault. But I've just had my son taken away.'

I burst into tears. She was still silent.

'All right, all right,' I coughed hastily, 'where do I get a case number from?'

'From your case worker.'

'How do I find my case worker?'

'From your case number, mam.'

'Stop this. Please. I don't have either. So what do I do?'

'Mam, you get back to us when you do.'

I put the phone down on her. I called through to the same office again. I was sure that I would get someone different, who would guide me through the maze. Find that helpful, knowledgeable person who would say it had all been a terrible mistake. But I didn't. The man, who took my call, led me more brusquely down the same cul-de-sac.

By now, I was sitting on Josh's bed, clutching his Roo and with his white rabbit under my phone arm.

I called Nancy.

'Hello, Anna,' she said, evenly.

'Nancy, what is going on? You said you would sort everything out with Social Services. Instead they have taken Josh away.'

'No, Anna, they haven't. If you must know, I worked tirelessly on your behalf. Tirelessly. And the compromise is that Josh remains with a close family member until they have completed their investigation. When you calmly think this through, you will realise this is a fabulous outcome.'

I heard the echo of Jessie's words. It was as if they were all in on it together. Paula, Jessie and Nancy. I breathed. I was going mad. It was a stressful situation. I was imagining it, obviously.

'Nancy. Josh is our son. He has been taken from us. How can it be a *fabulous* outcome?'

She sighed. Again I heard the tone that indicated that I didn't quite get the point. 'He is with Howard and me. Anna, you do have to calm down.'

Before I could think of a response, she continued, 'now . . . on to more practical matters. Do bring over any of Josh's toys or clothes you think he's particularly attached to. And I will organise the rest.'

I started to cry. 'Is he very upset? Can I speak to him now?'

'Of course you can dear. Josh, would you like to speak to your mom?'

'Mummy.'

'Josh,' I choked. 'Are you all right darling? This is all a bit mad. But I'm going to sort it out and you will be back home in a day or so. Don't worry.'

'Am I having a sleepover at nanna's?'

I grimaced at the name. 'Yes, just for tonight.'

'Oh, OK.'

'Do you mind? Sorry sweetheart, just for tonight . . . a sleepover.'

'OK. Bye.'

Nancy was back. 'Anna, I suggest you bring over just his essential things. And then you can see him and put him to bed. Would that be nice?'

I mumbled an agreement. Of course I wanted to be there. But at the same time, I hated to acknowledge that she was sounding reasonable.

I sat on the bed, clutching Roo and rabbit. Lost . . . not wanting to pack up Josh's things.

The phone rang. It was Jessie.

'Hello,' I said limply.

'Darling,' I heard his voice of appeasement. The voice of a man trained to make the Israelis feel it was a good deal for them and not the people of Gaza. 'Nancy's just told me you had a lovely chat. And you're going over to take Josh's things and settle him for the night. It's all great, isn't it? Yes?'

I didn't disagree. It would only start a row. So I did something I had never done with Jessie before. I totally hid my feelings from him.

'Yes . . . great, darling.'

*   *   *

Day One . . . without Josh.

Nancy had often mentioned her lawyer, Harry Finklemann. And he wasn't hard to locate. His office was on the ground floor of a building on 5th Avenue at the corner with East 59th Street. I had imagined it would be shiny and powerful like the image Nancy projected, but it reminded me of my doctor's office. Not surprisingly, because it emerged that Nancy was also at school with Harry Finklemann.

'Is Nance OK?' he asked, as he walked rapidly towards me.

I had insisted that I must see him right away. I hadn't phoned first, worried he might evade me or give an advanced date. I had told the receptionist it was about Nancy Wietzman and I was her stepdaughter-in-law and he had immediately emerged from his office. He was a tiny man with white, short shaved hair and a shiny energy.

As with my doctor, I was struck by how affectionate he felt towards Nancy. I couldn't bring myself to imagine that she inspired such warmth and loyalty. Though, with hindsight, I realise that she did. I held my hand to greet him but he ignored it and gave me a hug, which was positively unnerving in light of the purpose of my visit.

I had got up just after five this morning, manically worried.

106

After several coffees, I had forced myself to believe that getting Josh back was simply a process of attrition. I had to act and keep acting, until it happened.

I went to see Josh arrive at school in Nancy's black Lincoln car. Then I had sat on the wall outside the classroom and had called the only family lawyer I knew in London, the son of friends of my parents. Tim was warm and enthusiastic. I had explained it was totally confidential and that I couldn't bear to worry my parents about something which would be resolved in twenty-four hours. I had told Tim the whole story. He was concerned and supportive but had insisted he knew nothing about American law. I needed an American lawyer, if I needed one at all. I was convinced I did. And Nancy's lawyer seemed like the best place to start.

I hadn't told either Nancy or Jessie that I had intended to visit Harry Finklemann. I knew what they would both say. But I wasn't prepared to wait and trust their verdict after what had already happened.

Harry Finklemann's large, airy and otherwise functional office was heaving with gilt-framed paintings. At first I assumed they were cheap prints put there to cheer up his legal clients. Seconds later, I realised they were genuine. He had a good Canaletto, an early Monet and a Kandinsky drawing.

'You are a collector?'

'Yes, it's my weakness. I've overflowed our house and our place upstate, so some end up here.' He smiled warmly. 'Do you like art?'

'Yes, I studied art. I was a painter,' I said, with a slow shrug, ' . . . well, I suppose I still am.'

'Oh, wow. Have you done anything here?' He was genuinely interested.

I was totally thrown.

'No, I haven't. It's tricky here.' I squeezed my fingers around the phone in my pocket. This was the moment. I gulped, 'You've probably heard about my son, Josh.'

Why was I scared to bring it up?

'No. Sorry that sounds very rude. I'm sure he's a lovely kid.'

He didn't know, did he? I sighed with a certain relief that I could tell him the unadulterated story and get his honest opinion. I paused. How best to explain everything?

He gently helped me. 'So, Anna, what's going on?'

'Social Services have taken away my son.'

He was shocked, appalled. 'Sorry, let's just get this straight. He has been taken into care?'

'No. He has to be with a family member until everything gets straightened out.'

'Right . . . '

'He has been staying with Nancy since yesterday afternoon,' I folded my legs nervously. 'But I've done nothing wrong. There were a few minor incidents at school. Silly, childish things.'

He scribbled something on the pad in front of him. 'What were these things exactly?'

I explained the incidents as matter of factly as I could, careful not to criticise Nancy.

'Anna, if the facts are as you've explained then I'm sure there's no matter for concern.'

'Mr Finklemann,' I started, agitated.

'Harry . . . Harry.'

'Harry, I've had my son taken away for no reason. There must be something you can, we can do.'

It was a dull day. What early morning light there had been was fading fast from his office. He bought himself some time and lit the two modern steel floor lamps and the brass lamp on his desk. The receptionist knocked and peeped her head around the door.

'Yes I know, I'll be a minute. Ask him to please wait.'

She gave him a questioning smile.

I continued desperately now. 'You do understand? I was hoping you could help?'

He studied me. I sensed he read my mind. 'Have you talked this over with Nancy?'

'Yes, of course . . . ' I petered out.

He shrugged and looked hard at me again. 'But she doesn't know you're here, right?'

'She thinks we should wait. I can't wait. Obviously . . . he's my son. I just wanted your opinion. Your advice, as to what I should do next. I mean I don't know any other lawyer here.'

I could feel him staring at me. I saw the face of an understanding man.

'Now, I totally realise how you feel . . . I'm a parent – of grown-up kids though. But Nancy's right. You have got to follow due process with Social Services.' He gave a brief smile. 'And . . . Josh is with Nancy. He's in totally safe hands. Really.'

He grinned.

'It feels like . . . it feels to me like she's kind of kidnapped my son.'

I shouldn't have said it.

Harry Finklemann stopped smiling.

*   *   *

I was in a demented state of denial.

Mary had wide grey-white plaits which lay on either side of her ears and stretched down the front of her shoulders. Her tights were a cross between salmon and mauve. They bore no obvious relationship to her dress, which was orange and green and one of the many Laura Ashley style full-length brushed cotton ones I had seen her in before. Her wool tights were thick, even for the autumn weather. It had arrived last night, instantly zapping the humidity and tension out of the air, leaving New York with a coolness, a lightness of being, which matched the startling blue sky.

I had seen her standing on the sidewalk smoking. When I had discovered from Sharon that she was a therapist, she had become another colourful New York anecdote. I had laughed with Jessie. Who on earth would go to a therapist who was an overweight chain-smoker?

Nancy had already paid the first dozen sessions for me. An hour after I had left Harry Finklemann's office, Jessie had called to say Nancy had 'brokered' this appalling deal with Social Services. When I had satisfactorily completed therapy, I could have Josh back. It was unclear how much I needed, how many weeks it would take. I couldn't argue, though I was sure there was a quicker way to get Josh back. I would find it and do it.

It wasn't even twenty-four hours since Josh was taken away. I missed him constantly in a frantic, desperate way. I was terrified that this situation might become permanent. I was terrified that he was with Nancy. I was terrified of what she might do to him.

Jessie didn't see it that way. He was worried about Social Services' involvement, but he was still not concerned about Josh living with Nancy. I insisted again and again that we should involve the consulate and invoke our immunity.

Jessie was adamant we didn't. 'I am half American. I have an American passport. If we involve the consulate, the whole issue of my dual nationality and my place at the UN might come under question.'

This morning, we had argued on.

'Oh, Anna, stop this. He's with my family, our family. You have got to get a sense of perspective.'

'He's with Nancy, a crazed Upper East-sider you hardly know. You said yourself she's a manipulative bitch and evil with it.'

'Thank you for flinging my angry words back at me,' he had said crossly. 'She is trying to help. It's not her fault this has happened.'

'I think it is. *She* called Social Services.'

'Anna, don't be ridiculous.'

'I am serious, Jessie. We either need to sue Social Services or Nancy. There are only two options.'

He had walked out of the kitchen and had silently left for work.

I had moved abroad to try to escape the comfort of my home. Only losing Josh made me skid into the arms of Nancy's therapist. Well, a therapist Nancy's friend had apparently recommended. The supposed rebel part of me thought it would be a laugh to go along. It was Woody Allen's New York. The life experience I had been rattling on about for so long. But now, it was my life with Josh that depended on this psychobabble.

New York had caught me up. Or I caught up with New York. I wasn't sure which it was.

When I had glimpsed both Darren and Dirk, I was self-conscious that the entire street would know where I was going. The only relief was that I didn't see my telltale neighbour. It would have been the final humiliation. I appreciate how pathetic this sounds from someone who thought she wanted to stand out from the crowd.

My long lens snapshot of Mary had been wrong. Close up, she was smiley and pretty in a full bodied way, perhaps younger than I thought.

Mary started every session with 'free association'. Basically, I had to say a word and then another that I associated with the first and so on. That way she could get a full picture of what was going on in my mind.

'All New Yorkers are barking mad. No wonder they need shrinks.'

I didn't manage to keep the aggression out of my voice.

She laughed easily. 'Yeah, you needa lot of therapists in Manhattan.'

'Why do these people pay a therapist to live their lives? God, even their children's?'

I expected her to say this was beyond the terms of our session, like they do in Hollywood films.

But she leaned against her armchair and wrapped her toes around each other – her brown leather sandals had long been abandoned under the stool – before reflecting: 'You have to earn at least $500,000 to live up here on the West Side. They are used to paying for services – nannies, cleaners, laundry and meals. It's another service, employing another person to iron out the things about their kids they feel uncomfortable with.'

'Like fact – they're kids.'

She laughed. 'Normally, it's the parents who are disturbed. They say I'm gonna make my kid perfect.'

I nodded vigorously. This was what I wanted to hear.

She smiled. 'New Yorkers are very narcissistic people. They cannot tolerate their child's personality, especially their dislikes, or, God forbid, criticism.'

I warmed to Mary. I was righteously enjoying her critique of New Yorkers, because it married with mine. Maybe this common-sensical woman was Nancy's alter ego.

I frowned. 'Josh is my son. He can't be forced to live with his monster of a stepmother. It's crazy and it's wrong.'

'Do you think it is crazy for Josh to stay with his step-mother?' she asked.

I couldn't bear to think about Josh and Nancy. So I lightened the subject to protect myself.

'Where are you from?'

'California,' she laughed cheerfully.

I leaned forward confidentially; confident she would agree with me. 'I'm reluctant to be here. It's like admitting guilt. My son Josh's a typical four-year-old boy. He does naughty things. But it is totally wrong that he's taken away from me. You can see that, can't you?'

'What I think is irrelevant. What I care about is what you think, Anna.' She smiled easily.

I wondered whether New Yorkers were paying to have someone who had all the time in the world for them, because everyone else around was so busy striving to be a success. I realised Mary was waiting for my 'association'.

I coughed: 'Nancy . . . New Yorker . . . skinny . . . neurotic . . . manipulative . . . evil.'

She didn't move or smile. Her limpid gaze coolly met mine. 'That's how you describe your mother-in-law. How do you describe yourself?'

I gave her an exaggerated 'if-I-must' smile, which was churlish and immature. 'OK, me . . . mother . . . devastated . . . lost in another culture . . . adventure gone wrong . . . '

'Don't structure it. Relax, and say what comes into your mind.'

This was harder than I thought. I stared at my jeans.

'Err . . . childhood . . . joy . . . happy . . . wild . . . free . . . isolated . . . adventure . . . experience . . . irresponsible . . . dangerous . . . worried.' My head shot up. 'Sorry, I don't mean I am worried. I mean everyone around me is worried. Making me worried about them being worried . . . you know what I mean?'

What did I mean?

'Let's take a break. I'll go for a smoke. You relax.'

I couldn't relax. I stood and paced around the rug, worrying about what I had said. What did I mean? It was a mad old Freudian technique. I didn't need therapy. Of course I didn't. It was obvious to any sane person. And Mary appeared to be very sane. But I was afraid she'd think I did mean what I'd said. Then how was I going to persuade her that I was normal?

113

When Mary finally opened the door again, I darted guiltily back to my armchair.

*　　*　　*

Day Two . . . without Josh.

I waited for Nancy in Sarabeth's on Central Park South. Nancy was the only person who could get Josh back now, rather than wait to the end of my allotted course of therapy. I was sure that she was at the centre of this whole situation, though I couldn't explain how exactly. After another unsuccessful call to Social Services early this morning, I called Nancy. She suggested that we met for brunch at Sarabeth's.

To Upper East Siders, it was the place for brunch. The frescoed ceiling sported a bright blue sky and child clouds, which clashed with the fake trellising and trees. The 'court-yard' garden was a gentrified slab of lightless space. Their customers were coordinated: large leather bags, matching belts, matching shoes. Well-done hair, well-done nails, well-done make-up.

I barely noticed them. I decided that I needed Nancy to testify to Social Services. And I had to persuade her to do that.

I had a manic energy that hadn't left me since Paula's phone call. I wasn't tired, I had no desire to sleep or eat, but I felt physically invincible. I wouldn't feel tired until I had Josh back. In the middle of the night, I had made some notes in a red leather diary my mother had given me as another leaving present. Somewhere to jot down the great adventures we had, she had said. I re-read my nocturnal notes now to remind myself:

1　The 'incidents' were normal boyish actions.
2　Josh is happiest at home with his parents.

Of course he was. Children are happiest at home with their natural parents. Though I hated to admit it, he had settled in

114

easily with Nancy and Howard. I reassured myself he couldn't really be happy.

3   Jessie and I miss him so much. We are both very unhappy without him.

I sensed this argument wouldn't necessarily work with Nancy.

I distracted myself by looking at the two co-ordinates to my left, in the corner banquette, which were louder than their camel colours. 'It was so awesome, super-delish. I mean, gluten-free – we had the best mock-duck and grilled Seitan tofu ever.'

'It sounds divine.'

'What's more, it works on the 100-Mile Diet.'

Her friend was trying not to look confused.

'It only serves produce grown within a hundred miles. It's a crucial distinction for modern health.'

'Only you won't be able to go there in the winter. They'll only serve squash.'

To my right were engaged beaux. He had a long shoulder length mane of blonde hair and she was equally shiny in her crisp white shirt and trousers. Her ring towered over her tiny hand, a feat more than a feature. He was eating his muffin, home fries, scrambled eggs and bacon; while she was arranging her fruit bowl into neat piles: strawberries at one o'clock, the bananas at six, all the citrus at eleven. He didn't seem to notice she wasn't eating.

Then Nancy arrived. She had an escort. Even though this was her favourite and regular brunch place, it was inconceivable that she would move through the restaurant without a waitress in tow. This poor girl was a few steps ahead of her, scouting anxiously for me. When I acknowledged her, she was relieved to pass the responsibility for Nancy on to someone else.

There was Nancy, very fragile yet fierce and strong. She was wearing a black silk shirt which flooded her arms. Her wrist bones poked out as if they were wishbones in a chicken. All in black, Nancy was unbelievably immaculate. Like all highly sophisticated women, she had this ability to look as if everything she was wearing was straight out of the tissue, never worn, never washed. As I eyed her shirt which, on reflection, was clearly a blouse, I saw the detail, the trim, the narrow arms expanding into wide cuffs.

I wasn't going to be weakened by her wardrobe. I wanted Josh back. It was all I wanted. And she could make it happen. All I had to do was persuade her.

I pushed the table gently in her direction so I could get up to greet her. Despite the awfulness of my situation, I was struck by her vulnerability. This was a tough city and she didn't seem quite tough enough.

'I always have the "Baby Bear" porridge. It's perfect: plain and simple with milk and honey, yummy,' Nancy intoned, before even sitting down.

Nancy's childish enthusiasm for oats made me determined to bond first, and then ask for her help.

'That sounds good,' I said, even though I had barely eaten since Paula's call.

I needed to get her at the right moment.

'I'll have the Four Flowers juice . . . ' she paused. 'No, I won't. I can't believe it is now five dollars, seventy-five cents. No, I'm going to have the grapefruit juice – plain and simple.'

I stared at the menu, not quite able to believe Nancy was going to deny herself the Four Flowers juice to save twenty-five cents.

She ordered with a promptness which stated she was a busy working woman, grabbing a grapefruit juice before she power-walked into her office.

Her tone prompted me to indulge her first. I asked about her work. 'How is your new project going with the Lincoln Center?'

'Oh, I am so glad to be involved. They do fabulous work. I simply love it . . . '

I waited for her to continue, only her voice trailed off.

She almost greeted the juice, as it was placed carefully in front of her with a neat serviette decorated with the name, Sarabeth's.

Into the silence between us she echoed, 'I do. Yes, I do.'

I tried to imitate her forced enthusiasm. 'It must be fantastic to work with such beautiful things and clever creative people.' I paused, expecting her to help me. 'Getting to see opera and ballet all the time. The New York City Ballet, the New York Philharmonic, the Met. You're involved with such worthwhile projects.'

I was exhausted by the last forty-four hours. And I had exhausted my stream of drivel.

'Yes it is,' she finally said, before cooing with a longing that overwhelmed me. 'Oh, my Baby Bear.'

She pulled the honey spoon out of the white bowl and dribbled it in a straight line, which she then abruptly turned upwards. It was only after she had dunked it back in the bowl and lifted it out again that I realised she was writing N, in honey, over her porridge.

In that moment I confused my sympathy with hers. Was she trying to ruin my life? Or was I going mad? Maybe she was trying to help.

'Nancy, as you can imagine . . . ' I paused, I hoped, delicately, ' . . . we're devastated by the situation. I desperately miss Josh. Jessie and I desperately miss Josh.'

'Of course you do. He's a fabulous boy. Howard and I love having him to stay.'

Nancy didn't look at me. She was busy, furiously stirring as if every oat had to be comprehensively coated in this elixir of the bees.

'That's great. Thank you. We're obviously so grateful to

you. But we're extremely worried about the situation. We just want to get him back home where he belongs as quickly as possible, to sort this mess, this misunderstanding, out.'

I could hear my voice scratching upwards.

Nancy lifted the spoon, intending to wave it over the bowl, only it got stuck somewhere between the porridge in the bowl and the air above it, a gloopy Leaning Tower of Pisa. 'Oh, it will get sorted out, believe me.' She swayed the spoon as far as she could in my direction. 'If I were you, I would take this opportunity to discover myself. Who you are; what you want in life.'

'I just want my son back.' I breathed in sharply, 'Josh is my son.' Not yours, I wanted to say. 'I hoped you might be about to help me with Social Services – you understand the system here so well – you know how to testify on my behalf.'

Did she sneer? Or was I getting paranoid?

'I won't meddle further with Social Services. I have already negotiated that if you complete your therapy, they will allow you to have Josh back. I have done all I can. I am respected in this city; I won't jeopardise that.'

The implication was I won't meddle further for you. Hadn't she boasted she could breeze through New York bureaucracy?

'Please. Please, Nancy, this isn't right. You know that. Please help us.'

'No I won't. Now look at that Baby Bear. Aren't you a lucky girl.'

My porridge was slid in front of me. I didn't acknowledge it or thank the waitress as I usually would. I was crying without making a sound. Tears were seeping out of the corners of my eyes as quickly as I wiped them with my napkin.

She glanced at me, before sighing confidentially. For a moment, I wondered if she was going to relent. She waved her spoon-free hand and said, almost under her breath. 'You know the biggest pressure in life? Money.' She said it as if it were a curse, worse than losing your son. I wished Jessie were here to witness this.

I was silent. I wasn't going to oblige her by replying.

She stirred her porridge again. I realised she was going to play with her Baby Bear. Possibly divide it into corner piles. Possibly eat a small portion at one o'clock, but not the whole goddamn bear. She stopped churning the mixture.

Nancy looked up at me decisively: 'No one takes you seriously.'

I was even more afraid of Nancy's fragility than her strength, so I wanted to lift the conversation. 'Which is why you love your philanthropy. You are taken extremely seriously.'

We would turn out of the cul-de-sac of Nancy's insecurities. I had nearly finished my latte, fruit bowl and Baby Bear porridge. And Nancy clearly wasn't going to finish hers.

'You have no idea,' Nancy let go of the spoon, which sank gradually into the sludge that was now the content of her bowl. 'I am not taken seriously. I am not taken seriously.'

'Surely you are?'

Why was I trying to rescue her?

'No, no. I am not. I am not.' This was the kind of morbid turn that conversations took when one person had been drinking many depressing spirits and then spilled their lives like a split shopping bag. Only Nancy wasn't even drinking coffee, let alone strong stuff.

'I am not . . . ' She sounded as shrill as a low voice could. She started playing with the cluster of gold bands on her ring finger, 'I am simply not.'

I decided silence was the best option. I looked up desperately, willing the waitress to come back. A few minutes later, she did.

'Cheque,' Nancy said, curt and professional again.

She plunged back into her porridge finally, exhaustingly, spooning a mouthful through the narrow cavity between her lips.

119

She appeared to swallow it. She must have, because she spoke with her clear, clipped voice obviously free of any impediment.

'But I am not going to live with it any longer.'

I nodded. I wasn't really listening. She wasn't going to help me. What could I do next? There was only one answer now. I had to call the consulate. Hopefully, Jessie wouldn't find out. I was now impatient to get out of this restaurant, find their number. I wondered whether it was near here. Then I should also call Harry Finklemann again. Or maybe, there was an embassy lawyer who could help me.

'I am going to set up my own foundation.' It was effective. The beaux both eyed her. 'The Nancy Wietzman Foundation for Native American Prose.'

I was lost for words. Everyone was looking at Nancy. And she was waiting for a response from me.

'What's your connection with the Native Americans?' I finally asked.

She waved her hand and let it rest above her black silk breast. 'I feel a connection. You know, I've been to many Native American retreats in Arizona. I have this spiritual bond with the people. I am part of them; at one with them.'

I nodded, hoping it was brief enough to put an end to the conversation.

'And I have one hundred and eighty million dollars to put into my Foundation.' She was boasting. Unaware, or choosing to ignore, the fact that she was buying her way into being taken seriously, using her money as a weapon, as a tool.

The numbers were just too outlandish for me.

'Well, it's your money. Go for it,' I said grudgingly.

Maybe I should call Social Services again in case I got through to someone more helpful.

'And Jessie is going to run it for me. Give up that stuffy old job of his. A real job, managing big money for a big concern.'

She stood up, swung her black Chanel bag over her shoulder

and turned away from me. I couldn't respond because I wasn't expecting another blow from her after the porridge confidential. Her ability to be simultaneously vulnerable and ruthless was stunning. It stunned me into silence. When she walked, as if she had the Bible on her head, back through the restaurant, I decided to say nothing. Jessie wasn't going to give up diplomacy to work for Nancy. Was he?

Anyway, I didn't even want to think about it. I had to get Josh back.

*   *   *

The pressure lifted as I entered the British Consulate General.

I had jumped into a cab from outside Sarabeth's. The automated phone message had said the consulate was open until 12 p.m. to *assist distressed British nationals*. They dealt with these situations all the time.

I relaxed, almost smiled, as I heard British voices murmur through the reception hall. Everything worked smoothly here. I was back on home soil. And I was soon in front of a child protection expert.

Everything about Jane Bennett was comforting. She was wearing a no nonsense sage-green skirt suit. Its cylindrical descent down to her mid-calves insisted that she didn't care for the vanities of most New Yorkers. She cared about facts and her British citizens.

I didn't rush my story. I heard my measured tone. This was me at my best because I was at home with people who truly understood me, saw the world the way I did. What a relief. Why had I waited almost forty-eight hours to come here? Jessie's insistence that we didn't contact the consulate only tickled my mind. I didn't care. Once Josh was home, Jessie wouldn't mind either.

I slowly finished my story.

Jane Bennett looked at me with compassionate consideration.

'Mrs Wietzman, I understand your tremendous concern. But this isn't a case of child abduction.' She paused. 'Abduction is when a child is taken overseas by a parent or a relative. Joshua is still in the United States.'

I shook my head. 'I know, sorry, I used the term 'abduction' loosely. What I'm trying to get at is he has been taken away from me with no concern for the fact he is a British citizen. He has a British passport. And we shouldn't be subject to New York State Social Services.'

She nodded. Yes. I was clearly making sense.

'Ordinarily yes, you are right, of course, especially with your diplomatic immunity. But unfortunately, since Joshua is also an American passport holder on American soil, he is subject to New York State jurisdiction.'

'Can't you appeal?'

I didn't feel anxious because there was something about Jane Bennett that suggested she would work meticulously through all the options. She was the advisor I had been unconsciously searching for.

'No. I mean we would never directly appeal on behalf of a British national. All we could do would be to advise you to try and get a UK court order to overturn the decision of the American Social Services. But this would be difficult to get enforced in America.'

She was still comforting. Jane Bennett was sense itself.

'OK, right. So what would you advise me to do?'

Here we were. She was going to give me the answer that was unfathomable to me.

'In the circumstances, it would be worth considering our lawyers.'

I almost smiled. 'Yes of course. I had thought of that actually. The embassy lawyer, yes, I would love to speak to them.'

'Here's the list.' She moved a piece of paper on to my side of the table.

UK in the USA Foreign & Commonwealth Office.
Lawyers List for New York.

'It's just a list of names . . . ' I was slightly overwhelmed.

'No, not exactly. As you can see . . . ' She moved an un-manicured finger down the list. 'Their specialisation is listed below. See here, *General Practice*. Or this one, *International Family Law*.'

Peter Murray, an Attorney at Law on Park Avenue, I read. I was definitely daunted now. 'Do you have one you recommend?'

'Absolutely not. It clearly states at the top of this piece of paper that this list is provided by the British Consulate General to aid you in your search for a lawyer, but we accept no responsibility for their competence or probity.'

Her blandness stopped her from appearing callous.

'I totally understand,' I leant forward. 'Off the record, who would you suggest I try?'

'I cannot make any comment about any of these lawyers.'

I pushed one last time. 'Have you heard of anyone using any of these names?'

'No,' she was adamant.

Subject closed. I had been so sure that I would find confident clarity from the British system. I was deflated. I suddenly felt exhausted, and incredibly alone.

'Why don't you discuss it all with your husband?' she added, calmly.

Before meeting Jane Bennett, I had imagined that the Foreign Office was full of rule-bending chaps. Someone would call a contact in Social Services and Josh would be back home. But the consulate didn't actually do anything for their British nationals. They merely advised them what they might do. I had failed to mention to Jane Bennett that Jessie didn't want to take any action. I couldn't employ a lawyer without

Jessie being on board. Where would I get the money for an American lawyer? I could move our savings over from the UK. But we didn't have more than one and a half thousand pounds. How many hours advice would that buy me? And I couldn't spend the money in our bank account without Jessie noticing. I could call my parents. But I didn't want to. It wasn't just a question of pride. They would be devastated, worried sick.

Jane Bennett had been sitting impassively as I processed these facts. When I looked up, she gave me a warm smile.

'There is no rush for you to decide what to do, Mrs Wietzman. After all, Josh *is* with a relative.'

Three hours later, Nancy was waiting by the lockers outside Josh's classroom.

Yesterday after school, she had been waiting in the car with the driver. I had collected Josh out of the classroom, returned with Nancy to their apartment and stayed until Josh was in bed.

Now, as I arrived, she took me by the elbow again and led me gently through the heavy glass doors back into the courtyard.

'Anna dear, it's rather confusing and exhausting for Josh if you are with him every minute. He has to settle into our home on his own.'

I didn't say anything. I was terrified.

Thinking she had gained ground, she quickly added, 'Of course you must come and see him at bedtime tomorrow. That would be lovely.'

'I do want to come back with him today. I've missed him. I've been so looking forward to seeing him.' My tone was begging.

As if she couldn't hear it, Nancy continued. 'Now, I have the most wonderful little treat for you here.'

She dug out an envelope from her Chanel bag and winked at me. 'It's a gift from me to you.'

She was almost flirting with me. I opened the envelope, only to buy myself time. Four hours of treatments in the Mandarin Oriental Spa. This afternoon. She was buying me off.

I made one last pitch. 'You are so kind, Nancy. And I will definitely enjoy your offer. But I would rather delay the booking until tomorrow morning when Josh is at school, because I want to be with him this afternoon.'

She frowned quickly. And I saw the wrinkles in her lips. 'Sorry, Anna. It's not possible today. Tomorrow definitely.'

She opened the door and closed it in front of my face.

Seven

Day Three . . . without Josh.

Mary had fairy lights looped round the white painted branches in a tub to the right of her front door. She had probably strung up the lights as holiday decorations years ago but like the rest of New York had never bothered to take them down. Inside the front door was a stone statue of a nymph, which also had fairy lights on it. I hadn't noticed it the last time I had come.

I have to admit, I was looking forward to seeing Mary. It was a break from the ordeal of trying to get Josh back. She was the one person I felt I could trust. I could confide in her. I couldn't talk to my parents. How could they ever understand what had happened? Since Josh was taken, I had avoided their daily call. I was afraid that talking to them would only make me panic, and I had a vain hope that I would wait and speak to them once I had sorted everything out.

Instead, I talked to Mary about Nancy. About her cruelly dismissing my desperation to get Josh back, in Sarabeth's, and about her refusal to help me.

'She wants Josh for herself,' I insisted.

Mary's face rounded into a smile. 'Really? Why do you think she would want Josh?'

'I don't know. It's not logical, but I know it's true.'

She paused. 'We need to try hard to concentrate on separating your feelings from reality.'

'She wants to make him her own – she's dressing him in cashmere.' I closed my eyes, imagining that preppie yellow crewneck I saw him wearing yesterday.

Mary continued evenly. 'Well, a lotta rich kids in this city wear cashmere. Is this an issue for you?'

I chose to ignore her. 'Yesterday she stopped me from picking him up from school. She won't even let me put my own child to bed.'

'Have you asked her if you can stay to put him to bed?'

'Of course,' I said bitterly. I twisted my fingers into my palms. 'I am his mother.' I scanned her face desperately. 'I am his mother.'

Mary sighed sympathetically. 'Of course you are. And you are clearly a great mother.'

Any mother wants to hear those words, but particularly me at that moment.

Mary barely moved. 'Let's try and talk about you as a mother.'

But I wouldn't let it go. 'She taught him to pee sitting down, even before she took him. For God's sake, it's so emasculating.'

'Do you think so? Why is that, Anna?' Mary's face was impossible to read.

I whispered, leaning forward. 'Mary, the truth is she's trying to take over my family. I'm so scared.'

It did sound crazy, even to me.

Mary didn't look horrified. And her reaction reassured me. 'Anna, imagine the worst thing that can happen?'

I was silenced. Not because I couldn't imagine a doomsday scenario, but because I was too scared to.

Mary distracted me with her ready smile. 'Let's take a step back from the situation for a moment. Let's think about Josh. Do you think what he did was wrong?' She hadn't changed her slumped position. Her tight feet were across the stool.

Still, I sensed there was a change in her attitude to me.

'No, not wrong. That's so strong a word.' I found myself playing with my hair, imitating Jessie's one nervous tick. 'He shouldn't have done it. But they are so obsessed with controlling children here.'

Was I obsessed with not controlling Josh? God, I was getting into this therapy?

'Who's "they", Anna?'

'Everyone . . . ' I unfolded my legs and shifted forwards to qualify what I had said. 'Well, I mean, obviously, not everyone.'

Her face was eternally sunny. If I told her something terrible, would it change? I leaned forward to look at her more closely. She didn't seem to ever move in these sessions. She stayed leaning against the back of her armchair. I wondered malevolently what it would take to make her jerk forward.

'What about you?'

I heard an echo of our first session, and froze. Silence. What was I doing here?

'What do you actually feel?'

'About what?'

'Josh's behaviour.'

I was still silent, sensing this was a therapeutic trap. Was I paranoid as well as everything else?

'Once he nearly stabbed himself in the eye with a branch; he did climb on to the terrace. How do you feel about exposing him to danger?'

'It's not danger. It's life,' I scratched the side of my cheek, unable to contain my irritation.

She was silent. She waited, still the sunny, smiling face, though this was leading somewhere.

I struggled to crystallise what I thought. 'I was allowed to climb trees, build bridges. It made me adventurous.'

What had it made me?

'And you have been adventurous enough to move country and culture, right? Do you want Josh to be like you?'

'No . . . obviously. I question myself . . . ' my knees rubbed against the needlepoint, brushing against her bobbled tights. I leant forward, whispering, 'I even opened Mel Levine's book.'

I wanted some guarantees. Of what, I wasn't sure. I couldn't think about it, because I was worried whether there was a follow-on question. Not so much what it was, but when it would come. Sometimes Mary left the most unbelievably long silences, which I was expected to fill.

'Did you do that because you want Josh to succeed?'

'No!' I was horrified. 'No, Mary. I suppose I was wondering whether my parenting was right. Living here has made me doubt myself.'

I was lost in my own argument. I wasn't even sure what it was. I felt a rising panic. She didn't bale me out. Even now she was smiling . . . infuriatingly. The back of my armchair was itching against my bare legs. I tried to move them away, but only hit the stool. I pushed the armchair back a foot. Then I worried it might appear I was being defensive, and still Mary didn't hurry on. She never hurried.

As always, only her mouth moved, as she slipped in, 'And what do you think your husband feels?'

Her mention of Jessie made me feel dehydrated. His flirtation with the sausage king darted into my mind, swiftly followed by Pamela's perfection.

'For example . . . about the terrace incident?' Mary persisted.

I had to speak. 'He has a slightly more American, New Yorker approach to things.' I was stalling because I was aware I couldn't deflect her. 'About danger . . . about money . . . about Social Services.'

I felt a tightening in my neck from sitting constrained and semi-still for so long. I pulled at my neck, moved my shoulders, hoping this would force Mary to move. She was still. I waited.

'He was less American in London somehow.' I trailed off because I couldn't quite believe I was confiding in a therapist about Jessie. I felt disloyal. I wanted to say, 'How dare you invade the sanctity of my marriage uninvited.' But I had a terrible sense of defeat and disappointment. Was my lovely, perfect marriage flawed? Even discussing it was dragging me on to a landslide.

She nodded, 'Now he's back with his tribe, he can sense the possibility. Is that what you mean Anna?'

'No. I mean his co-workers here are British. He's half-British himself. His mother's English.'

My neck was definitely stiff now. I had to move. I had had enough. Mary didn't say anything. It was going to be one of those endless silent spaces. I couldn't bear it.

I conceded: 'He's aware of the big possibilities here.'

My words hung between us.

'How's tricks?' Darren, the doorman, mouthed from a distance as I dragged myself from Mary's back past ten or so brown-stones.

'Fine thanks, Darren.'

I wanted to get into my apartment, close the door and climb into bed.

'Where's Josh been?' Darren continued.

I looked quickly over to him, wondering if he knew. 'He's staying with his grandmother for a few days. On the East Side.'

Please stop talking to me.

'Oh, he must be loving that.'

I didn't saying anything. Dirk was sitting on my stoop. It was a temporary relief to see him there.

'Cumin,' he burst, as I approached.

I was blank.

'The spice in the soup, right?'

I had popped a bowl of soup out to Dirk when he was sleeping on the steps further up the block, four nights ago. The night before Josh moved to Nancy's. I was suddenly weepy and fragile at the thought of the last three days.

'Yes, sorry. It was pumpkin with cumin, butter and lemon.'

'It's the lemon I could taste.'

'Yes?' I managed.

After all that had happened, I was discussing recipes with a homeless friend. Talking to Dirk, I had always sensed here that a couple of hard-knock weeks could put you out on the same street where you grew up in an apartment. Well, that was what he had said. He had never explained exactly how he ended up homeless. I hadn't wanted to ask. Anyway, Dirk wanted the recipe. This discovery was uplifting, despite everything.

New York does that to you. One minute, you are flying with the gods of cultural diversity, social energy and the eccentric joy of it all. The next minute you are sinking, drowning – or being drowned.

*   *   *

Day Seven . . . without Josh.

As Jessie and I pulled up in a cab outside Nancy's apartment I noted, not for the first time, that it was exactly a week since I lost Josh. I had this sense of guilt and failure. The days had mounted up to seven, and I was no nearer to getting him back. I had called Peter Murray's office on Day Three. However, I couldn't get an 'initial consultation' with him for two weeks – Day Seventeen. And it would cost a thousand dollars. I didn't call another lawyer on the list because I had decided Peter Murray was the one. He dealt with family law, child custody, child abduction and the Hague Convention. Overturning Social Services' decision would be easy. In the meantime, I had transferred our savings from our account in the UK into our American account. It would take seven days to clear.

At least I was seeing Josh tonight.

Nancy's house could have been in Eaton Square. Or Cheyne Walk. It was immaculately, accurately English from the Colefax & Fowler wallpaper to the Osborne and Little curtains. However, unlike those original SW addresses, Nancy and Howard's home wasn't a house but a floor in one of the most luxurious apartment buildings in New York, 740 Park Avenue. It was a sombre but grand citadel designed by Candela & Harmon, who had designed the Empire State. Brokers mentioned Candela in their adverts because people paid a premium to live in one of his buildings. Or so Howard claimed the first time he gave us the guided tour, which included their personal wine cellar and maid's quarters. The building was impossibly grand, in keeping with the rest of Park Avenue. Nancy boasted it was 'sheathed' in limestone – her words not mine – with a hint of Art Deco in the granite entrance, only a hint because any more in the Thirties would have been in extremely bad taste. Art Deco at the time was trendy on the West Side but seen as plebeian by the gentry of Park Avenue. It was one of those buildings that was too posh to have a doorman waiting outside. An invisible team emerged through the shadows in the hallway.

There was an obvious conflict between the architectural greatness and the English pastiche interior which somehow, to me anyway, summed up Nancy.

Every time the liftman opened the door right into the 'entry hall' – as Howard called it – I was over-awed and intimidated by it. The first time we visited, the lift reached the penthouse quicker than we imagined and our puerile giggles echoed round the room. There were Howard and Nancy, the immaculate if artificial foreground.

Tonight, Nancy and Howard weren't waiting for us in their customary position. Instead, their Malay housekeeper, Sing Sing – I was never sure if that was her real name – led us towards the drawing room's double doors at the other end of the 'entry hall'. I felt nervous. I was afraid if I upset Nancy or Howard in any way, Nancy would take her revenge on my access to Josh.

Jessie's ease extended to opening the door himself. And he walked ahead of both Sing Sing and me.

'Hiyyyya, it's us.' He greeted them with a loud confidence that I had never heard in him in London.

Both their faces radiated a smile in return.

'Hey you!' Howard intimated with the jocularity of a gap-year student dressed as Santa Claus.

They were sitting on a chaise longue on either side of Josh. It was early evening. Normally, at home, he would be damp and pink from his bath, already in his pyjamas, the ones with the wide cream and red stripe, or the checked ones with the sailing boat on the top. But he was wearing a white frilly shirt, aubergine velvet waistcoat and navy knickerbockers. He looked like a late eighteenth century French aristocrat's son posing for a painting. A still life, a statue. Not my boy. It hurt so much to see him in these ridiculous, somehow demeaning clothes.

'Joshie, hello darling,' I moved quickly over, crouched in front of him, squeezed him towards me. I couldn't help saying. 'What are you wearing?'

Nancy rose up from a chaise longue without shifting any part of her spine, shoulders or neck out of perfect alignment. She was wearing an impossibly delicate cream silk dress, a slip of a thing with tiny, tiny straps, which blended in with her collarbones. It sashayed to her ankles.

'I'm dressed for drinks,' Josh stated.

'Well, you certainly are dressed up.' I pulled playfully at his waistcoat, desperate to take it off. 'You look French.'

Thankfully, he grimaced. 'What's French?'

'Someone from France.'

'Joshie! Hello darling.' Jessie hugged Josh. 'Nancy, you look fantastic,' Jessie reached forward to hug her and drew quickly back.

He scrutinised her for a brief second. I saw him take in the Spartan straps trailing over her shoulders, the delicate nature of the silk that emphasised her childlike body underneath

133

which showed the upright curve of her breasts, the prominence of her nipples, the flatness of her stomach and the narrowness of her pelvis. Nancy's body was a showcase for her wealth.

'What a fantastic dress,' he murmured.

She gave him a broad smile that disappeared into a giggle. A young man was admiring her wardrobe. Her child-sized arm reached towards his hand. 'Calvin Klein, I'm not normally a fan, but you've made me change my mind.'

Jessie had no idea what the correct response was so he nodded and turned to say hello to Howard, inevitably in his uniform blazer, checked shirt and chinos. Jessie moved beside him and into a triangular conversation with a short man with unflattering red hair and a square face, sun-red and coated with wild freckles. He had squeezed into his suit, a wrestler, stiff-necked in more formal wear.

No one seemed to think of introducing me to him.

Sing Sing returned with a silver tray of Martinis and stuffed green olives. I took one of each, before turning back to Nancy. She had replaced herself on the edge of the Louis something chaise longue, with her knees tightly crossed, her legs parallel and folded beneath the furniture as Queen Elizabeth II was doubtless taught to do in photographs and portraits. I tried to fold myself down beside her with some sort of similar decorum. I was suddenly tired. Exhausted, I couldn't make social small talk. Instead, I hugged Josh under my left arm and gulped my Martini. The drink dulled my sense of loss, the pain of being separated from him; the pain of Nancy dictating Josh's wardrobe and habits.

'Is something bothering you, Anna?' Her lips were pursed defensively, which sat a little oddly with the question, while her chilly hand seized mine.

The physical approach and concern threw me. My eyes welled. I had to blink hard to see her face at all.

'Yes of course, I desperately miss Josh,' I stated, squeezing

134

and smiling at him before gulping the last mouthful of my Martini. 'I want you back home, don't I darling?'

Sing Sing immediately moved towards me and replaced my Martini with a fresh one.

Nancy waited with a patient expectancy. And I wondered what she thought.

'Now, Josh, tell your mommy how happy you are.'

Nancy's tone was indignant and sharp.

'I got a Nintendo DS today,' he grinned, before jumping up. 'I'll show it to you.'

He ran from the room as Sing Sing went to answer the door.

I gulped half of my second Martini. Despite knowing I shouldn't criticise her, I snapped, 'Nancy, we don't let him have computer games.'

'Or guns I suppose.' She laughed.

For the first time, I saw Howard eye her with appreciative love. 'Can we join in? It sounds fun.'

I always wondered if Howard had married Nancy for her money. Only because he was a large jocular, sporty man who wouldn't, surely, fall for a skinny, refined philanthropist. But the look I saw spoke of something else, something hidden. A sexual excitement between them.

'You can,' she gave him a look, which can only be described as salacious.

Pamela walked in. Or rather her legs, wrapped in invisible sheers, forked in. She was wearing the shortest sequin sheath dress, perfect for late night clubbing, but somehow refined and purified on Pamela. Everyone danced forward to greet her. No one had mentioned to me she was coming over. I tried to see Jessie's expression, but failed. Jessie and the redhead immediately followed Howard, shifting away from the Steinway Grand to position themselves in an arc on either side of Nancy and now Pamela, who bent her impossibly perfect legs and squatted in front of Josh.

'Hello, Josh, I have heard so much about you from your Daddy.'

Josh was armed with his Nintendo DS so he only gave her a cursory acknowledgment.

Jessie stepped in. 'Josh, say hello. This is Pamela and she is working with Daddy.'

'Hello,' he said, while staring at his DS. But I didn't want to upset him by making him put it away.

Pamela moved her attentions on to me. 'Anna, I can't say how wonderful it is working with Jessie. He is fabulous.'

She gave me the widest smile before transferring it to Jessie.

He smiled back at her easily. 'It is wonderful having you at work, I have to say.'

Maybe I did read too much into this congratulatory chat. I hadn't drunk anything since Josh was taken away. Two Martinis on a stomach full of sorrow sent my head spiralling. I leant forward, turned away from Pamela, trying to focus.

'Oh hello I'm Anna, Jessie's wife,' I stated to the redhead. 'I'm sorry, we haven't been introduced in all this excitement.'

'Connor Flint,' he said, as he squeezed on to the chair beside me.

Flint's bangers. I was starting to feel unstable and sick.

'You invented sausages. How extraordinary,' I managed to say automatically. Only Jessie saw my wide eyes and exaggerated facial expressions. He knew I was faking it. His eyes flashed back furiously.

The banger magnate wasn't aware. 'That's me. I came over from Ireland to make my fortune. My ancestors landed in Baltimore.'

'How adventurous,' which was the truth, I suppose.

'Yeah, I am adventurous.' He grinned again.

Sing Sing came round with more Martinis, but no more olives. The second cocktail was already singing inside me. I reached for another. I wanted to get drunk. I heard but did not register the conversational turn.

'Yeah, I agree. The war was the right thing,' Howard said. 'We had no choice.'

I had always believed Howard and Nancy were what the papers described as 'limousine liberals'.

'They got us on our own soil. We had to get them back.' Sausage King said. 'Hunt 'em down.'

Who was this Conor Flint? Who held these views in New York? But then he was from Ohio.

I gulped my Martini and observed Jessie. We were both anti-war. We agreed utterly. Funnily enough, it was the one subject Jessie was more outspoken on than I was. He got frustrated by the argument even though we didn't know anyone who was more than lukewarm in favour of it. We had never ever come across this outrageous viewpoint.

'We had to get 'em before they got us again, the whole lot of 'em.' Sausage king repeated, as if we might have misunderstood him.

It's strange but when someone's saying something so unpleasant, their whole face seems to change. His was redder, wider, uglier than before.

I didn't saying anything.

Nancy did. She clasped her hands to the middle of her breastbone, forcing the silk to tighten over her now visible nipples. 'Oh stop it. That's quite enough cowboys and indians chat. We want to talk about something far more interesting than the war.'

She paused expectantly, before turning to look at Jessie. 'Connor, tell us about the fantastic job you're giving Jessie.'

Pamela grinned and clapped.

*　　*　　*

Day Eight . . . without Josh.

I careered down the steps leading to the Hudson River, pounding under the bridge, turning the corner, which opened up the vast vista of water, houseboats, tug boats, tankers and Washington Bridge. A hopeful, tranquil New York. It was a beautiful view of New Jersey's grey suburbia. The water was sometimes a flat grey lake, sometimes a forceful sea. Today, a sharpened HB pencil had drawn the lines of the river. A clear straight line divided the water and the bluest of skies. I felt the lightness of wearing flimsy clothes in mid-October.

But my mind was racing, caffeinated by my huge sense of loss, emptiness and loneliness. When I was away from Josh, I felt completely disconnected. Lost. I had lost him. I felt my life was out of control. Jessie's move fast-forwarded that feeling.

He would now be protecting the rights of hot dogs, not trying to negotiate some sort of stability in the world. OK. I had a dewy view of the United Nations. But then I fell in love with Jessie and he ultimately believed in the institution's ideal. It was more honourable than politics, indeed above party politics. They were working for the 'peaceful settlement of disputes' particularly in the Middle East and Afghanistan. Jessie had even been out there since we had moved to New York. The UN were the defenders of human rights, the environment warriors. Jessie had a special counter-terrorism brief which he found fascinating and obviously important. He was too junior to be shaping policy, but he was present at high level negotiations which gave him a taste of the kind of the real international power that he believed in.

There was a more cynical view, our London friends always shouted. Jessie was merely a civil servant doing the bidding of the British government, defending the national interest, be it good or bad. Maybe it really was no better than looking after Connor Flint's interests on the East Coast and his expansion into Europe. But it was more important and vital to the state of the world.

The bottom line was that talking borders with presidents and prime ministers was more alluring than talking pork fat content with Ohio farmers. Surely?

But Jessie had said yes. Right there, leaning against Nancy's Louis-fucking-armchair. He hadn't said, 'Thank you, I've got to think about it. Chat with Anna,' as he would have done because that was the way he was. The way his considered and considerate nature worked. No, not this time. He had smiled appreciatively at Nancy and Howard, grinned at Pamela and given Josh's hair a playful rub. They had all glowed back at him. And he had said an unequivocal 'yes'.

I normally would have said something right there in front of Howard, Nancy, even Connor. But I sensed Jessie had surprised himself. He got extraordinary power from breaking with his own traditions, breaking out, doing something different, being radical. In the cab home from Nancy and Howard's, I was detached from what had happened. I always felt flat after leaving Josh behind. Nothing else mattered. And I was able to ask Jessie questions about his decision as if it had nothing to do with our lives, or our life together.

'So, you're going to leave the Mission?' My matter-of-factness made me feel calm, but it acknowledged an aching gap opening between us.

He grinned, leaning forward as if to talk to the driver, even though we were going the right way, shooting through the Crosstown tunnel in the middle of Central Park. 'For $525,000 a year? Too right.'

Of course, he was doing it for the money. But I chose not to understand the power of the dollar or the importance of money. I chose to see his attraction to it as crass and ultimately, American. I had always thought that about Howard and Nancy. Their richness was unattractive. I had assumed our early jokes

139

about them were based on that assumption. But now I realised there was a large part of Jessie that wanted to be them.

'Money doesn't make you happy,' I said, with unintentional primness. I heard my mother. I heard the solid middle class stamp of my country childhood. Materialism and money was all rather vulgar. Unless it was hard-earned savings or sensible investments reaped with prudence.

Jessie no longer agreed. 'Don't be so naïve.'

I was silenced by his aggression. My mind couldn't help diverting back to Pamela.

'Money will give us a fresh start.'

'We don't need one,' I said.

Only he did, and by moving to New York I had implied I was up for it.

'How long do you think you'll do it for?' My bland question gave me back a sense of control.

Jessie raised his voice slightly. 'Two, maybe three years. I don't know. Depends on when Nancy thinks I'm ready to run the Foundation.'

He knew about her long term idea, though he had never mentioned it before. But then I had never mentioned Nancy telling me about her Foundation plans over porridge.

We had both become devious.

'Are you worried you have no experience in the Arts?' Or sausages, business or America.

He chose not to hear me and faced the National History Museum looming ahead as we reached the Central Park West traffic lights. 'I love this city. I love it here. We don't ever have to leave now.'

Had I missed out on a conversation? Did we discuss staying in New York for ever? Jessie had moved on and sensed the only way to take me with him was by complicity, by stealth, by avoiding the face-to-face, the heart to heart. Normally, we both vocalised every decision. There weren't great big

140

silences between us. I couldn't quite believe we wanted different things. I actually refused to believe it. That coloured my behaviour.

'It's great we're not going to leave. Isn't it?' Jessie said again, more to the cab driver than to me. He wanted confirmation of that fact. I wasn't going to challenge this big decision of his. I wasn't confident enough any more in my judgment, or in what I wanted. The silence between us was uneasy.

'As long as you're sure you want to leave the UN? I sense there's no going back.'

'You sound concerned. Don't be concerned for me.' His tone was that of the alpha male.

'At least we can stay in the apartment,' I said. Our apartment had been strangely comforting even without Josh.

'No, we'll have to give the apartment back. But Nancy will find us something. She is already on to it.'

I felt heavy on the seat of the cab. As if my stomach was bloated.

Jessie continued, 'She knows everyone here. She can make anything happen.'

My impotence enraged me. 'Why doesn't she get Josh back for us then?'

'Oh don't start that again.'

New Yorkers couldn't bear children reeking havoc with their real estate. All New York kids parties were held in a 'venue' – a word Josh pronounced with confidence. This Saturday afternoon birthday party was in a kid's gym on Amsterdam Avenue. As usual, all the dads and moms were there. And they were redundant to the party. They didn't drink the bottles of champagne or eat the platter loads of canapés laid on by the parents. They merely stood with their backs to the neon lit glass wall, which made the whole party visible from the street, beautifying the proceedings. Impossibly cheery girls in pony tails and loud boys repeated the formula that applied indiscriminately to every single gym venue birthday party, no matter which kid's parents had forked out a small fortune.

'OK, OK. Let's get ready for a birthday *paarty!*'

The red sweat-shirted team danced manically to the music they had put on, while shouting: 'It's Peter's birthday today. Let's give him a big shout. Happy Birthday Peter!'

Jessie and I were lost and alone waiting for Nancy to appear with Josh. I wanted to see him so desperately I felt physically sick. My hangover wasn't helping. I had run it away this morning. Now it made me fragile.

After five minutes of dancing with the frenzied entertainers, some of the children, particularly the girls in their long pale party dresses, started to wander towards their parents. Not acceptable, not part of the routine. Not spending time with your parents at birthday parties. 'Come back here'. We gonna line up. Line up. Make a train. Come here. Choo, choo.'

Josh appeared in front of Nancy, who was holding him protectively by his shoulders. He was wearing a checked shirt buttoned up to his neck, thick navy blue corduroys and navy loafers. Nothing substantially wrong with those clothes I agree. But they weren't clothes I had chosen and bought for him. They were too prim, too smart, even for an indoor gym party. Nancy was wearing obviously 'casual' clothes: black skinny trousers with silver ballerina flats.

The hostess, Jennifer, who was in a full-length silver dress, approached Nancy eagerly.

'Mrs Weitzman, so good to meet you.'

Nancy gave one of her beneficent smiles and delicately removed the white Apple bag from her black and white striped shoulder. 'A little *cadeau* for Peter.'

'Wow, you speak French.' All Jennifer's teeth came out to gush over Nancy. 'You must meet my husband Bill.'

'Hi and bye, Josh,' Jessie parroted, smiling at Josh as he

waved to us and moved away to join the birthday train. Jessie took a swig of his beer.

The train of children snailed off to the farthest side of the gym away from the street, and where the climbing wall, trampoline and other soft bright plastic equipment was kept. The parents were penned near, but not beside the gym equipment, mere spectators of their children's enjoyment. The kids were organised into neat groups and instructed how to roll on the trampoline, only twice, before queuing to climb the wall with a safety harness – obviously – and then over the inflatable coloured bricks.

Jennifer had managed to guide Nancy towards her husband without touching her. 'Bill, honey, this is Mrs Weitzman.'

Bill, a burlesque, gymed banker who always wore shorts at weekends, grinned at Nancy. 'Pete is always talking about Josh. Josh, Josh, Josh. So it's great to finally get to meet his mom.'

Jessie didn't seem to hear Bill. I stood staring at the patch of floor beneath my feet, unable to move and unable to explain.

Finally, Jennifer said gently, 'Oh, honey, Mrs Wietzman is Josh's grandma.'

'Oh, Bill,' Nancy touched his arm, 'I'm so flattered. Thank you.'

He appeared genuinely surprised. 'Oh, I refuse to believe it, you're not his mom?'

It was as if Bill wanted to torture me.

'Oh, thank you, Bill. To tell the truth, I feel like his mom. I was intimately involved in his conception – he was our IVF baby,' Nancy raised her almost invisible eyebrows higher than their usual position.

'Really?' I heard Jennifer whisper, turning to Bill. 'Gosh, you are amazing, Mrs Wietzman.'

I felt all the oxygen leave my head.

Nancy continued in an exaggerated hush. 'Anna, his real mother, couldn't get pregnant on her own.'

I sat down on the floor with my head in my hands trying to breathe.

'Josh is living with me at the moment. There have been significant problems at home, as you probably know from the school. But we're all one big family.'

'Are you all right, Anna?' I heard Jessie say, and someone say something else.

I nodded and tried desperately to find Josh's face in the crowd. The children were lined up again and trained back to the fishbowl near the street.

'The pizza's been delivered,' shouted one of the cheerleaders.

There he was. I smiled hard at Josh, even though he didn't seem to have seen me. I stood up and moved slowly in his direction.

He ran headlong towards Nancy, who did an exaggerated backward move as if he was a truck approaching. 'Careful, darling.'

'There's pizza, nanna!' Josh howled, holding Nancy's hand and pulling her in the direction of the cardboard boxes stacked up beside the low long kids' table. He jostled with his friends to find a vacant spot at the table and grabbed a juice. 'Juice box!' he called out.

Nancy stood behind him with her hands resting lightly on his shoulders. I couldn't stop staring at her hands.

Birthday tea was always pizza ordered in. I registered this obsession with pizza, but to Josh, my Americanized son, it was normal. I could already see him playing basketball after school, swearing allegiance to the Flag and eating take-out on his way home from college . . . and living with Nancy and Howard for ever. I glanced at Jessie who was leaning against the glass wall at the other end of the table, nodding at something one of the other Dads was saying, holding his half-drunk beer by the neck. Nancy moved slowly to stand next to him. She was holding a glass of champagne, but not noticeably drinking it.

Happy Birthday started in an uneven, but loud chorus. And then, the predictable: 'How old are you now?' The cheerleaders rang. 'Are you one?'

The collective shouted back, 'NOOOOOOOOO!!!!'

I noticed not only was Josh shouting back, but also Jessie and Nancy.

'Are you TWO?' one of the blonde cheerleaders was in danger of losing her voice.

'NOOOOOOOO!!!!!'

Jessie and Bill grinned at each other after cheering.

'Are you THREE?'

'NOOOOOOOOO!!!!!!'

Jessie was having a good time.

'Are you FOUR?'

Josh was having a good time.

'NOOOOOOO!!!!!!!'

'Are you FIVE?'

'YEEEEEEAAAAAAHHH.'

Eight

Day Nine . . . without Josh.

At breaking point, I finally called my parents.

'Darling! Thank goodness you called. We were beginning to worry. How are you?'

'Good,' I said.

All children do that, even when they are as grown-up as I was. Make it clear there was a problem, push for their parents' concern.

Usually Mum would pick up the signal. Today, instead, she called to my sister Sophie. 'Soph, it's Anna on the phone.'

Then she was back to me, but distracted. 'Sophie's here with all the children. They're in the kitchen making chocolate biscuits.'

I imagined my younger sister's Volvo wedged between the wall of my father's garage and the compost heap. I instinctively smiled at the thought. Even her car was endearing somehow, with its spontaneous mess and clutter inside. A strap of a bag, or coat, would be hanging out from the boot, a jumble of clothes and plastic supermarket bags visible through the back window. Its windscreen wiper stuck, or broken, half way round its usual arc of cleaning. But Sophie couldn't care less. It was what I loved and admired about her.

Sophie worked briefly for a couple of companies in a couple of jobs, but never found her role until she got married and had children: Izzy, Oscar, Sam and Sara. She was born to be a mother, relaxed and calm despite the surrounding crisis, mess and impending damage, which her four children regularly inflicted on their surroundings and each other.

Sophie's children, and the entire contents of two boxes of toys mum had accumulated, would spread across the kitchen

146

floor. Sophie had a child a year for four years. There was no plan, no grand scheme, just a series of happy mistimings. Her husband Ned was laid back. He accepted every unplanned birth with equanimity, even though they lived in a pokey three-bedroom cottage and he was working intermittently as a free-lance web designer.

I loved Sophie's lack of caution. She was never going to move to America – she wasn't adventurous in a modern way. She lived six miles away from where she grew up. But she was confident enough to accept the roller-coaster life delivers, without needing to control its every move.

Mum continued. 'Oh, she's changing Sara. How's Josh?'

'OK.' My eyes stung. I wanted to tell her. I just couldn't.

'Anna.' I imagined Sophie's long streaked hair waving over my face and then her arm brushing mine: the tight, warm circle of my family. I missed them so much.

'How's New York?' Sophie's voice was enthusiastic.

'Good. How are you?'

'You don't sound good?'

'No?' I managed.

'You sound low.' Sophie was always in tune, always sensitive.

'I'm tired, that's all.'

She was silent for a minute. 'You always wanted an adventure. Do you remember making a list of all the places you wanted to visit? You were only about nine.'

Sophie remembered all the tiny details of our childhood. I often wondered if I had amnesia.

'Did I? Was America on the list?'

'Oh yes it was.'

Mum called out, 'Along with Papua New Guinea, Antarctica, Russia, China, and Iran.'

'Maybe I need to move to Alaska,' I quipped. 'Maybe, that's the answer.'

'What's wrong, Anna?' asked Sophie.

'Nothing . . . Nothing at all.'

Having avoided telling Sophie the truth, I felt more alone and lost. I had the whole of the day, a Sunday, to get through. Nancy and Howard had insisted that they had a day trip planned for Josh. Jessie had disappeared early, keen to do a protracted run and gym session. He was determined to run the New York marathon in November. It was ridiculous in the circumstances for him to start training now. But I was relieved. I couldn't talk to him about Josh. There were so many gaps in the story between us now. I still hadn't told him about going to the consulate, contacting Peter Murray about an initial consultation, or about diverting our savings to New York. I kept worrying that Jessie might get a cash point statement and wonder why we had extra money in our account.

So I was desperate to talk to Mary. I left a rambling message on her mobile not expecting a reply on Sunday morning. But she called me twenty minutes later and suggested I came over.

I had two lattes wedged into a cardboard cup-holder in one hand, and a white cake box containing two fresh fruit tarts in the other. I had walked up a few blocks to the French-styled Café Lalo, an Upper West Side institution famous for its cakes, teas and the fact Meg Ryan met Tom Hanks there in *You've Got Mail*. I was standing outside Mary's basement door. I didn't want to eat cake or anything else for that matter. But I bought them as a token towards establishing greater intimacy.

Mary let me in, enthusiastic about my takeaway deserts. She opened the box, exclaimed enthusiastically and started on one of the tarts. She took another bite as if she needed to eat it quickly. We smiled easily at each other. I felt this bond. She was my surrogate American mother who, unlike my own, could relate to what was happening to me in New York.

Her smile was open, without even a therapeutic glint. 'How's your husband doing, Anna?'

'He's busy at work, enjoying it all.'

The spectre of his resignation flashed like a demonstration banner. But I didn't have an image of Jessie.

Mary waited.

'He loves it here. And he's involved with interesting security issues at the moment.'

She waited. I hated the hole in the conversation and had the urge to fill it with fluffy chat. But I stubbornly remained silent.

Her expression hadn't changed. There were crumbs around her mouth, which she didn't even try to wipe away.

I leant impulsively forward. 'Actually, Jessie is going to resign from his job.'

'Why do you think he is doing that?'

'Nancy's got him a job with this sausage magnate. The idea is he will then work for her new Foundation. It's all down to bloody Nancy of course.'

'Do you think he is choosing to do it of his own free will?'

I chose to ignore her.

'Nancy is completely taking over my life.'

'Do you think she is actually doing this?'

'Yes, yes I do. Yesterday, someone asked if she was Josh's mother. It's mad, it's crazy. And she is making me crazy.'

'Are you saying you think that Nancy claimed to be Josh's mother? Why do you think she would say that?'

'She didn't actually say that. Well, I mean, she didn't deny it quickly either.'

'Do you think this is something you might have imagined? Or her lack of denial was a reality?'

I felt panic, like nausea, in my mouth and grabbed at Mary's arm. She instinctively moved back. 'You think I'm imagining it, don't you, Mary?'

'I am not thinking any such thing, Anna. I am not the

subject here. As I have said before, I am only interested in what you think.' How could she stay so still for so long? 'Do you think that you are imagining these things, Anna?'

'I'm not. Really I'm not.' Suddenly, convincing her became everything. Only she was never going to let me know what she thought. How could I do it? All I could do was physically hold on to her. 'You have to believe me, Mary. I'm losing my mind.'

I was losing my mind. It wasn't a phrase. It was the physical state of one's mind slipping away. I was losing any sense of reality. What was reality? My daily life was insane. There was no normality.

My eyes were rigid, forcing her to acquiesce. 'I'm not imagining what Nancy is up to.'

But Mary never would.

'Anna, why do you think you are loosing your mind?'

Without thinking, I fell across the needlepoint stool and flung my arms around her neck.

I wrapped my duvet under my body on both sides. I lifted my feet to tuck the end under my toes. I was wrapped like a mummy. The way Josh liked to have his duvet moulded around him. My face was underneath it too. I lay there still, and empty of any constructive thoughts for the first time in the last nine days. I had given up. All I wanted to do was sleep. I comforted myself that I could do this today. There was nothing I could do on a Sunday. I could hide away. I was going to stay in bed all afternoon. I closed my eyes, but of course I couldn't sleep.

*   *   *

Day Ten . . . without Josh.

The weather abruptly changed. As if determined by some fixed date in the diary, sun-soaked Fall lost its warmth. November 2nd was dramatically cold. Not English chilly but downright 'butt-burning'. I opened the door on to my stoop to find Sharon squeezing her arms around her black down duvet coat. I barely hid my annoyance. I had to make a list today and every day. Things I could do, at least three, to try and get Josh. I mustn't loose it. I must focus. The last thing I wanted was Sharon wasting my time.

'Hi, Anna, how are you?'

'Fine.' I hoped my minimal reply would drive her to a quick hello and goodbye.

I was depressed after lying in bed all yesterday afternoon and into the evening. I had only just raised myself this morning with guilt. I had to fight to get Josh back. How could I give up like this?

'Well, I am worried right now,' Sharon continued as if she couldn't see my expression. 'I am a concerned kind of person. And I'm feelin' really concerned right now.'

She paused. And I paused, sensing there was a PS.

'Do you want to have a breakfast or something?'

I didn't want breakfast; I didn't want to be with Sharon, or anyone else. I had thought I would try and prepare some notes for my consultation with Peter Murray, but I realised I had nothing to prepare. I knew so little about the situation, despite what felt like an extraordinary effort on my part. And I still had seven days to wait until my meeting with Peter Murray.

Sharon would at least distract me. I reluctantly walked with her to an empty stylish brunch place on 72nd Street. We were seemingly their first customers of the day. As she sat down on the aubergine banquette, I was aware she appeared to have physically shrunk since I last saw her on our terrace. Her lime polo neck flopped away from her tan skin. She appeared listless. Her hair, which usually waved elegantly on to her shoulders, hung down and her fringe frizzed up. There was something tired about her. The waiter hovered. Her order didn't come tumbling out. She hesitated, blank in the face of the menu she clearly knew well.

I fought the hysteria I could hear inside myself. I had lost my son. How I could just sit here and peruse a brunch menu? I should be grabbing Josh out of school, racing in a cab to JFK and home to my parents in Kent.

He wrote down my order, but Sharon was still undecided.

She looked up at me for help. 'What shall I have?'

Her uncharacteristic hesitation stopped me from answering.

The waiter lurched into action. 'We have a good mushroom soup today or eggs Benedict? Fresh bread and jams.'

'A latte.'

Sharon put down the menu. She was inert, as if her manic energy had been sucked out.

Another silent minute passed.

I had to ask, 'Sharon, are you OK? You don't seem yourself.'

The idea of her relatively petty worries reassured me; or rather, the fact I could ask her about them showed I was still connected to some sort of reality. I had a friend; I was sharing confidences. Well, she would share. I couldn't imagine telling Sharon what I felt about Nancy and Josh. But then I didn't need to; I had Mary to talk to.

I expected my concern would snap her back into her concerns. The conversation would fly.

She focused on her napkin, which she started folding into a fan. 'The thing is, I have always tried so hard to hold everything together. I am the one who does that, you know.'

I lent forward, 'Are you talking about Nathan and his therapy?'

'Nathan,' she paused, 'Nathan.'

She sounded bitter. She finished fanning the napkin and let go of it.

'How he has let me down . . . '

'What has he done? What happened?' I was at a loss to imagine how this 'gifted' but practically silent child could cause offence.

152

Her eyes were watering. 'I can't tell a soul. I can't even bear to think about it. It'll break me.'

She stopped talking as the waiter brought our coffees. She held both sides of her coffee cup as if she was warming her hands, and focused on a distant spot on the furthest wall. 'I suppose, I can tell you. You don't care about Josh's education. I mean, you have so much bigger issues with him right now.'

Her brutality struck me, but I stopped myself from saying anything. It was my fault. What was I doing sitting here with Sharon when I needed to get Josh back? Was I that desperate for human interaction?

'Anyway, you have Nancy to get you into any school you want.'

I laughed. Her bluntness was almost endearing. Except it reminded me how alone I was in New York. Nancy knew that. I didn't know anyone or anything. She could take my child and I couldn't get him back. What was I going to do?

'Nathan.' She stopped, gulping repeatedly, as if a baton of carrot was wedged in her throat. 'Every single one has rejected him.'

She couldn't look at me.

'Are you talking about schools?' I sighed. I didn't want to discuss education with Sharon. It was so trivial compared with Josh's freedom.

'All twelve. They have all rejected him.'

Her eyes were wide and scared. I leaned forward, tentatively touching her hands which were clasping the coffee cup.

Automatically I stated, 'Surely Mona can make a few calls? I mean she's the education consultant.'

'Monica. Monica,' Sharon shrilled, as if the name brought her back to life. 'She has so let us down. She promised she'd smooth the way; she advised us which schools to apply to. She guaranteed results. Guaranteed results!' She was glaring at me. Her hands pressed into the tablecloth. 'All she can say is he's not ready. He's too young. He didn't communicate in the interviews.'

'Well,' I murmured, thinking Monica sounded sensible. 'He is young for his years. And he is a quiet child.'

Sharon's green eyes flashed fierce. 'All gifted children are quiet. He is more mature than his peers. I expected them to be able to see that.'

I shifted slightly. I wanted to help Sharon but I realised I could easily become her target. 'Well, it's difficult to tell he's gifted.'

I busied myself with my omelette.

'They can tell.'

'Maybe Monica can call them back.'

'I have called her and called her.' Sharon's eyes were now soft and vulnerable. 'She has stopped calling me back.' Sharon lurched forward and squeezed my forearm for emphasis. 'I was hoping you could call her. I mean, you are totally ignorant about New York education. I appreciate that. But tell her I need to talk to her. It's vital. This is my son's life we are talking about. I am begging you to get her to understand. She has to take my calls.'

She was crying. But I didn't think this guru would even accept my calls. 'I don't know what help I can be.'

She bit at her lip and wiped her eyes with her napkin. Then she passed me a card, which was already on the table. The writing was in a handwritten font.

Monica Clements.

Manhattan Private School Advisor.

The competition knows what it takes to get their child into the right school.

monicaclements@yourchild.com/ 646 292 5622

Sharon squeezed my arm again. 'I want you to call her right now.'

What could I say? I was damned either way. I imagined an answering machine; I imagined a haughty girl acting as a filter to those without twelve thousand dollars spare. What I didn't imagine was the educational guru of New York would answer her own phone.

'Monica Clements.'

It was farcical. But I was staring at Sharon's face wrought with distress. This wasn't farcical, for her. And strangely, I felt sympathy. I knew what it felt like to be cornered, damned.

'Good morning, Monica. We haven't met before. I'm Anna Wietzman.'

Sharon moved off the banquette and took the chair right next to me.

'Hi. I'm acquainted with a Nancy Wietzman, but I don't expect you're related.'

It always came back to Nancy.

'Well, if she lives on the Upper East Side and is married to a Howard, then I am. She's my stepmother-in-law.'

'Haahhh, the wicked stepmother-in-law,' she gave a warm throaty laugh. 'Nancy Wietzman, whatta girl!'

This gave me confidence. And made me warm to her.

'So what can I do for you?'

Sharon was gesticulating madly as if Monica was about to hang up.

'Well, I'm sure my son Josh could do with your help airlifting him into the UN school,' I said, trying to make light conversation.

Sharon whispered in my phone-less ear. 'You've got to tell her how brilliant he is.'

'But I'm not calling about me. No, it's about my friend, Sharon Rosenbaum's son, Nathan.'

'I cannot talk about my client's son.'

I moved my chair back, praying Sharon hadn't heard her.

'Oh I understand that. But Sharon Rosenbaum has specifically asked me to call you.'

'She needs to call me directly.'

'Well, I believe she has tried. She is very worried and concerned that Nathan hasn't got into a single school after their and your efforts, not to mention a vast sum of money.' I spoke in one long sentence to get it out.

Sharon got a notebook out. She wrote hurriedly. 'He IS gifted. He should have got into EVERY school. She has to MAKE them take him.'

'What was your name again, Wietzman?'

'Anna.'

'OK, Anna,' she sounded as if she was drawing on a cigarette. 'You sound like a kind of sane woman. Unlike these rabid parents I deal with.'

I stood up. Sharon stood up too. While the waiter hurried over with the bill.

'Yes,' I murmured, hoping Sharon hadn't heard her.

'This is the situation. Her son is socially autistic. He is unable to communicate because he's been pressure-cooked. He's uptight, and therefore is seen by the schools as difficult to teach, a poor member of class because he won't make friends easily. He is a loner and he is socially immature.'

She breathed in sharply. I was sure she was smoking.

'And your friend, unfortunately, is unable to see this. She imagines he is gifted because she wants him to be gifted. But he isn't. Well, he may be at a later date, but he's an ordinary kid. No, actually, he is not an ordinary kid because he does not play or hang out like an ordinary kid. He isn't ready to go to Kindergarten. He needs another year with more time in the Park, and some play dates. Then hopefully he'll do OK next year.'

Sharon was waving the page at me again.

'Yes I do understand. It would be extremely kind if you could explain this to Sharon.'

'Sweetheart. You obviously don't know this woman very well. I did explain all this to her. But I'm not a therapist. I advise couples about the range of educational options and schools. And I make introductions. Period.'

'She is finding this very difficult.'

Sharon's face contorted.

I ploughed on. 'She believes he's gifted.'

That was it.

Sharon shouted loud enough for Monica to hear every word. 'He is gifted. Oh, for God's sake what is that woman saying?'

'Oh Jesus! She's not on the line is she?'

'No, no,' I said hastily.

'Listen hon . . . If she tells her husband, and they come and see me together, I will talk to them. But otherwise I can't do anything for her.'

'That would be great.' I gesticulated to Sharon, 'Isaac and Sharon will come and see you. When is a good time?'

Sharon grabbed her notebook off the table.

Monica sighed, 'Well, what about I come to them tomorrow evening, seven o'clock?'

'Not Isaac,' Sharon scribbled.

'It'll only be Sharon.'

'No way. Listen. My last word. I am being so patient here. She has to tell her husband the truth. When she has done this, we can talk. OK. You call me back Anna.'

The phone went dead.

I turned to her. 'You haven't told Isaac?'

'NO. NO. Of course I haven't.'

'Why not?'

'Because she is not telling the truth. He is gifted. He is. She's getting at my Nathan because she has not done what she promised.'

'Shouldn't you tell Isaac?' I ventured quietly.

'How can I tell him? We spent twelve thousand dollars on Monica and another thousand on applications.'

'It's one of those things. He's too young. Next year he'll be fine.'

'I can't tell Isaac. I can't.'

She was sobbing. I didn't have the energy to make her see the truth. Despite our distance, Sharon's inability to talk to Isaac made me feel a renewed closeness to Jessie. There was nothing like other people's marital problems to give you strength.

'I can't.'

Her head was flat on to the table. I stroked her hair. 'It's not that bad. God, it's only money. Believe me, you haven't lost your son.'

But Sharon was inconsolable.

*   *   *

Day Eleven . . . without Josh.

Nancy, Jessie and I were sitting on the tiniest of children's chairs opposite Josh's teachers, also sitting on the tiniest of children's chairs. There was a tiny children's table between us on which there was 'Josh's Portfolio'. Jessie had planned to go into work a little late so that we could come to the parent conference together. Nancy had invited herself. She had called me yesterday evening to announce it. I had immediately voiced my objection to Jessie.

'Anna,' he had said, as if I was too stupid to get the salient point, 'Nancy is looking after Josh at the moment. She needs to be involved.'

'It is a parent conference Jessie,' I had returned, without much vehemence.

I was too exhausted to fight Jessie or Nancy. I hated the fact she was going to be there. But what could I do? I was cornered.

Fredericka and Finela, Josh's form teachers, had allotted forty minutes to each child. There was no school today because of the conferences. We had already been here over fifteen minutes and had yet to get beyond discussing Josh's friendships.

'There was this special moment when Josh hugged Zachary.'

As if by magic, a digital photo of the hug was produced by the teacher's assistant, Finela. Jessie and I leaned even further forward than we had to anyway. Sure enough, Josh was hugging Zachary, a child with some 'issues'. Actually, he had a mother and father who worked full time, and commanded his baby-sitter to take him from after-school class to class. He didn't get home until six-thirty in the evening.

'Mmm,' said Jessie, dismissing the photo, 'so how's Josh actually doing?'

Finela checked the teacher, Fredericka.

'Well. What we would love to do is look at Josh through the eyes of our core curriculum values. So first of all, we would like to look at him as a 'thinker'.

'Fabulous,' cooed Nancy, 'what a great approach.'

Fredericka and Finela gave her an appreciative smile. They had barely considered me since we arrived. I sensed, post the biting incident, I was still in the bracket of unfit mother.

'Well, he is a big thinker. We love his stories about England and his travels. And he always entertains his buddies.'

'Great. Fantastic.' Jessie rolled impatiently round on his chair.

Fredericka and Finela gave Nancy visionary smiles. 'He thinks about his environment.'

'He definitely cares about big issues. All our family do,' Nancy stated.

I had to add something. 'Yes, well the other day he said God can't be everywhere. Not in New York and London, all at the same time.'

I laughed in a way you do about a story about your own child. Fredericka and Finela briefly narrowed their lips. I was sure I could see Nancy's lips widen into an amused smile.

We were in competition with each other. And I was losing.

Fredericka and Finela quickly recovered. 'So,' Fredericka managed to smile a little wider. 'He is obviously a great communicator. Often his photo ends up on the "communication" train.'

We all obligingly considered a painted train, with carriages behind it, hanging on the wall. Each carriage was marked with either: 'thinker', 'communicator', 'inquirer', 'risk-taker' or 'caring individual'. Josh's grinning photo was stuck to the communicator train.

Finela tossed her long straight hair over both shoulders. 'I remember when he told us how you make lemonade Nancy.'

'It's a family recipe. Josh loves my lemonade.'

I felt this thudding pain in my head. Was she being insidious? Was I imagining it?

'He told us. And he was, like, able to share all the tiny details with his class.'

'Yeah, it was fantastic,' Fredericka added.

Jessie was kicking his foot up against an imaginary ball situated somewhere in the air above the table.

But I was relieved. It was hardly a chore to hear lovely, if kitsch, stories about Josh.

'He's able to communicate well with everyone, his teachers and his peers.'

'Fantastic,' Nancy repeated. 'Of course, I absolutely love our little boy.'

I wasn't imagining it. She was taking over Josh. How could I stop her?

I smiled, and met them half way, 'He does love talking.'

'Anyway, moving along, I'm sure you've got so much on today Mrs Wietzman,' Fredericka said, looking at Nancy, not me.

'Yeah,' Jessie raised his head. 'Nancy, you are so good to come.'

I frowned at him, but he didn't look in my direction.

'OK. Let's move on to look at Josh as an "inquirer".'

Finela piped in. 'One day he saw the pipes above our head and started asking about the heating and how it all worked. He was exploring his environment in a really neat way. And we were so happy about that.'

'He loves pipes and equipment, all that sort of thing,' I added to participate, and because I felt they were being very sweet, even if it was insubstantial and rather pointless.

'Yeah he does,' said Finela.

'Please feel free to come back on anything. We're in a two-way process here,' said Fredericka.

'It is all very clear,' Nancy smiled appreciatively, glancing in Jessie's direction to prompt him to add something. But he was absorbed, texting.

'Moving on to another one of our carriages on the train . . . ' They both giggled.

'Risk-taker.' Fredericka paused to let the word sink in. She briefly eyed Finela, who was no longer smiling.

'This is a value that sometimes Josh takes a little too far.'

Fredericka glanced at Finela, who nodded. 'Let me explain. He sometimes struggles with transition times. Say we're transitioning from 'Dot Time' to 'Carpet Time', he finds it very difficult to contain himself.'

'Contain himself?' Jessie pushed slightly aggressively I thought, bearing in mind we were on tiny chairs in our child's classroom with their docile teachers.

'Not in a bathroom way, no,' she said hastily. 'He has a tendency to take from the high energy in the classroom. He then finds it difficult to be more structured.'

'He's badly behaved?' I asked.

'I mean, if I ask him to sit down, he will. But he grabs his friends, lies on top of them, pulls at them. He is not aware of their feelings.'

'Tell him not to do that. I'll also talk to him,' I insisted.

'We have talked to him. We have explained to him that his behaviour is not safe and also not kind to our friends. But he has not been able to make the 'caring individual' train.'

'The caring train?' Jessie was being rude. He was texting and looking down as he talked to Fredericka.

Nancy touched Jessie and piped up before I could. 'It is an issue, Jessie. He hasn't got on the caring train.'

'There is an immediate solution,' Fredericka interjected reassuringly.

I waited.

'Linda, our child expert, has been observing the class as she always does.' She paused. 'And she feels Josh would benefit from a weighted vest.'

'Sorry?' I said

'It's a vest, which provides proprioceptive input to a body that is having a hard time calming down. It provides weight to a body that is in constant motion,' said Nancy calmly.

'You're planning to weigh Josh down?'

'Not all morning,' Finela injected.

'Yeah, a few hours a day when he's having a hard time sitting down.'

'That sounds sensible,' said Nancy. 'He is a bouncy child.'

I ignored her. 'I'm sorry, but adding unnatural weight to his body sounds extremely punitive and not something I imagine is even used on abnormal children these days.'

'Excuse me?' Fredericka frowned. 'I am not saying Josh is abnormal. No, I am not.'

'Anna, she most definitely did not say Josh is abnormal. Please, don't exaggerate.'

Nancy's voice was like a ringing in my ears.

'Though the circumstances are difficult,' added Fredericka.

162

'Anna is still in therapy, though it will help resolve the issues soon,' Nancy said.

I wanted to shake her, slap her and force her to leave. But I needed to sort this out. Josh was never wearing a weighted jacket.

'I am bizarrely, as you know, having therapy because Josh, a normal boy, bit a child at school and you and Nancy, in your wisdom, involved Social Services.'

'I am outraged at that suggestion,' Nancy's voice wobbled dramatically.

'Anna, apologise to Nancy.'

'No I won't, Jessie.' I was shrill, close to scream. I had to focus. I breathed sharply in. 'Weighting him down is an outrageous suggestion. It's your job to discipline him. Not torture him.'

Jessie put a hand on my arm and managed this very relaxed sounding laugh. 'Yes, I am sorry, we're not happy with that.'

His words calmed me. We were a couple, a force together. Even Nancy would listen to him.

'No, we're not,' I echoed.

'How else are you planning to ground him?' Nancy asked. 'And in the circumstances Anna, you are not able to help him, are you?'

'Oh yes, yes I can, Nancy. I can help him by insisting he isn't weighted down.'

'It does work, believe me.' Fredericka insisted.

'We definitely support you.'

'Excuse me, Nancy, but I don't. And I am his mother. It sounds outrageous to me.'

You are outrageous, Nancy. You are all outrageous.

Fredericka and Nancy exchanged sympathetic glances. 'Anna, I am gonna set up a meeting for you with Linda. We're so keen for you to be comfortable with it.'

'I am not comfortable with it. At all. Sorry. I never will be. No one would be. Would they?'

I turned to Jessie desperately for support. This was insane. He could see that.

But Jessie held up his hand as if he was adjudicating between us, not one of the parties. Diplomat, not Father. 'Anna will obviously meet Linda. It's always good to discuss things.'

Fredericka was clearly grateful. Her smile spread back across her face. 'Well, if there's nothing else. Have a great day and thank you for coming in.'

'Thank you,' Nancy insisted, delicately holding out her fragile fingers to be squeezed by Finela and Fredericka. 'We'll work on Anna.'

I got up and left, without saying goodbye to any of them. Nancy got into her car having kissed Jessie on both cheeks, but ignored me.

I paced in an arc round the corner from the school building, waiting for Jessie to get off the phone. My heart was pounding. How was I going to stop them using the weighted jacket? They must need my permission. Surely?

'Pamela, I'll be there in thirty minutes. This tedious meeting at school over ran.'

'It's Victorian. My God!' I paced in an arc in front of Jessie.

'Sweetheart, don't worry about it.' He squeezed my shoulders.

'I am terrified. We cannot let them do that to our child. Nancy was encouraging them.'

Tears burst out.

'Oh, Anna, come on, Nancy was just being open-minded.'

His impatience struck me.

He relented slightly. 'It'll resolve itself. Go and see Linda anyway. No point antagonising them.'

'Antagonising them? They're antagonising us. Nancy's antagonising us and controlling our child.'

'Stop this, Anna. Poor Nancy is trying to help.' His tone was sharp, but he softened it slightly before adding, 'Listen, I've got to get in for Pamela, or she will have nothing to do.' Did he look slightly sheepish? Or was I paranoid about Pamela?

I raced on. 'You don't fancy her do you?' What sentient man wouldn't? Only a man in love.

I know it was gauche, hardly the approach to elicit the truth. And I got the answer I deserved.

'Anna . . . God, don't be so ridiculous. She is obviously a beautiful young woman, but what an insane suggestion.'

He didn't add I am too madly in love with you. The only person I fancy is you. He didn't reassure me. He deflected my delusions, nothing more.

Nine

When I got back from school, I got a phone call from Sharon's husband, Isaac.

'I am sorry to call you like this . . . '

Like what, I wondered.

'But Sharon confides in you.'

I was exhausted at the thought of Sharon's distress. I couldn't get involved again. I had too much worry and stress to deal with myself. The vision of the weighted jacket was tearing me apart, especially as I had barely slept the night before. I had finally settled in Josh's bed. I could still smell him in the bed. The smell of baby shampoo mixed with an earthy kind of park smell. I had wrapped his single duvet round myself like he did.

'She finally told me everything.'

I tried not to let my sigh filter down the phone. 'He's young,' I said, more wearily than I intended.

'Yeah, you're right. Immature, closeted and over-analysed.' His brusque, succinct words surprised me. He was less beige than Jessie and I had thought.

Jessie. My mind drifted away from Isaac. Jessie was finishing work at the UN tomorrow and starting with the Hot Dog King two days later. It hurt. But not as much as missing Josh.

'We've got to figure out Nathan.'

'Mmm.'

'It doesn't help him that Sharon and I have split up.'

Why hadn't Sharon told me yesterday? Then I felt guilty. She had called me four or five times yesterday afternoon. And I had ignored her.

'She has lost her mind. Being a mom has been too much for her.'

I didn't say anything. I felt this deep resentment that both of them used me as an additional therapist. I felt aggressively selfish.

'Listen, I ought to go.'

Without changing his tone, Isaac continued, 'Last night she tried to end it all.'

'Sorry? Are you saying . . . she tried to kill herself?'

I didn't think I could react to anything any more. It was almost a relief. A jolt, a reminder of the fundamentals: life and death. I was still alive.

'She's OK. She's gonna to be fine.' He was trying to reassure himself.

The last eleven days, I had been in a dark place. I have to admit I had even dreamed of being dead, or seriously ill in hospital to escape Nancy and everything going on. But I had never considered killing myself. My sense of self-preservation, and of Josh's, lifted me. It mattered. Even if it was all I had.

Isaac hurried on. 'She's gotten you involved in the whole Monica thing. That was too much. I am so sorry. But I would so appreciate it if you would visit her.'

I was silent. Scared. What would I feel like, visiting Sharon? I would feel more desperate. The thought terrified me.

'Honestly, you are the most kind, decent, loyal friend she has.'

I felt so guilty. Of course I had to see her.

I was outside New York Presbyterian. Only six months before I was admitted to Emergency. I was a different person back then. This time, I didn't notice what the other people were wearing. This time, I glided straight into the main entrance.

I was clutching an extravagant bunch of flowers from the proper florist on Amsterdam. Lilies, roses, tulips, anemones in the gentlest of whites and pinks edged with dark green foliage, cellophane and a knot of raffia strings. They were like a shield in front of my chest. My black former work trouser suit helped me feel on top of the situation.

I was nervous about seeing a suicidal Sharon. My only friend in New York, who had reached the edge, leaned right over and had been snatched back by the soles of her shoes. Would I almost envy her? At least she had the courage to jump.

Sharon was sharing a room, but Isaac had explained there was currently no one in the next-door bed. I paused for a moment before knocking on the door. She didn't answer. I waited for an appropriate moment and then opened the door about a foot and squeezed the right side of my body round it. Sharon was supported on a triangle of pillows reading a magazine. The room was lit with flowers. Sharon appeared angelic in her white hospital gown, drenched in the setting light which soaked through the ceiling to floor windows. Her face was pale but surprisingly 'normal'. What I mean is, she was herself. Her hair blow-dried and she was wearing mascara.

Her changed mental state was only noticeable when she spoke.

'Anna,' she said deliberately.

It was as if attempted suicide, or the drugs they had subsequently put her on, had slowed her right down. She was calmer and happier than I had ever seen her.

I emerged fully into the room. 'Sharon. How are you?'

She flicked a hand towards me. I saw the thick patch taped to the inside of her wrist.

She saw me look at it. Her new self-awareness and sensitivity was unnerving, especially when I wanted to hide away from any questions. I was scared of questions.

I was already regretting this visit.

She held both wrists out, and upside down. 'Look what a mess I made.' She laughed.

What can you say to someone who has had enough? 'You

have so much to live for Sharon'. Knowing how I would feel about sympathy, I couldn't give Sharon platitudes. I shrugged my shoulders. I almost told her that I had dreamed of doing the same thing. But I didn't. Probably because I was a coward.

I sat limply in the armchair beside her and put the flowers gently down on her legs. 'Well, I brought you flowers. But you already have such beautiful ones.'

'Yeah. Guilty flowers. From Isaac.'

Mine were guilty flowers too. I refolded my legs nervously. 'I'm so sorry I never called you back yesterday. I will always feel utterly terrible about that.'

'No, I understand,' she waved a hand again.

I could only see her wrists.

'I shouldn't have gotten you involved.'

'No, honestly, you didn't. Please don't worry, at all.'

I had done nothing to help Sharon. I couldn't help her. I couldn't even help myself.

She turned to stretch for a bottle of Evian sitting on the cupboard beside her bed. I leaped up to get it for her, happy to have a role to play. After refilling her glass and passing it back, I sat down again. She didn't need to confide in me about Nathan's therapists and school applications any more. I wondered if this visit would descend into silence.

She took several thirsty gulps of water. I was conscious of my fixed, closed smile.

'It is relaxing being here. I haven't had time out since I had Nathan.'

I was grateful for the chance. 'Did you spend long in hospital with him afterwards?'

'It was kinda complicated. I had an emergency c-section. He had stopped breathing.'

'How scary . . . How is Nathan? And Rachel?'

'They're fine. Isaac's been given compassionate leave. Weirdly, they seem happier without me.'

169

Her face fell for the first time.

I gingerly touched the top of her hand. 'That's not true. They're probably just being brave.'

There was a directness to her reply, but her green eyes didn't flash.

'I like being institutionalised. It's a rest,' she repeated.

Her hospital therapist had probably planted that idea in her head. But it was clearly comforting.

'Isaac is so worried about you. He does care, you know.'

She gave a half smile. 'Which is a good sign, right?'

She was no longer dependent on my answer.

'Anyway, how are you, Anna?'

The glazed eyes refocused on my face.

I was struck by the question. 'OK.'

I was OK. That was the most striking thing about the whole miserable situation. I was OK. I wasn't going to kill myself.

She gave a quiet laugh. 'You don't look it.'

I laughed. 'You look better than me.'

That was weird. We both laughed. I nearly told her. I nearly confided in Sharon about the weighted jacket. But I was afraid I would drag her down further.

She pointed one hand towards slightly mismatched flowers – white lilies, pink gerberas and blue rhododendrons. 'They are from Monica. Two-faced bitch.'

We both laughed again.

Her eyes drifted from Monica's free-for-all to Isaac's carefully stated vases. 'His biggest guilt is that he doesn't love me any more.'

I moved forward quickly. 'That's not true. I'm sure he does. You've got to give it time.'

Her eyes trailed back up to mine. 'Time isn't gonna change anything.' She gave a slow but sure smile. 'But that's OK.'

*　　*　　*

That evening, after I had seen Sharon, Jessie looped up our inner stairs two at a time, obviously excited. He was triumphantly brandishing a copy of the *New Yorker*. I couldn't see the cover as he was holding it open on a page titled: EXTREME CHOCOLATE. Beneath the title was a photo of two men in bandanas, floppy cotton shirts and dirty jeans. They were in the Amazon.

'This article has changed my life.'

'Has it?' I didn't care about features in the *New Yorker* right now, or anything. I was constantly thinking about what Peter Murray was going to say and do. When I was feeling positive, I was sure he would resolve it immediately, a simple phone call to the right person. Now though, I felt worried. Worried he might not be able to resolve it, worried about the weighted jacket issue. Worried . . .

'This man, this druggie hippy, who started making his own chocolate has sold his company for seventeen million dollars. Can you believe that?'

'Yes, I can actually. There are so many entrepreneurs here,' I said automatically, slumped down on our sofa. The stress of trying to get Josh back was exhausting.

'Exactly. Twenty-three million in 2005.' Jessie was standing in front of me with a rolled *New Yorker*.

'Sorry?'

How could he think about things like this when Josh was living with Nancy? I had given up railing against his disinterest. All that mattered was my meeting with Peter Murray.

'The number of entrepreneurs rose to 23 million in 2005. It's probably higher now.'

'Is it the chocolate, or the entrepreneur that has changed your life?'

'Both.' He stood pointing the end of the magazine at me. 'You see, what's extraordinary about this story is it takes in all elements intellectual and international. I had no idea that one of the rarest kinds of chocolate is the South American Porcelana, or that the hottest chocolate beans around are Madagascan. Did you?'

'No.'

Jessie was absorbed. 'This is a story of discovery, of geography, of history, of adventure. It's real, it's out there in the world.'

He stood up above me.

'I am so glad I'm not a spectator any more, but a participator – a player on the world stage. Not an office boy trying to make sense of the mess other people have made of the world. And I can't wait. I will actually be out there.'

'What's working for Connor Flint, the ultimate in corporate America, got to do with entrepreneurial chocolate?' I couldn't help saying.

'He was that entrepreneur once. He built his business from scratch into a global phenomena. I'm part of that big dream.'

'His big dream. Not yours . . . or ours.'

I thought of Josh. As I always did, all the time. Everything came back to him.

Jessie sensed it. He didn't answer.

It was soon clear the reality of working for Connor Flint was very different. His offices were up in White Plains, a forty-minute drive into New York State. Jessie had bought a second-hand silver Toyota Highlander, a big SUV. We had lost our tax-free status, diplomatic car, plates and paid-for parking space. New York had become infinitely more expensive. So it was the Highlander. I was sad about Jessie going off to join the out of town commuters on the Henry Hudson Highway. That he was no longer looking across the East River and a panorama of dazzling glass buildings. He was no longer living and breathing the dream that was New York.

*   *   *

Day Fourteen . . . without Josh.

Jessie left the apartment extremely early with a contained enthusiasm. I also felt his annoyance. There was his tired wife in her drab pyjamas, worrying about her son and the weighted jacket, when the wide world, the market of 300 million Americans, was waiting for him.

There is a harshness to successful people. They feel they see the blunt truth about the world and the way it works. They are impatient with the dreamy and their tinted glaze. Jessie had been trying to play that part.

He left without saying goodbye. I heard the emptiness in the flat before I realised he had gone. He came home more relaxed, but less enthusiastic than I imagined. It was quarter to nine. It took him over an hour and a half to get back. There was a translucence to his skin and a green tinge under his eyes.

'Did you love it?' I said, as soon as he had taken his winter layers and boots off.

He wandered into the kitchen and opened a bottle of wine, pouring us both a large glass.

'It's interesting. No, it is.' He was convincing himself, not me. 'It's a different environment.'

'Did you meet some interesting people?'

'I spent most of the day with Connor. We went for lunch.'

'Was it delicious?'

'We went to a local diner.'

I heard his disappointment. His multi-millionaire ate fast food. That wasn't Jessie's American dream.

'We talked about my role as ambassador. When there are any policy issues in Washington or New York or any other place, I'll be airlifted to help deal with them.'

'Are there a lot of policy issues with sausages?'

I raised my eyebrows.

Jessie rubbed his forehead. 'There are. There are. Foreign imports are a huge threat; there are issues about cheaper

173

competitors undercutting with pork substitutes; it would be good to get policy change on water content; there's packaging wars. No. There's a lot to do.'

He didn't seem excited about it. He kept rubbing his forehead upwards into his hairline and then twisting the front of hair into a tight knot.

I sipped at my wine. 'Are you a little disappointed?'

He shifted himself to bring his other leg on to the sofa. 'No,' he insisted, 'it's only day one.'

The next night of Day Fifteen without Josh, Jessie was visibly disappointed. He studiously avoided discussing the details of his day. Instead, he polished off a couple of bottles of wine in front of a film.

I was almost delighted. Here was my answer, finally, after days of trying to find a way of getting Josh back. If Jessie hated the job, left and returned to the UN, he would no longer be useful to Nancy or, crucially, beholden to her. I sensed that if he asked, she would call Social Services.

'Listen,' I said in my most persuasive, gentle voice. 'To be honest, the job sounds disastrous. Maybe you should think about leaving? I'm sure you would be able to slip back into the UN.'

'No. I'm not going to quit. I made this move with my eyes open. This was my decision. And I'm not going to leave. I promised Connor I'd do at least two years. And I will do that. Then I can run Nancy's Foundation.' He was desperately worried. 'And it will give me time to decide what I want to do. Nancy's happy to back any idea I have.'

'Really?' I couldn't help my bitterness. 'What about the idea of getting your son back?'

He sighed torturously. 'Anna, we can't keep going over this.'

I snapped. 'You make it sound like our finances, or flight details. I'll keep nagging about getting Josh back. Sorry it's getting tedious.'

He turned away from me. 'Nancy will help.'

'You keep saying that. When? When will she help?'

'I don't know. But she will. I'm sure.'

His confidence didn't reassure me any more. What did he know? He had gone to work for Connor Flint. Then he was surprised that he hated it.

*   *   *

Day Sixteen . . . without Josh.

I met Linda the school's 'child expert'. She couldn't have been less like Mary. She was an earnest looking woman with a dark straight fringe which reached down to her round black glasses. She was pale, especially for a New Yorker, as the city's Siberian wind was beginning to give a raw flush to everyone's skin. Linda must have taken a cab or driven everywhere because she was unnaturally white. She had the sort of whisper of a voice that made you want to shout back at her. But I didn't. I was desperate to show that I was a calm normal mother with a calm normal child.

She seemed to be convinced.

Until she said, 'I am so glad we've had this chat. Because we both know Josh is a great little boy. We both want to make sure that his behaviour doesn't affect his opportunities in life.'

'His behaviour isn't bad. He's not violent or abusive,' I heard my scratchy insistence, and tried to calm and lower my voice. 'Well he bit a child, but he was frustrated, having a particularly bad day. He hasn't done it again. He's four. He's a little boy. He needs to be simply told "No".'

'Well, the teachers have done that. But they can't keep doing that.'

'Why not? That's their role.'

She recoiled slightly.

I added, hastily, 'What I mean is, I'm sure it's a phase he's going through.'

'I understand what you're saying,' she smiled, placating me. 'I do.'

I wasn't sure she did. But what could I say to convince her? I was useless. I couldn't even help my own child.

I nodded.

'Thank you for your time, Anna. This has been valuable for me, and I hope for you.'

I smiled and thanked her back. I didn't understand what the conclusion was. Keen not to press any advantage I might have gained, I didn't ask. Or maybe I was too fearful of the answer.

To distract myself, I went shopping. It was a strange thing to do. But I had got to the point where I was so worried all the time I couldn't find an answer. I was spiralling and direction-less, in every sense. Totally lost.

So I started in Bloomingdales. The problem with depart-ment stores is you need to be even more confident as a shopper. They are so large, so full of choice but with so many possible errors waiting to be made. I wasn't working any more. I wasn't spending my own money. As a very occasional shopper, each purchase was crucial, its significance so huge I was paralysed by indecision.

I covered every floor. I walked and walked until it was clear that in the state I was in, I needed to get out. I was on to Lexington Avenue, which wasn't friendly either. I started walking briskly towards Madison Avenue, a designer paradise, and one expensive boutique after another. In this street of all streets there was a Zara, a Spanish chain store. Its familiarity cheered me up just as I was beginning to think about Josh and the bloody weighted jacket, and maybe I should start heading back across town to school. I was always afraid that if I arrived on time, Nancy might have left early with Josh.

All chain stores are the same yet simultaneously location

specific. Zara was no exception. This Upper East Side branch had less in it, wider aisles, more polished glass and more eye-catching collared pieces. The women shopping in the store had multiple designer bags puddling around their feet. They were in Zara for that cheap, cheap extra; to feel good about a bargain when they had already spent a small fortune. A couple of beige Armani model types in their twenties were getting guidance from their mothers, which seemed very strange as I had been independent of my mother's sartorial taste since I was a teenager.

I half-heartedly considered a yellow printed silk top, which was seventy-eight dollars. I saw a tall dark girl out of the corner of my eye looking at a fantastic wide collared red jacket. That was the sort of thing I should buy. She held it up, not against her but out in front of her. She scrutinised the stitching, the cut, and the material. She put it down and picked up the same jacket in pale beige. She was wearing a white polo neck and white tight jeans and an exquisite cream, fur-lined Puffa. I hastily returned the yellow silk top. I watched the girl. I was curious as to whether the beige jacket was good enough. It was flung over her arm as she moved round the racks.

As I realised who she was, I saw who was with her.

Nancy wrinkled her nose at the jacket and swung an off white silk-looking shirt on to Pamela's arm. She didn't hold it up for inspection this time, but against her, for Nancy's approval, which she immediately got.

Nancy and Pamela. Nancy, Pamela's shopping godmother. I felt total dismay. Pamela was doing a little shopping with Nancy on Madison Avenue. What was Nancy up to? Did she always shop with Pamela? For a mad moment, I imagined she might be grooming Pamela to be Jessie's second wife. I suddenly couldn't see them. I hadn't got the stamina or confidence. I quickly turned from them towards the shop doors. Without thinking, I walked downstairs into the menswear.

After three assistants asked if they could help me, I started picking out clothes with Jessie in mind. I spent fifteen minutes choosing a pair of trousers and a jumper for him and then realised I only had an hour to get back across town to meet Josh before Nancy took him home. I paid for Jessie's clothes and quickly ran up the stairs without looking properly into the store. I turned sharp right towards the door.

How likely was it that two rich women would stay that long in Zara? How many items could possibly be acceptable to buy? It was about thoroughness. I realise that now. Nancy and Pamela covered all the racks and all the possibilities in every store they visited.

Pamela recognised me. How unlikely was that. But when fate's falling against you that's what happens.

'Anna! Anna! Nancy, it's Anna, Jessie's wife.'

I kept moving. I pulled open the heavy glass doors, bumping the security guard with the metal handle, I was so frantic to get away. I hoped Pamela would assume I hadn't heard her call, or that it wasn't me. And I would be out. I had the door wide open as Pamela reached me. She gently, gingerly touched my arm. I had to turn round. I felt every centimetre of my tense face as I took in her immaculate tan, newly acquired since I met her at the opera.

'Pamela . . . hello. Have you been away?' I focused intensely on her face to avoid looking at Nancy.

'Oh yes, Turks and Caicos. I needed a break after I finished working with Jessie.'

I didn't look even vaguely in Nancy's direction.

'Hello, Anna. You look dreadful. Are you all right?'

I expected to be brushed over. This cruel comment was worse. Then I wondered whether I was misinterpreting her.

'I'm fine. I'm on my way to school shortly,' I said, automatically.

Nancy didn't offer to drive me there, even though she would

178

be waiting in the car when I came out of the classroom. She stood behind Pamela. One hand on one of her shoulders, proprietorial somehow. Pamela couldn't see Nancy's expression, so the face she made must have been for my benefit alone. She gave a slow smile that ended up as what could only be described as a wicked grin.

I got there early and picked up a coffee and bagel around the corner from the school. It was an odd thing to have for a late lunch. Anyway, I don't remember letting go of my coffee and bag, with the cream cheese and salmon on the wholemeal, sesame seed bagel, the plastic cup hitting the pavement, the bagel oozing, the curdled mess of coffee and cheese. My Ugg boots hot, wet and stained. It all must have happened. I have to include these details. But I didn't experience them at the time. All I remember vividly was my face pressed against the cold glass, like Josh had often done from the other side. His nose squashed, his lips wide as he breathed on the glass. My face was hard against the window now, as if I was trying to push through it, into the classroom. I pressed my hands so hard against the glass that if it had been an old-fashioned English school window, I would probably have cracked it. But this was New York. This window was reinforced, safe and secure.

Josh was sitting at one of the huddle of tables. I remember exactly what he was doing. I found myself absorbed by it. He had a purple pencil in his left hand and he was outlining a third person on a white piece of paper. It was obviously a person to me – I was his mother – a straight line for the body, a straight line for the two arms, no feet and a round head with big eyes, no nose and a wide smile. His pencil grip was ginger and the 'person' he had drawn was barely visible, faint purple lines. Josh was focused, seemingly happy and calm, which made everything worse somehow.

When he had finished, I was forced into the situation. My

eyes were drawn back to the tan waistcoat. I couldn't actually see the weights. But they were there inside the jacket, pressing him down.

I moved along the glass, afraid to loose sight of him for one moment. When I finally had to move round to the door near the 'cubbies', I rushed. The door was locked. Security, to keep bad people out, which only enraged me more. The bad people were inside. I frantically waved at the classroom assistant in the other class. She came smiling to the door, only realising as she opened it that I was furious. I didn't even thank her. I ran into Josh's classroom. Several children turned to look at me.

One child, I don't remember who, said, 'It's your mom, Josh.'

Josh then screamed, 'Mummy.'

He didn't get up. He couldn't. If it had been possible, my anger would have mounted. But I barely had the physical body to contain what I already felt.

Fredericka moved towards me. 'Hello, Anna.' She didn't immediately look worried.

But I ignored her. I moved in one action to Josh's little table. 'Josh, Josh.'

I fumbled with the buttons of the jacket. I couldn't seem to open them. And I couldn't wait. I started pulling the two sides of the waistcoat apart. The buttonholes started to give way. Two buttons released.

'Mummy, that's hurting.'

I stopped and fumbled with the top button. It opened. I don't remember it but either I took the jacket off, or Josh did.

'Anna, can we step outside for a moment?' Fredericka said quietly.

I ignored her. Finally Josh was free. It was all I cared about in that moment. Everything I cared about.

I grabbed his hand.

'Where are we going Mummy?'

'We're going home. We're both going home.'

Ten

The cab ride was comforting, the way it predictably jolted and creaked through every set of lights from the cars and vans we trailed eastwards, out of the city. I asked the driver to put the heating on. It blasted through the black radiator, pumping the cab with warmth.

Josh was excited. He loved journeys, probably because I did. That whiff of possibility, adventure and magic. Though this time, I wasn't remotely excited. I kept nervously unzipping the inner pocket of my handbag and digging out our passports, which we had picked up from home. I fingered their plum covers, repeatedly opening them up to double-check neither had expired.

I called my mother from the cab and told her about the weighted jacket. She uncharacteristically shouted down the phone. She was so upset that she had got my father on the line from his study upstairs. I was right to bring Josh back. Mum was not a person to suggest a woman abandon her husband. She had been a dedicated, traditional wife for thirty years.

'Come home for a break. Josh can run around in the fields and you can get some perspective.'

Mum was wise. And they were wise words. I was never going back to live in New York. Romney Marsh would be my home again, at least for a while. I had been so keen to escape parochial Kent, and now I longed to be back there. I imagined the fairy lights my father twisted around the vast horse chestnut tree in the middle of our square drive every year, on the first day of December.

The air in New York was as freezing as it was on Romney Marsh. I wanted to get there as fast as possible. I was already imagining my frustration on the plane. I would be unable to sleep until we landed in England. Like most of my generation, I had never been particularly patriotic. Now I couldn't wait to see the monopoly-sized terraces as we circled over Heathrow. I couldn't wait to be back in my own country.

As I had run out of the classroom with Josh, Fredericka insisted that Nancy had given her permission for the jacket to be used. She was Josh's temporary guardian, Fredericka had said defensively. Not any longer. The weighted jacket was Nancy's last victory over me. I knew what she was doing now. Any doubt was gone. Nancy was behind everything. I was sure of it.

I hadn't risked packing or going to Nancy's to get Josh's things. Jessie was at Flint Sausages; I found our passports and escaped. I tried not to think how my rapid departure would affect our marriage. Or think about Jessie. I had to get Josh home to England. That was all that mattered.

We didn't have airline tickets. But that didn't worry me. We could fly with Virgin, British Airways, American Airlines or Aer Lingus. The list was endless and even included Air India. One of them would be able to get us out of here quickly.

We bought tickets at the Virgin Airlines information desk for a flight leaving in four hours, VS04. It was only as I paid with a credit card that Josh asked why we didn't have any luggage.

'We didn't know we were leaving so suddenly.'

'What does that mean?' Josh gave me a penetrating stare.

A cab ride away from Nancy and the school, he had dropped his Americanisms and shifted back to being my perceptive, endearing boy.

'We are going to stay with Grannie and Grandpa. It's an impulse. Do you know what that means? It's without any planning or luggage.'

'Because school put me in a weighted jacket?' His bright eyes were piercing, shrewd.

Or was I choosing to imagine it.

'Yes, partly because of that,' I paused, thinking how to explain everything to him. I always tried to be honest. 'And because Mummy hates not living with you. I love you too much to do that.'

'Why isn't Daddy coming?'

'He will. I'm sure. Soon.'

Was I confident of that? Would he join us? If it was a choice between me and New York and Flint Sausages, who would win? I wasn't sure any more.

I did the self-service check-in. We headed through the first straightforward luggage security. My handbag went through the X-ray machine, along with Josh's school bag. And we were through, into the elongated departure lounge. There was no decent shop in JFK but plenty of places to get food. But I didn't stop there. I wanted to get through the more complicated and jammed final security and passport control and on to our gate. There was a bar beside it, and I planned to treat Josh to a burger, fries and ice cream, in honour of us leaving New York. A woman, stuffed into her uniform with her badge wedged on the upward curve of her breasts, was checking passports and boarding passes before the torturously long circular queue for the final security check. There was an American family with three kids behind us. I handed her our documents. She gave them a cursory inspection and nodded us silently through.

Josh was slouching a few feet away against the window of a shop just beside us. I called him over. The American family airlifted their pick n' mix of backpacks and wheelie pink and green suitcases and pushed forward.

'Mam, I need to look at those again.' Despite the 'mam', she sounded coolly assertive.

The American family pressed close to our backs.

'Does this kid have the permission of his dad to travel?'

183

The husband and wife glanced at each other.

'Of course,' I lied instinctively. 'We are just going to stay with my parents in England for a few weeks holiday.'

She eyed Josh's passport photo for a few long minutes. I felt nervous but ultimately confident. Children can travel without both parents present. There was nothing wrong. She was a job's worth. It was fine.

Josh piped up. 'Daddy's coming later.'

She didn't seem to be listening to him.

The wife behind us murmured, 'He's so cute.'

I smiled gratefully at her, reassured somehow.

I tried another tack with the security guard. 'I am so sorry, I need to get my son to the gate, he is hungry.'

I caught the eyes of the husband and wife again, rolling my eyes as if to say, what a hassle, airline travel.

Without saying anything, the security guard motioned me to the side of the long queue that was now forming behind us.

'Wait here.' She moved away from us and unclipped a radio from her waist.

I couldn't hear what she said into it.

'What's happening, mummy?'

'I don't know darling.' I managed a smile and squeezed his hand a little too tightly.

A few minutes later, another security guard appeared from inside the security gate and took her place checking passports.

She spoke into the radio again.

'Oh, they are probably checking your passport. It's OK.'

It was OK. We were British citizens returning home.

Her thick thighs brushed against each other, as she shifted back over to us. 'Mam, I'm afraid this kid can't travel.'

The couple behind whispered to each other, in that exaggerated, loud New York kind of way. 'Do you think she's kidnapping that cute kid? Oh my god, it's just like the Sean Chapman case.'

'Honey, Sean Chapman's mom ran off with him to Brazil. This woman's not Brazilian.'

The couple's conversation only made me panic. I raised my voice the way New Yorkers did to assert their authority in the land where customer was king. 'Excuse me? Of course he can. He's a British citizen. He has every right to return to the UK.'

The wife wasn't even pretending to whisper. 'Honey, I can tell it's one of those kidnapping cases.'

The officer repeated herself impassively. 'No, mam. He is not able to travel. He is a citizen of the United States of America. His temporary American guardian has specifically refused permission for him to travel. We have a note on the system.'

I was angry now. 'Don't be ridiculous. This is absurd. You are not telling me his stepmother decides whether he leaves the country or not? I am his mother.'

She was solidly resolute. Her expression didn't change. She saw angry New Yorkers every day. My paltry wrath wasn't going to move her.

'I don't know who she is, mam, but the kid can't travel.'

'Thank God,' said the woman behind.

'Mummy . . . ' Josh was extremely anxious. 'What's happening? Are you leaving me?'

'No,' I said squeezing his hand. I was going to talk myself to the other side of the security barrier. 'I need to speak to someone more senior.'

'They will tell you what I have just told you.'

'I don't care! I want to speak to someone more senior before I call my embassy.'

Of course, it was an idle threat. We weren't covered by diplomatic immunity any more. The embassy would probably just give me advice . . . yet again.

'Go back to his dad,' the woman behind cried, 'it's wrong what you are doing.'

185

I didn't want to go anywhere with the security guard. And I certainly didn't want to move back through the departure hall. Not backwards. I was going forwards. I was getting out of here. Whatever . . .

'Couldn't they come here? I don't want to miss our flight.'

I know. Mary would say I needed to separate my feelings from reality, but my only thought was if I persisted maybe, maybe, I would be on VS04 waiting to see those Monopoly terraces through the fog. My country!

My phone rang. I imagined it was Jessie. I almost shuddered. What had happened to me?

'You are not going without me, are you Mummy?' Josh was getting worried. I hated seeing him nervous and insecure.

'Of course not, Joshie. We're both flying to London.'

We were. I still had to believe it.

A big broad man in a uniform approached us. I was about to speak. I coughed slightly. Ready.

'I'm going to have to accompany you out of the airport.'

'I have just bought two full price airline tickets to fly. I have my boarding passes . . . ' I paused.

He didn't react. 'You need to take up that issue with the air carrier. As I said, you have to accompany me out of the airport.'

I crumbled. 'I just . . . please I want to take my son home.'

*   *   *

I was defeated, battered, broken, angry, upset, even violent. But Josh was sitting beside me in the cab. His minute hand enclosed in mine, his clear eyes searching my face for answers. I wasn't going to let him down. I wasn't going to be crushed by Nancy. I wasn't going to let her cage us both up. I was going to fight her.

We got out of the cab at 20th Precinct, that grey concrete-and-brick rectangle; that flagpole on the roof, holding up that

186

flag. Only I wasn't intimidated today. I didn't need Eliot to translate the New York-isms. I had been driven into sounding like them.

'Hello. I need to report my stepmother-in-law. She is trying to steal my son.'

Of course, the officer on the other side of the counter didn't look surprised. Stolen identity, credit card fraud, stepmothers stealing kids; nothing could shock her. This was just another confession. This was New York, the home of the confessional.

She politely asked me to take a seat. Staring at the vast drinks machine on the admin side of the reception desk, I felt safe and comfortable. It was like being on an NHS ward having had Josh. We all have our routines, but none are as fixed as state institutions. There was something about the semblance of order that appealed to me.

A policeman, thankfully not the brute with red hair from my previous run in with the NYPD, but a jocular, skinny black man with an easy smile spoke quietly to the policewoman, while never taking his eyes off me. Finally, he came round the counter towards us.

'You need to chat. I'm Jim and I deal with domestic issues.'

I sighed. I was relieved. We followed him into a room that was as nondescript as the main hallway. It was cold and I shivered slightly.

He had a pad and pen and a tape machine, which he turned on.

'So you are?'

'Anna Wietzman.'

'And you live in London?'

'No. No I live here, 153 West 82d Street, between Columbus and Amsterdam.'

The thought made me suddenly sad. I had lost so much in the last six months.

'Right. And who is this?' He ruffled Josh's hair.

187

'I'm Josh. This is my mom.' He was straight back into his Americanisms.

I didn't want Josh to hear what I was going to say. But I was too terrified of leaving him alone in the reception.

The gentle skinny policeman spoke. 'What seems to be the situation?'

I breathed in. 'I know it sounds mad, but my American stepmother has systematically taken over my life. She has just stopped me from going on holiday to England with my son to see my parents. We are trapped here. Josh, why don't you go and sit over there?'

There was a chair and table in the corner of the room.

'Hey you, take this pen and paper and make me a picture of Central Park.'

I smiled gratefully at the policeman as Josh moved.

I whispered. 'She has custody of my son. She involved Social Services, on behalf of his school, because he bit another child. I mean my son is actually British – even though my husband has dual nationality. But we've lived in England all our lives . . . until a few months ago.'

I was having trouble ordering my thoughts.

'I need a lawyer. I mean, I have found one, but I haven't seen him yet. Not until Day Seventeen. Which is actually tomorrow. But it will be too late.'

'Whoa. Hey . . . let's start at the beginning. Right . . . take me back there.'

'Aah, I suppose the very beginning was when the NYPD came on to our balcony because Josh was out there late at night. Josh was jet-lagged,' I rattled on, afraid of him stopping me before I got everything out. 'Anyway, the balcony is completely safe – it's walled. They imagined we had locked him out there, which, of course, we hadn't done.'

The policeman didn't react. I was pitifully grateful.

'Anyway, Nancy seized on this as a sign of my irresponsibility.

When school said Josh had bitten another child, she called Social Services. They made her his temporary guardian and she took custody of him. I've got to satisfactorily complete a course of therapy. Which I've been doing, but I don't know whether this means I can still have Josh back.'

The policeman let me speak. He was making notes and his Dictaphone was whirring, but I sensed he was really listening to me.

'Then she persuaded my husband to leave his job, well, his career in the British Foreign Office, to work for Connor Flint.'

'The Hot Dog King.'

'Yes.' His enthusiasm stopped me. 'What was I going to say?'

'You were talking about your husband.'

'Yes, she wants him to run her Foundation.'

'Right.'

'You see,' I sensed he understood. 'She's controlling everything: she has my son living with her, she found my therapist, the school, the Social Services, my husband's job, even my travel out of the country.'

'OK, I get it. She's a scheming bitch,' he laughed warmly and leaned forward, twirling his pen through his fingers. 'There are so many of them in this city. Jesus. But I fail to see what she has done that makes this a police issue?'

'Taken my son. It's not right,' I continued hastily, 'or legal. Surely? He and I had done nothing wrong, nothing worthy of involving Social Services.'

The policeman spoke gently. 'But it was their decision, not hers, to have custody of your son?'

I struggled for words. 'I feel she put them up to it, persuaded them somehow.'

I was close to the truth.

'Right, but I'm afraid that isn't illegal. I'm sorry.'

'Please. Look at Josh. He should be with me.'

I was crying now.

He touched my arm gently. 'He's a great kid. And you clearly both love each other very much. I want to help you. But I can't.'

I was crying uncontrollably now. Josh came and stood beside me and held my hand. I looked at Josh and then at the policeman.

'Please, you have got to help me. I have no one else I can turn to. I want to get back to England with my son. Please help me.'

'Hey, buddy. Don't worry. Your mom's just a little sad right now.'

He stood up. 'You know, you should take this up with Social Services.'

'They don't even seem to know about it.'

'I'm so sorry I can't help.'

I built a Lego tower with Josh. It steadily rose in red, blue and yellow. The Lego pieces fanned around me as I sat on the wooden boards, my legs tucked beneath my knees. They were protective somehow. My mind felt blank, empty. I should have taken Josh back to Nancy's. But I simply couldn't. We had nowhere else to go.

The phone rang. It echoed round Josh's large empty play-room. I wondered if it was Jessie, or Nancy. I didn't care. It finally rang off. A few seconds later, it started ringing again.

'Hello,' I said, flatly carrying the handset back through the playroom.

I sat back down carefully in the gap between the Lego pieces, into the space where I was before. It gave me a certain strength.

'Hi, is that Anna?' said an uncertain voice.

'Yes it is,' I said dully. 'Who is this?'

'Isaac Rosenbaum. You know, Sharon's husband.'

'Of course.' I didn't try and engage with him. My tone implied, 'What can I do for you? Why are you bothering me?'

'Is this a bad time?'

I laughed high-pitched, mad even to myself. 'Yes, yes, you could say that. A bad, bad time. A fucking bad time.'

Josh didn't look up, but focused more intently on his Lego. Isaac went silent. 'Sorry, look I better go.'

'No, I'm sorry. I'm having a terrible day. Not just a terrible day even; a terrible, terrible time.' My eyes watered.

'Sharon's . . . Sharon.'

I waited, not really listening, imagining he was looking for the therapeutic expression for her mental state.

'Sharon killed herself this morning.'

I didn't say anything. I could barely breathe. I watched the door of the playroom nervously. Like there might be someone lurking behind it listening, knowing what was happening to me. Isaac took my silence for shock. He carried on, grateful for my reaction. 'I brought her a cake yesterday. You know one of those great Russian cheesecakes from Café Lalu. I brought in a sharp knife with it – the biscuit base is always a little tough. I didn't think. I didn't think. I . . . she was so calm, relaxed . . . more than usual. I thought . . . I thought everything was all right.'

He was crying down the phone. I had no urge to cry with him. I could only think how Sharon's death brought me closer to mine. Don't we all do that? A large part of our grief is our selfish fear of our own fragile mortality.

'She slit her throat right across.'

Even the detail didn't shock me. I held the phone slightly further away from my ear and sat back down by the tower. I smiled at Josh as he showed me how much higher he had made it. I started picking out more red bricks for his next floor.

'Why did she want to end it?' Isaac continued through his

191

sobs. 'Why? She had everything: two great kids, a husband. We were good. How could she think otherwise?'

'Happiness is all in the mind,' I intoned, not to Isaac but to myself.

'Sorry?' Bizarrely, he burped.

'Is anyone happy here? I am totally unhappy.'

Isaac was finally silent. He was shocked, hurt, by my self-obsessed comment. My social good sense would have stopped me making such an inappropriate statement even a few days ago. But now, why should I care? Josh and I were trapped in this crazy city.

Half an hour later I opened the door. Jessie and Harry Finkle-mann were standing on the stoop. Harry Finklemann was no longer genial. I noticed this in passing, but I focused on asking Jessie a trivial question to buy myself time.

'Hello. Have you forgotten your key?' My voice sounded strained and false, even to me.

'Anna.' Jessie said, with visible disappointment.

'What?' I stalled.

I had been waiting for him, or Nancy to turn up. She would know that I had tried to escape. And she would punish me. Of course she would.

'How could you do it?' Jessie scrunched up his eyes as if to say it is unbelievable . . . you are unbelievable.

'Let's all step inside,' Harry Finkelmann insisted.

We squashed into the tiny square space before the next flight of stairs.

'Where is Josh?' Jessie blurted.

'He's upstairs of course. I should have called you, but the school had put him in the weighted jacket without our per-mission. I shouldn't have just gone to the airport. But it was appalling. I was in shock.' I reached out to touch his hand.

He moved it suddenly out of my grasp.

Why was I apologising? I was scared by the presence of Harry Finklemann. What did it mean? What were they going to do?

'You kidnapped Josh,' Jessie sounded disgusted, as if I was abusive or a murderer.

'Don't be ridiculous. He's my son. I just wanted a break from all this craziness. That's all.'

I remembered the woman at the airport. Did it look like I was kidnapping Josh? Was I kidnapping him? I had no intention of returning to America. But he was my son.

'Now . . . ' Harry Finklemann sounded as if he was adjudicating between two kids. 'I don't want to witness a scene because everything is plain to see. We all have to be very straight about this.'

Jessie pretended to focus out of the window at the trees.

'Anna, you kidnapped Josh. Social Services and, more importantly, the United States of America takes a dim view of that kind of action, especially in light of the Sean Chapman case.'

Oh my God. They were as mad as that woman at the airport. I was terrified. Even Jessie had turned against me.

I could only witter my defence. 'I just wanted to go home for a holiday with my parents. It's hardly illegal.'

I gave a dry laugh into the silence.

'You tried to take Josh out of the country without Jessie's permission.'

'But it wasn't Jessie who stopped me, was it? Nancy's behind all this. She has put an embargo on me leaving the country. She is the devil and you both are subservient to her.'

Jessie turned slightly to look at Harry Finklemann. They exchanged looks, which declared that I was mentally unstable. I suddenly panicked – they were going to have me committed. Declared mad, when I was sane.

'It's very simple, Anna. I don't want to argue with you. From this point onwards, you are denied access to Josh.'

'No. No, no you bastard.' I grabbed at Jessie, pulling at his jacket. 'Who are you? How could you do this to me? Nancy put you up to this. God!'

He shrugged me off, the way you might do to a dog when you are allergic to animals.

Josh came to the top of the stairs. 'Mummy? Are you all right.'

His voice tore through me. I understood those mothers who would rather kill themselves and their child than live without them. It was an unbearable moment. I stared at Josh, wanting to tattoo his face on to mine. I ran upstairs. Jessie and Harry Finklemann were close behind me, but I got there before them. I wrapped my arms around Josh and held on tight. I dug my own finger nails into my palms to stop them from taking him. I couldn't hear him or them any more. I couldn't hear at all.

When I came round, the apartment was darkly silhouetted and empty. I was stiff and sore and lying at the top of the stairs, alone.

Eleven

The background was a burning orange, like ginger highlights set alight. The torso was beginning to emerge. An aggressively muscular body with arms splayed wide like a crucifixion. The body was sweating, oiled, dark brown. The face and head were hairless. The eyes were black and looking to the right of the painting. It was a body under strain, a body on the edge. I crouched down, looking at it sloping from the brick wall to the floor of Josh's playroom. The first canvas I had worked on over three months. I turned it carefully round to face the wall.

I used to recount the days without Josh as I waited for Mary to open the door. I wasn't counting any more. What was the point?

I never turned up for my 10.30 a.m. 'initial consultation' with Peter Murray on Day Seventeen. There had only been a day to go until the consultation. But then I saw Josh sunk by kilos of lead. In that moment, everything had changed. How could I see Peter Murray and explain away the accusation that I had kidnapped my son? Or that I was now denied access to him? I was afraid, my badge of hope, Peter Murray, would turn on me and make things worse.

I was physically overwhelmed, even tugging off my Ugg boots. Mary took off her shoes. I crossed my legs and folded my feet underneath me. I wanted to tuck up close into myself. I was exhausted. I couldn't pick my feet up. I was weighed down with lethargy.

She looked surprised, even slightly worried. 'What has been happening, Anna?'

I gazed at her, not thinking about the question, but whether I wanted to answer.

'Anna?'

'What's not happened to me? What's not happened to me, Mary?' I jabbed my finger at her.

Normally she slumped backwards, with her hippie dress splayed like a dying rose around her chair. But she sat forward, leaning towards me with almost visible concern.

'The school *weighted* Josh down with this jacket,' I banged the needlepoint stool with both my hands as if to demonstrate the heaviness of the injustice.

'Proprioceptive input,' she said softly. 'Not usually recommended for a normal child.'

'You think so?' I said.

Finally, her opinion when it mattered most. She was a voice in the wilderness.

'Nancy made it happen.' I couldn't hear my voice. Had I actually spoken?

'Why do you think that Nancy would want Josh weighted down?'

I was silent. Of course I didn't know. I just smelled it. It was feral.

She finally added, 'What does your husband think?'

'What does Jessie think? What *does* Jessie think?'

'Anna, do you think you can concentrate on answering the question?' She said it evenly.

My eyes roamed vaguely. 'I only wanted to go home. Take Josh home. But they wouldn't let us fly. Nancy wouldn't let us fly.' I paused. 'Of course, I didn't want to leave Jessie. But I didn't want to stay here. I wanted to take Josh home.'

'Were you planning on separating from your husband?' she asked solemnly.

I rounded on her. 'No. I just told you, I didn't have a choice. We are trapped here.'

Her head dipped closer to mine. She had heard the venom in my voice. I was reassured by her reaction. At least I had Mary on my side.

196

'Why do you say that sweetie?'

She had never called me that before. She touched my hand gently.

'They said I tried to kidnap Josh. Now he is gone completely. Completely gone. I can't see him; I'm not allowed to see him.'

I surveyed my hands. They were dry and worn. I had this sudden urge to bite them, bite deep into them.

'What are you actually saying Anna? Are you being denied access to Josh? Is that what you are saying?'

She sounded anxious. Or perhaps I was imagining it. I didn't know.

'I hid outside school this morning,' I remembered, almost eagerly. 'I was right down behind the wall in the courtyard. *They* couldn't see me,' I focused on the watercolour print in a gilt frame above Mary's head. 'I saw Josh. I could see him. I wanted him to know I was there. But I couldn't think how to get his attention without getting everyone else's.'

Tears poured out. They weren't even mine any more.

'I was on my knees. I was low, low down and I stuck my head round the brick. But he couldn't see me.'

'Anna, I am so very sorry,' Mary was genuinely disturbed. 'Why don't you consult a lawyer?'

'Oh, I've tried. I have tried. Peter Murray, attorney at law. Sounds good, doesn't he?'

She just nodded.

'Oh, Mary, I almost forgot to tell you. My friend Sharon . . . '

Mary was now leaning forward with her knees wide apart to allow her to reach both my hands and squeeze them. 'Anna, we are trying to talk about you and your access to Josh.'

'You know the one, who tried to commit suicide?'

'Yes, Anna, you mentioned her.'

'She slit her throat.' I ran my left index finger along my neck. I could imagine it being welcome. At last, a real sensation.

197

And, in that moment, the reality which must have bludgeoned Sharon finally hit me.

'Things got so bad for her, she actually killed herself,' I smiled at Mary, almost brightly.

Mary interjected, 'I am very sorry for your loss.' She gulped slightly, 'Do you think your negative feelings about Josh and the situation may be coloured by what has happened to Sharon?'

'No,' I was suddenly definite. 'No. Sharon has made me realise I am going to die here.' I was decisive. 'Nancy is planning it now. My death.'

There was no other way out for me. It was so clear.

'Anna, these feelings of yours are not to do with reality. Do you understand what I am saying Anna?'

I stared at her. I didn't know any more.

'I don't even have "access" any more. That's what she's done. She's denying me my own child. That was her plan all along. Of course it was. Why didn't I realise?' The thought of Nancy weighed me down. I wanted to lie on the floor in a tight ball on my side, close to myself. 'What can anyone do against her?'

'Obviously, I don't normally get personally involved with clients. But in the circumstances, I am happy to give a call to Mrs Wietzman and say you are psychologically fit. Let's see, Anna, maybe I can even testify on your behalf at the Family Hearing.'

I couldn't quite let myself think that was possible.

As if she sensed my feelings, Mary added, 'Don't loose heart, Anna.'

It was the most encouraging and warm sentiment she had ever uttered to me. It created a silence between us that was calming. It gave me space to stop thinking and worrying for a moment, a break from the endless whirring in my head. The relief left me with nothing else to say. Mary waited for me to continue. She shifted back in her armchair. Her gaze was impervious and neutral. Her silence reminded me she wasn't a friend or an aunt. This wasn't an intimate situation, rather something else masquerading as one. Therapy was for people who didn't have friends to confide in.

The front doorbell rang. Mary glanced at her watch and stood up. My time was over.

*   *   *

Snow had been falling since dawn. Its gentleness hid the speed and size of its onslaught. It marched up our windows; it drowned our stoop. Cars and bicycles were soon completely buried. By seven in the morning, the street had disappeared. In my British experience, snow had never been more than a sprinkling of fairy dust. This was more chaos than Tinker Bell could imagine. A dump, dropped on Manhattan unceremoniously and with little warning. Upper West Siders knew it was on its way. 'It's going to be a big one,' said the white haired owner of the hardware store as I passed. 'A real northeaster.'

This morning, New York did stop briefly in its tracks. Even cabs stopped moving. The streets were silent. I watched the snow scaling our windows. Josh would be excited. Snow in New York. We had dreamed of this. But he would be tucked up in Nancy's baking hot apartment, instead of on the plastic sledge I had bought him from the toy store further up Amsterdam Avenue.

I would walk through the snow and stand outside Nancy's apartment. Maybe they would take him out sledging. Maybe I would see him, happy in the snow, having a snow day even without me.

Jessie came up behind me as I continued to look out. We hadn't spoken for over twenty-four hours. Not one word since he took Josh away. He had clearly stayed at Nancy and Howard's that night. I hadn't asked. I didn't care what he did.

He coughed slightly to alert me to his presence, though I continued to ignore him.

'Nancy and Howard have suggested we meet for lunch.' He said it formally, without any trace of emotion.

I didn't respond. It was an outrageous suggestion. How dare she suggest we eat together when she had kidnapped my son?

'Anna, did you hear what I said?' It was Jessie's new aggressive tone.

'I did. But I'm not going to eat with people who have taken my son away from me. You have forced me to put up with so many awful things here, but you can't force me to go to a restaurant with that woman.'

'Anna, I'll ignore that comment. Nancy would like to meet because she is no more happy with this situation than you are. She wants to help. As she always has done. Do you want to regain access to Josh or not?'

Jessie and I struggled across town, getting soaked either side of the subway ride and arriving drenched at her chosen restaurant, *La Grenouille*, on 52nd Street between Madison and Fifth Avenue. I hadn't ever expected to see her with my hair dripping out from the edge of my hood and the damp patches on my black trousers sticking to my legs. Only now, I didn't care.

On New York snow days, everyone in the street was wet, red-faced and cold but happy and exhilarated. There was an unwritten New York rule that the fur boots were brought out of the closet and you were bulging with padded ski clothes.

But Nancy was unique. I can say that about her. She was all in new white. A white fur-edged fitted jacket, a white silk shirt, a white cashmere jumper, white jeans and white snow boots.

As if he read my mind, Jessie crowed, 'Nancy, all in white. Perfect for the snow.'

I hated him as much as her. I hated being here. I hated the

fact that Jessie had dangled what I already imagined was false hope. Nancy wanted to talk about resolving 'the situation', he had insisted.

Now Nancy ignored me completely, but she flashed Jessie a smile. She dangled her booted feet in the face of the bending cloakroom attendant who swiftly pulled off her boots and placed them behind the counter.

Jessie kept gushing. 'This is a wonderful place. Trust you to know somewhere like this.'

Out of her white Todd's handbag, she airlifted a pair of white satin sling backs, probably Manolo Blahnik.

Once the attendant had taken her jacket off, Nancy finally turned to me. '*La Grenouille* opened in 1962 during a snow-storm, *n'est pas*? Very fitting for our lunch, don't you think?'

I didn't concur. I was determined not to speak to her until she told me exactly what she would do to help. Seeing her, I was painfully aware that she was more likely to punish me for trying to escape. My wetness was turning to coldness. I was the only sodden reminder of the weather in this gilded salon shining with mirrors, low table lamps, plum banquettes, white linen, impeccably suited managers, white jacketed waiters and a red carpet, all surreally untouched by the snow outside.

There were two children sitting with an old dame. The boy was wearing a suit and the girl had a pale blue silk dress on with a matching bow in her hair and a matching pair of delicate pale blue suede boots. Everywhere I saw children. Everywhere I saw Josh. Where was he right now? Who was he with?

Nancy moved forward, almost on to a man in a dark navy suit and elegant pink tie. They talked intimately before he bowed and tipped a step backwards to allow her the floor into the salon. Nancy moved through it to the table, which was clearly her regular and designated one.

'Why don't you sit there?' Nancy pointed her black painted nails to the chair backing into the salon.

I sunk silently down. Nancy took the banquette space next to Jessie, only after a waiter had pushed the table against me in his haste to get Nancy secured without so much as a brush of white on white. We were all passed a menu. I hardly heard the specials of the day. I did notice that Nancy was unusually quiet, distant. She examined the menu for a long time, bearing in mind they came here regularly for lunch. I bent over it too. The 'déjeuner' as I was sure Nancy was about to call it, was resolutely French with not even the vague acknowledgement of its host state.

'*Alors, nous sommes prêts?*' Nancy's French had a clinical accuracy. '*Garçon!*' she commanded to a man who looked closer to my dad's age than Josh's. '*Allons-y.*'

She gave her order and her menu back decisively and started to remove imaginary fluff from the silk edging her cashmere cuffs.

'Well, unlike her, I'm wholeheartedly American,' Howard smiled genially. 'I'm gonna have the corn crêpes and the pan-fried calves liver. Can you gimme your wine list?'

'Pan-seared sir. Is that good?'

'Pan-seared, pan-fried, panned. It's all good to me,' he grinned.

Nancy usually giggled at his feeble word play. Today she kept fretting over her cuffs.

Jessie abruptly added his order. 'A dozen oysters, and the lobster.'

I couldn't help myself. 'That's rather extravagant. You don't even like oysters. Are you celebrating something?'

He ignored me and thrust his menu at the waiter. He was showing off. There was no other way to explain his behaviour. I could only think it was because he was entering that world, their world, the world of billions of new Hot Dog money. He thought he needed to eat differently.

'Better be a bottle of champagne Jess?'

'Yes, why not? I'm not working today,' Jessie grinned. Howard had that effect on him. But his smile was brief. He too had noticed Nancy's silence and he was watching her nervously.

Howard was strumming his fingernails against his wine glass. He, too, was suddenly tense. 'Jessie, how's it working out with Connor?'

Jessie didn't reply.

Howard repeated his question.

'Good, good,' Jessie insisted.

I watched Nancy. Talk of Jessie's new job would draw her into the conversation. But she was utterly preoccupied. It would have made me anxious even a few days ago. But I had nothing to be anxious about any more. The worst had already happened.

Our starters arrived. I had ordered the split pea soup like Nancy, only to avoid having to choose food.

Nancy stirred her soup several times before rapidly lifting a spoon to her mouth. 'Guaranteed perfection,' she said. 'There are so few of guarantees in life, aren't there, Anna?'

I didn't reply. Silence was my only weapon. I was determined to use it to force her to talk about Josh.

Nancy spooned her soup in a production line between her bowl and mouth. Why was she eating so fast? What was going on? We all hurried. Nancy was setting the pace. It was a signal to otherwise unhurried looking staff, and they quickly cleared. The main courses arrived swiftly. Jessie and Howard circled round business, Connor Flint, and philanthropy. They didn't have the natural rhythm of father and son.

Then I heard Nancy's voice. 'Oh, Anna, I spoke to *your* therapist.'

She didn't use her name. She disassociated herself from any link to Mary, even though she had organised it through a contact. I blushed enough to feel hot and sweaty for the first time that day. She had been hurrying through lunch to get to this point. Jessie was trying to make eye contact with Nancy. But he caught me looking at him and frowned.

Nancy continued, oblivious. 'I think you've made all the progress you're capable of. Don't you?'

It feels strange writing this now. But I was suddenly worried about not seeing Mary. She was the only constant in my life. I relied totally upon her. And now Nancy was taking her away. She didn't want me seeing the one person who was supporting me. She *was* set on ruining me.

All I could do was fight. 'Nancy, I want to talk about Josh, about how you agreed to have him weighted down, banned him from leaving the country to have a holiday with my parents, his grandparents, and how you are denying me access to my own son.'

She only turned her eyes in my direction, the way you do when you see someone interesting on the subway but you don't want to appear to stare. 'Am I?' she said, as if she was curious about the answer.

'Stop playing games with me Nancy. Jessie said you wanted to meet because you wanted to help me get Josh back. Do you, or don't you?'

'Put in that particularly charmless way of yours, I most definitely do not.'

Nancy stood up, slid her ridiculously skinny body out through the gap between the table and the banquette and walked away.

I turned to Jessie, who turned away from me. 'Did she lie, or did you?'

He frowned, but didn't answer.

*   *   *

Nancy was pressed against the floor to ceiling windows of a 25th floor condo. The windows were sealed shut, shatter proof. Nancy admired it as if it were a view across Central Park and not the tip of another red brick tower and clouds. The broker stood slightly behind Nancy imitating her expression. She could have been thirty or forty. In the flesh, she was an identikit of her photo, which was alongside every property she was in charge of selling on the realtor's website. As if her face might be a deciding factor. She was immaculate and elegantly highlighted with the same shoulder length blonde waves as the other two brokers we had met earlier.

'It's triple mint.' She moved towards the door again. 'Miele washer/dryer,' she enthused, opening a closet by the entrance.

Nancy was still staring at the view.

The broker led me towards the stainless steel kitchen. It was in the corridor, or maybe the corridor was in the kitchen. She pointed with the reverence West Coasters have for the Dalai Lama. 'A window.'

I didn't see a window. I couldn't see this apartment.

Last night, Jessie had abruptly told me we had to leave our brownstone. The Foreign Office would reclaim it at the end of the month. Nancy would find us a new apartment. I didn't reply, or react. I didn't care where I lived any more. What did it matter?

My days were framed around spotting Josh. I waited behind the brick wall every morning, once all the other mothers had left. I risked rising up and peeping at him in the classroom. He appeared well and happy. Mostly I felt good about that. Thank God he wasn't suffering as I was. Other times, I panicked that he wasn't missing me. He was forgetting about me. A typical child wedded to the routine of each particular day: quick to move on.

The broker waited for an answer. But I was lost for words. I hardly spoke from one day to the next. Now I didn't even see Mary.

She sounded impatient. 'It has gotten a window. And, you can have your breakfast in the dining alcove.'

The 'dining alcove' was the three-foot squared space underneath the window where you might fit a couple of stools and tiny table for two.

But I looked at it without even a flicker of interest. New York was ready for the holidays. The decorations were elegant, delicate. White lights romanticised every street. I couldn't bear to see these signatures of happiness. I imagined Josh decorating a tree at Nancy's apartment. Then I actually saw him one Saturday afternoon waiting in the apartment block reception as two men laboured in a vast tall tree. I had been waiting too, for over three hours, to spot him. From the other side of the road, I regularly focused on the apartment entrance with a pair of binoculars that Jessie had bought for us to take travelling when we explored America.

The broker was regaling Nancy with details of the luxury residents club. 'It even has a pet spa,' she said triumphantly. 'The *pièce de resistance.*'

Nancy nodded.

'Shall we go and view the residents' club?' The broker posed the question to Nancy.

Getting no response, she was transparently annoyed.

Rightly, she realised Nancy had the money. Jessie had tripled his salary but he still couldn't afford to rent this red brick toy flat without Nancy's help. This soulless shoebox up on East 96th street, between Second and Third Avenue, was seven thousand dollars a month. Nancy's money bought her the right to interfere. It bought her everything.

'I think,' I finally ventured.

The broker eyed me narrowly.

'This is not right for us. You see, I have a young son, a boy called Josh. I can't see us living with him so high up.'

I wanted Nancy to deny that I had a son, for the fight to be out in the open. But she didn't say anything.

The broker frowned. 'This glass is safe. There has never

ever been a problem in these condominiums. Never.'

Nancy spoke. 'We need to get Jessie to have a look at it. To make the decision.'

It wasn't the first time she had undermined me. She had done far worse. But I was tired. I was so, so very tired.

'Nancy, this is going to be my home, where I will live with my husband and my son Josh at some point very soon. And we are not going to live in this tower block.'

I felt briefly brave and I turned to outstare her.

Nancy shrugged icily away. 'Then I'll keep Josh. And I'll make sure you never seen him again.'

The fight was out there. Finally. 'Are you blackmailing me, Nancy? Because that is what it feels like. My life for my son.'

The broker moved rapidly away from us back to the front door, where she busied herself ostentatiously opening her brief-case and pulling out a miniature MacBook Air.

Nancy pursed her lips as I heard the front door close.

'Oh, I have every intention of doing that.'

Her light had vanished and she looked grey.

Twelve

Life is suspended in a hair salon, especially when you are having your colour done. I wanted that suspension.

Since Christmas I found it unbearable to stay in the condo. Even the smell had started to get to me. Despite the freezing weather, I walked for hours, and blocks in between, trying to spot Josh. I had managed to wave at him this morning. I had waited weeks for this moment. When it happened, he just waved back as if I was going to see him after school. As if everything was normal. And it hurt. It hurt in a way I thought it couldn't any more. Sometimes, like today, I covered twenty blocks without remembering walking them, what I had seen, even what was in front of me. I constantly felt tired, but I still walked all the time.

Today somehow I had got from the Nineties, where the condo was, to the Sixties. I suddenly noticed 61st Street for no apparent reason, not as a landmark or turning point. I turned down it into the overshadowed, dirty part of the street between 2nd and 3rd Avenue. It was freezing and dark. I had no plan; I never did these days. I tipped my head up, which was an odd thing to do in this tunnel of a street. And there it was. *Ken's Salon* was stencilled in black on the windows, a back street hairdresser's. It appealed like nothing had done today, or yesterday, or any other day, for so many weeks now. My calf muscles hurt as I climbed the worn carpet stairs.

Ken was streamlined even by Japanese standards. His pencil frame was distinguishable only by the ginger streaks coursing through his black hair. Ginger highlights were popular in this salon. The two other hairdressers had them and so did one of their clients. Behind the bulbous white plastic reception, the lady was neither Japanese, nor young or slim. She was a red-faced lady with an amoebic body and a vibrating Bronx accent.

'Hi, how ya doin'?' she squawked at me.

I shrugged. I wasn't able to do small talk. 'Can I have my hair cut and coloured by Ken?'

I only asked for Ken because I had seen his name stuck on to the dirty window. And I didn't want a conversation about hairdressers.

'Sure, sure. Ken's free in ten.' Her two paws took in my elbows. 'Gawd, ya so cold. Kinda wanna the heat to come, don't you? It's too butt cold for me.'

I was empty of words.

'Well, make yourself at home.'

This scruffy salon felt more like home than our condo.

A tiny super smiley Russian girl with bleach blond hair bent her head towards me. 'I wash your hair.'

Despite her miniature fingers and frame, she pressed every pressure point on my head as if she was drilling into them. It was excruciating.

'OK. Is the pressure good for you?'

I nodded and closed my eyes. My body and mind were still. After five minutes or so I started to feel a light headiness. When I finally lifted my neck out of the sink-rest, my head felt disconnected and empty.

Ken called me over to a swing chair by the window. His streaks made him look more edgy than he was. He stood behind me and peered studiously over my hair in the mirror.

'Someone has put some layers in the back here.'

I nodded.

'It doesn't add smoothness. What length?' He held the ends of my hair.

'Whatever you think . . . ' I was unable to make even the smallest decision.

He nodded, staring at the top of my head.

'Well, you need some highlights, but toned down.'

I nodded. I wanted him to start, to close my eyes under a mass of wet hair. I was thankful when I was glued to the seat, with my head tipped down towards my knees. And Ken wasn't chatty. He worked slowly, and I sensed painstakingly, pasting my hair to a foil and folding it into tiny wantons. I rhythmically turned the pages of a hair magazine. Bright photos of tanned, happy girls with ironed hair, chignons, twists and plaits, crops and curls. I felt pale, fragile and ill in their reflective glow. The faster I flicked, the more they all looked the same. When Ken finally said I could unfold myself, I was a foiled rag doll.

Ken cupped the sides of my foils in his hands, as if to check them. 'I'll leave you for a moment.'

I got up to go to the loo. To avoid turning into Ken, I circled left round a metal foot stand. I gazed vaguely out through the stencilled *Ken's Salon*, at the street below. A Chinese lady was pushing a metal laundry cart, a city type was hurrying and texting, swerving around a couple without looking up.

They were holding hands – only holding hands. Their touch was light enough not to restrict the momentum in their arms, which were a pendulum of happiness. It is difficult to see a smile from far away. They must have been grinning. The two of them were now barely visible, half hidden by a van to the very right of the street near the corner with 3rd Avenue. They kissed. Two people kissing in a desperate urge to be one, thinking they were blocked by vehicles, unaware they might be watched from above, careful even in their passion. I could no longer see them precisely. They might never have been there. In a way, I wished for blissful ignorance. I wished that it wasn't Jessie down there. But I felt nothing, not even disappointment. No rage, no nausea. All my emotions had been used up.

I looked down again. But they were gone, completely and absolutely gone.

I continued looking out of the window. More people filled my view. A van had stopped on the other side of the street. The driver came round its navy side and unlocked the back doors. His passenger opened them wide and climbed in. He slid a full clothes rack towards the driver. The dry cleaning bags covering each piece billowed as the rack descended. The two men lifted it down and then up on to the sidewalk towards 2nd Avenue and out of view.

New York had already moved on.

*   *   *

My foils were freezing. Or rather, it was the gaps between them that let the unforgiving wind rage up 3rd Avenue and tear into my head.

I had stood at the window for a few moments, before it became clear what I was going to do. I hadn't stopped to collect my coat from the receptionist. I had grabbed my handbag from the floor beside the hairdresser's chair and left. Strangely, no one had called after me. Maybe they had thought I was going to have a cigarette; maybe they hadn't cared; or maybe they had called after me, only I hadn't heard them.

I wasn't going to miss this moment. I was fully aware. I was fully conscious. I stayed a block behind them, knowing what I was doing. I was going to follow them all the way. This thought didn't frighten or upset me. On the contrary, it was the moment of truth I had been waiting for. As I trailed them, I realised I had always known what was going on. It had been so visible. I had chosen not to look.

Finally, they turned into a building. I knew it was a shabby midtown hotel before I got to the door. It was all so predictable. I felt in my handbag for my purse to see how much paper money I had. I imagined myself paying off the receptionist. But I only had fifty dollars. I wasn't sure even the underpaid in midtown could be bribed with so little. Maybe you could get your way with a credit card, I didn't know. I slowly opened the white laminated door. They weren't at reception. Nor was anyone else, including the receptionist. I was stuck, suddenly uncertain. The *Chrysler View* probably only had a few rooms, and even fewer occupied. Would I be able to hear them? I was freezing as I leant on the Formica freestanding table, only a poor nod towards an official reception desk. There was a large diary on the top. Of course, it was for checking-in clients. I turned it towards me. There were only two names down for today; neither of them was the one I was looking for. I flicked backwards. The hotel did less business than even I had imagined. I got to 1st January. No sign of the name. I rounded the table. There were no drawers underneath it. Where was last year's diary? The cupboard behind the chair was locked, but as I moved to see where else it might be, my toe nudged against a worn red version of the black diary on the desk. I still had to go back months to find it. Every day that it wasn't there, only emphasised how blind I had been for so long. It didn't make me angry or upset, rather resolute.

9 September. The day after we all went to the opera together. Obvious. Room 4. Would it still be the same room after all these months?

Old-fashioned door keys, with plastic rectangular numbers hanging off them, were hooked on to one of those wall holders, an open box with numbered hooks. It was that easy.

Standing outside the door with its brass 4 tipping to the left, I was strangely exhilarated. I had expected screams of excitement to echo down the corridor. Only there was silence. I wondered whether I had dreamt the whole scene in the street. I was in such a bad way I could have believed I was hallucinating. Only I wasn't, because it was true. It was the first thing that had made sense for months. I wasn't mad; I had been made mad.

Still I waited. I put my handbag down outside the door, bent down and got out my iPhone. I thought I was ready. I gently

212

unlocked the door, set up the iPhone ready to film, quietly turned the brass handle, opening the door with my left hand. My phone was up in front of my outstretched right arm. I didn't look at the scene on the bed. I watched it on the screen of my phone. Nancy was chained to the bed-head by her neck. Not handcuffed, but chained with thick industrial looking metal. She was naked. Of course, I had prepared myself for that. But she also had no pubic hair. And that fascinated me in a macabre sort of way. Jessie was also naked, half-kneeling on either side of her ankles. He was holding a black whip, which he was lashing against her breasts. As she moaned, he simultaneously rubbed her clitoris harder. I didn't take my eyes off my iPhone. The room was claustrophobic. My breathing was difficult, but I focused even harder on my phone. I stood my ground. I wasn't going to run from her now. I waited for her to look up at me, giving that malicious smile of hers. Only she didn't. I wondered how long this could go on and how long I could stand it before collapsing? Finally she came. Jessie threw the whip to the mauve carpet and loosened the chain round her neck. She gasped like a battery chicken given a last minute reprieve. But he was already on top, thrusting into her. As she moved her bruised neck to one side, she saw me. I stayed behind the phone. I watched her reaction on the screen. I expected a grin but I saw horror greater than mine. She tried to shake Jessie off. He only pushed harder with greater violence, pressing her wrists deeper into the polyester eiderdown.

'No!' she screamed.

He covered her mouth with one hand, pressing deep into the hollows of her cheeks. He kept going. She tried to fight him off. Only she didn't succeed.

It was my turn to smile at the screen.

When he had finally finished and slumped on to her, I turned and quietly shut the door.

I circled the metal stand of Ken's hairdresser chair and sat back down. He came over from where he was drinking coffee with a minimal smile. He checked a foil without a word, silently nodding. I smiled, stood up and walked towards the Russian girl waiting for me behind a basin.

*　　*　　*

As I admired my hair in the window of a shop, I called Mary. I left a message and then I took a cab to her basement flat. I pressed the buzzer several times before she answered it.

She seemed flustered. 'Anna, your hair looks nice. I'm with a client right now.'

'I have to talk to you.' I heard my assertiveness.

'I can't see you right now. Sorry, Anna,' she frowned.

'Please, Mary. I need to talk to you.' She was the only person I could tell such a dark truth to.

She gave me a dispassionate look. 'Anna, sorry, I'm with a client right now.'

I was thrown. She had been so kind to me the last time we had met, offering to testify. She had clearly talked to Nancy on my behalf.

I suddenly had a thought. 'Is it because I am no longer a client?'

She waved her hand with an unreadable vagueness. 'No, Anna, really.'

I seized on the unpalatable truth as I saw it. 'I'll pay you, obviously.' I suddenly felt like a man who has befriended a prostitute, only to realise she won't have sex with him unless she is paid. 'The going rate, whatever it is,' I added desperately.

'Anna,' she sighed and turned her head from me. I was so used to her permanently direct gaze, however impenetrable, that I knew something was gravely wrong.

I grappled, 'Have I offended you?'

Offending Mary mattered. It was a strange thing. In spite of the extremity of everything that had happened that day, my friendship with Mary was vital, my lifeblood.

'Noooo,' she said soothingly, sensing my stress. 'I really have abandoned my poor client. Anna, could you possibly come back later?'

'I can't. I literally can't.'

She was going to shut the door and leave me alone with my dysfunctional truth. I had to tell her.

'I have seen Nancy having a . . . doing, you know, S&M with my husband.'

I believed I wanted to believe her face altered. But it didn't change at all. She stood in front of her half-closed door with the same plaits, the same long dress I had seen her in so many times. Only this time, she was silent. She had no therapeutic questions to bat back to me. Or rather, she wasn't going to get involved this time.

'Jessie was whipping her,' I added. I wanted to get a reaction from her that I couldn't feel myself.

She was still silent. I was totally lost.

Finally, not sure what else to say, I insisted, 'I know you are going to say I am imagining it. I know I've been a bit crazy. But I'm not. I actually saw them. I was in the hotel room with them.' I paused.

Mary still didn't speak. She didn't look shocked, or upset or anything. Just numb. She was reflecting my own feelings.

I hastily swirled my right hand round the inside of my bag. 'I have it all on camera on my iPhone. Really.'

'I don't want to see it, Anna.' She finally spoke.

Her voice sounded shaky.

I stopped searching for my phone and considered her.

'You sound . . . ' I couldn't quite place her emotions. 'Well, I don't know. What are you thinking?'

I almost smiled. I was asking her how she felt. It was too bizarre.

Automatically she stated, 'This is not about me, Anna.'

But she didn't follow her statement with a question. Slowly, I reasoned it wasn't just because we were standing on her doorstep without the Berlin Wall of the needlepoint stool between us. Something had changed.

'You don't seem shocked. What's going on, Mary?'

She said ever so gently, 'I really think you should go now, Anna.'

Her dismissal hurt. I turned to go. I moved passed white branches dug into the deep pot, up the three steps to the black worn wrought iron gate and on to the street.

I will never know exactly why I turned back round to look at her. I like to think it was instinct, though it probably wasn't.

She had turned in towards her hallway. But she hadn't moved back down the corridor to her room and her client. She had both her knuckles pressed painfully into her forehead. She let out a pained sigh like someone trying to repress an anguished cry.

She did care. I felt the flush of warmth that friendship gives.

She seemed to be saying something to herself through grinding teeth. I couldn't hear the words. But I didn't need to. For the first time, I clearly read her face. I knew what she was thinking. I saw her emotion. The only possible explanation was guilt.

As I stepped back down, I lunged for what I still hoped couldn't possibly be the truth. 'Mary! Did you know Nancy was fucking my husband?'

I was right in front of her.

She didn't unclench her hands. She twisted her head from side to side, still pressed against them. 'Anna, please, please.'

'Tell me, Mary,' I whispered. My jaw was shaking uncontrollably.

'Please,' she insisted.

'Mary,' I shouted, anguished.

'I should never have seen you both. Never! It was wrong.'

I heard a new steeliness in my voice. 'You are Nancy's therapist.'

It wasn't a question.

She sighed through her nose. Her mouth was shaking too. 'I have been Nancy's therapist for twenty years. I'm so sorry, Anna.'

She couldn't look at me now.

It was up to me to ask the questions.

'You are sorry, are you?' I said coolly, 'What exactly were you thinking you were doing?'

'Honestly, Anna, I have gotten very fond of you. I was genuinely worried about you.'

She was concerned. But I wouldn't care. She had deceived me. Shaking her fat shoulders felt easy, enjoyable even. I felt the joy of cruelty that some children seem to recognise. The moment when you drop your rag doll off a seventh-floor balcony and watch it fall helplessly to the ground.

'Anna, please . . . '

'You knew what Nancy was capable of. You knew she wanted to take my son, my husband, and my life.' As I said those words I felt my loss. 'And you told me I was imagining it?'

'Excuse me, Anna, I never told you what you were thinking.'

She stepped further back down her corridor. I stood still with my arms crossed, which reminded me comfortingly of my mother.

'I came here to confide in you. The one person I've been able to trust in the whole of New York. That's laughable isn't it?'

She blushed.

'You know if I was American, I would sue you wouldn't I?' I laughed. The thought really did amuse me.

She leaned a hand towards my shoulder, which was meant as a gesture of concern. I ignored it.

She bit her lip hard enough to redden it. 'Nancy pushed me to do it. Honestly. I have had to live with that fact.'

How dare she try and appeal to me.

'I will always, always hold you to blame,' I prodded at her hard in the chest. 'You took my confidence, my life for money. Intending to destroy me, were you?'

I turned away from her, before glancing over my shoulder with a smile. The same one I had given Nancy. 'I am going to let you in on *my* secret, Mary. I am going to go public with my little film.'

'Why would you do that, Anna?'

Her stock therapeutic question – only this time, it barely masked her concern.

I spat. 'To get Josh back and give her what she deserves. I didn't deserve any of this.'

'Nor did I,' she whispered. 'I really didn't.'

She suddenly looked her age.

Thirteen

I hailed an independent cab, a black Cadillac. The old man driving was quiet and kind. He accepted my loose directions: 'uptown'. He curved the car round. I sat comfortably back on his black leather seats. My mind was empty, suspended somewhere outside my own life. I could have been a tourist, merely here to eat Southern cooking and spot Bill Clinton. It was a calm place to be, temporarily. We kept driving up to the 120s. By then, I judged it was time to turn round.

We arrived down at the southern end of the park, still on Central Park West. We were staring at the towers of midtown. I never tired of seeing them from the Park. It reminded me of the best view of New York, from the reservoir in the Park's centre. When we first arrived, I used to run round it several times a week almost losing my balance, as I watched the 360 degree view change, like a kaleidoscope, from the hauteur of the East side through the wall of midtown and back to the higgledy-piggledy brick of the Upper West Side.

The driver slowed down and turned round, gently. 'Where do you wanna go?'

There was only one place I could go.

The sleet had lifted into a deep grey light. 740 Park Avenue was more sombre than usual. The car stopped outside. As soon as I got out, I would be greeted, issued up to their apartment, perhaps to face Howard as well as Nancy. I leant heavily on the seat. I hadn't come here to talk to Nancy. What did I want to do?

'Ya gonna get out?' The driver said, more insistently.

'No. I'll pay you, but can you wait with me?'

He did a soft version of sizing me up. 'All right.'

He turned back and we sat there in a companionable silence. Nothing might have happened. Maybe that is always the way of human happenings. But then the man who usually stood in the hallway emerged. If he recognised me, he didn't give me that impression. He leaned towards the driver's window. My companion wound it down, but didn't say anything. There was a silent nod between them.

'Mam, can I help you?' His head twisted through the open front window in my direction.

I surprised myself by speaking lucidly. 'No. Thank you. I am waiting for someone.'

'Should I inform them you are here?'

I could have said no. But I couldn't be moved on. 'The Wietzmans. Nancy Wietzman.'

He nodded.

My head was thumping again. The thought of her physical presence. What was I doing here? Was I going to confront her? I leaned forward to speak to the driver. Then I saw her. All in pale grey; a grey suede full-length coat, grey trousers, a grey cashmere polo neck and a grey Chanel-looking bag. The loose tight face, the blonde hair. Despite my new-found power, I shrank from her. She was going to come up to the car. Probably explain away her behaviour. But she walked decisively from the granite entrance towards the corner of the cross street and got into a car.

As she stepped into her car and the driver closed the door, I realised what I needed was some sort of resolution, something to ease my pain.

'Please could you follow that car?'

It was the line from a film. It was insanely sane.

The driver turned back round. 'I am sorry. But I am gonna have to leave you here.'

'OK. No, I understand. How much do I owe you?'

'Listen. Let's say forty dollars.'

'OK.' Gypsy cabs were a rip off.

I gave him the cash and got out quickly on the side of the

traffic and stopped a yellow cab. It was only as it jerked vaguely trailing the black car, six or seven vehicles in front, that I realised I had left my coat in the other car. I noticed it, but I didn't react. I was shedding all of my life.

I had a plan to follow her. I didn't think beyond that. We finally moved to cross town at 79th Street and down Broadway. It was only as I saw the Lincoln Center that I realised where she was going. Her car stopped outside. She was let out to walk across the square in front of the main building. She moved slowly but deliberately. I paid my cab and got out. I was exposed without my coat. The air bit through my polo neck. I followed her slowly. She went through the main entrance and slowly mounted the red-carpeted stairs. She had disappeared by the time I got to the bottom door. I opened the door slowly and stood in the centre of the ground floor looking up at that chandelier and Marc Chagall, uncertain of whether I was going up after her. The building was empty. Finally, I crept up a floor. There was no sign of Nancy. I stood there for a while in the centre of the stairway. Then I moved slowly towards an alcove curving away from the stairs and sat down on the carpet cross-legged. I was desperate to sleep. I dozed until I heard voices. I couldn't hear what they were saying.

I heard Nancy's voice. 'That all couldn't be better. Wonderful. I am delighted by it all.'

I couldn't hear the reply.

'Yes, we must, very soon. It's been too long.' Nancy again.

She emerged. I could hear the other person going back upstairs. Nancy stood for a moment looking down, her grey pointed booted feet tipping over the edge of the top stair. Her hand wasn't on the rail. It was across her bag, which was barely balancing on the other silk shoulder blade. Her coat was loose over the other wrist. Her head was bent slightly down, bowed, penitent and her face was tauter than usual. For a second, I saw all this. I saw her in her entirety.

I leaped towards her. She looked alarmed, as if I was an aggressive burglar, a criminal. Her expression enraged me, but I stood my ground waiting, forcing her to speak, grovel. Those chicken-winged arms sprung out with her skinny hands, which grabbed me, below my elbows, ferociously for someone fragile. Nancy shook and pushed as if she was trying to wrestle me to the ground. I was almost too shocked by this bitch fight to defend myself. Finally, I planted my feet wider apart, as she twisted and yanked to the left and right of me in judo-style moves. But I was balanced and strong. She screeched with frustration through clenched teeth. Without warning, she swung out a leg in front of my calf and jerked it back. I was falling and snatched at the only thing I could. Nancy.

In spite of this desperate display, she was a mere frame. She had no real weight to put up serious resistance. I seized her, which steadied me enough to collapse on to the step below.

I didn't see her fall past me down the flight of stairs. I didn't hear her either. I must have closed my eyes and ears somehow. When I finally opened them, she was lying on the floor, a heap of bones. I was relieved. A pressure released from deep inside my head. But I instantly regretted it. The consequences of what had happened. I raced down many steps at a time. How could she be dead? Only Nancy would fatally fall one flight of stairs? She lay still, perfectly still. I gingerly lifted a hand and felt for her pulse. She was living, she was breathing. Her eyes half opened. I jumped back. The only way I can describe it was as if a Hollywood horror character had jerked back to life. I was terrified. I stood two feet away. Then I moved closer. I pulled down the neck of her polo and stared at the bruises. They really were there. She twisted her neck ever so slightly to get away from my touch. I squeezed her neck hard to add my own bruise. Her eyes were wide. A tear released itself from one eye. I assumed it was the pain speaking. She opened her mouth but I didn't hear her speak. Her mouth stayed open. I stood up.

Her fall jolted my emotions. I fumbled furiously for my phone in my bag. I dialled 911.

Her mouth snapped closed and she breathed heavily through her nose. 'God forgive me.'

I will never know if she said that, or indeed meant it. That is what I thought I heard.

*   *   *

The siren shrieked intermittently as the ambulance moved down Amsterdam towards midtown. I didn't watch it go. I walked away. I didn't bother getting a cab – I had time. I took in the horizon visible at the very end of Amsterdam Avenue. The looming rectangle of sky leaned down between the buildings, a ray of light and hope between the concrete. Despite everything, I still felt the pull of New York. I loved the walk across the Park. I circled past the zoo, remembering so many fantastic times there with Josh, when we had all been so happy.

My phone rang. I didn't hurry to get it out of my bag. It rang again. And slowly I delved for it. Should I listen to the message? I wasn't sure.

'Hi, it's Yolanda. I've got your creams. Give me a call.'

Did she really leave that message? I pressed replay.

'Hi, it's Yolanda. I've got your creams. Give me a call.'

I smiled, almost laughed with joy.

'Hi, it's Yolanda. I've got your creams. Give me a call.'

She sounded confident, casual. It wasn't me. I wasn't crazy.

'Hi, it's Yolanda. I've got your creams. Give me a call.'

No embarrassment, no guilt. I couldn't believe what I was hearing. It made me happier than I had been for weeks and weeks. And I kept playing back the message as I crossed the Park.

I called her. 'Oh, Yolanda? Hello, it's Anna Wietzman. I can't tell you what a relief it was to hear your message.'

'No problem,' she said coolly.

'You have got my creams,' I paused, trying to articulate what I wanted to say. ' . . . which is great because it means I'm not mad. But I don't need them any more. Thank you.'

I paused, and then said on impulse, 'Would you like to meet for lunch? I need to ask you a question and I have a few hours to kill.'

I was glad Nancy was in the New York Presbyterian Hospital, a fitting place to finish my story. I was not only going to vindicate myself, but also Sharon, who had killed herself because of the pressures in this city from people like Nancy.

The colour and make-up had drained hours ago from Nancy's face, leaving her the colour of porridge. She was uniquely exposed. As I walked in without knocking, she remained silent. I glanced at her cursorily before moving to the light at the window. I felt this physical flush of warmth from the sunshine outside and from the thought of being with Josh.

'I have to thank you, Nancy.'

She glanced at me, nervous and wary, possibly increased by the pain she must be suffering.

'I have learnt so much about this city because of you. About attorneys, the police, the school system, even a little about Social Services,' I turned to face her. 'And now, I am discovering about the press. I wouldn't have even known whom to sell a good story to.'

She coughed unhealthily and tried to move her hand to her mouth, only the drip feed prevented her. 'I'll obviously give up Josh for the tapes.'

'Silly Nancy,' I bent my head sideways with teacher-style disapproval. 'You are so out of touch for someone so sexually out there. Not tapes – copies.'

I leaned back against the radiator below the window and folded my arms. 'Sorry, Nance, too late I'm afraid.'

She tried to sit up, assert herself.

'Already sold to the *New York Post*. Fantastic newspaper – I didn't realise you had your very own salacious tabloid here.'

'What about Josh?'

'Oh Nance, you disappoint me. Such a plotter, making such a schoolgirl error. You think after the stills are in the paper that *you* would still have *access* to Josh? Even if there is a custody hearing, I will win over you and Jessie. Even your own dear Harry Finklemann says so.'

'I will claim I had a breakdown.'

I leaned over the bed. 'Oh, that old chestnut. Not going to help your Foundation or your contacts, is it? Not one bit. Madness. People are afraid it's contagious, especially in this city.'

She finally got her hand to her mouth as she coughed again. I saw the darkness in her face. She hated me as much as I hated her.

'You are so bourgeois, Anna,' she pursed her lips. She was drooling spit from the side of her mouth.

'Yes, do you know, I probably am. And I suspect the likes of Pamela's parents are too. They don't do scandal. They are a closed society. You're either in and play by the rules. Or you are out.'

She spat, almost rearing back to life. 'You haven't got high enough self-esteem to step outside the mainstream.'

'Oh, that's what you were doing? I had quite forgotten your bleeding corpse.'

She genuinely smiled proudly. The thought of her own S&M scene delighted her. She couldn't help herself. 'I have been told that I have perfect breasts.'

I looked at her pitifully. 'Do you know how sad and empty that boast sounds?'

'Do you know what it felt like to be allowed to whip Jessie's balls with a leather belt?'

I gulped. I nearly lost my nerve. 'All that money and power and all you really wanted was attention,' I turned away from her again. 'But you know, it just makes a much better story and for that, I'm extremely grateful.'

'We were consenting adults.' I could almost smell her desperation. I had her, and she knew it.

'Unfortunately, as far as the newspapers, your friends and Social Services are concerned you were both most definitely married, consenting adults.'

This was the end of my married life, the end of my journey with Jessie. From now on, we would be on opposite sides, never rooting for each other ever again. Despite everything, I felt a moment of loss.

There was a silence between us. Of course I had enjoyed being on top of this conversation, playing with and dominating Nancy for once. But it wasn't enough. I had wanted to see her guilt and shame. But she just didn't feel it. She was completely unemotional, completely indifferent to the common concerns of most other women.

'Why did you set out to ruin my life?' I asked quietly. It actually was the only question I wanted to put to her.

She paused, as if she was considering it. She licked her lips and then breathed uneasily in. 'I wasn't thinking about you.'

It was a statement of fact, not an apology. But I sensed it was the truth.

'No. You weren't,' I smiled. 'But you will be forced to think about me in the future, and in this moment.'

I absorbed her. Her elegance. Her skinniness. Her visible wealth, painted in the arrogance of her face, her blinkered sense of self-assurance. I took in the full horror of her for one last time. She returned my stare, but I couldn't read her expression, even now. I walked out of her room, leaving the door open.

Fourteen

I folded my copy of the *New York Post*. I suspected it wouldn't totally ruin Nancy. But it would force her to limp through the next eighteen months.

Our door buzzer screeched. When the porter had said I had visitors, I had imagined it was Jessie bringing Josh over. He hadn't come back to the condo since the 'incident' in the hotel. The use of that word finally made me smile.

It was Howard who filled the open gap of our front door. His checked jacket thickened his wide chest. His legs in navy chinos, tipped with matching slip-on shoes, were surprisingly slight. He was wearing a checked navy shirt under the brown checked jacket. His golfing blandness had been overtaken by sartorial schizophrenia.

I didn't want any further contact with Nancy or Howard. Then I saw Josh behind him. I couldn't speak. Howard moved aside and I bent down and grabbed Josh. I wanted to consume his touch and smell.

'Mummy,' he half-hugged me and then moved back. But I picked him up again. I tickled him, swinging him in the air.

He giggled rapturously, and he was back . . . I squeezed him and he giggled again. As I hugged him with one arm, I finally turned to acknowledge Howard. He could hardly get through the half of the door I had unlocked. I wondered whether to unbolt the other door. Was he planning to come in?

He spoke awkwardly. 'Obviously, here's Josh, but I also wondered whether you could do with some brunch. Not anything fancy. There's one heck of a diner round the corner from your old place.'

We walked into the diner together, visually companionable: grandfather, mother and son. It was about ten on a bright

227

February morning. We all sat in a booth of shiny red banquettes. I was wedged beside Josh, so I could feel him brush up against me and hold his hand.

Howard ordered blueberry pancakes with a double portion of fries and a side of bacon. I wondered whether he did this all the time, sneaked away from Nancy to brightly lit diners for a high-carb, high-fat meal. We made small talk about the weather, which were the authentic diners in New York. I wondered whether Howard would ever say what he came round for.

We got our meals. Josh had a plate of bacon; I had eggs Benedict. I ordered more coffee. When the man arrived with the glass pot of filter coffee to fill my mug, Howard got a refill too.

'I used to come here as a kid with my grandma. It was a kinda real treat, having the ice cream float.'

I wondered whether he was only mentioning this because he wanted to find a way into discussing what had happened. I had nothing against Howard. Indeed, I felt sorry for him, but I couldn't help him out.

He pulled his paper napkin out of the collar of his shirt. 'I've been wanting to talk to you. Hey, Josh, why don't you sit on that high bar stool and do the colouring sheet they gave you?'

Josh turned questioningly to me. 'Darling, just for a few minutes.' I stood up to let him out, hugging him as he went to the bar stool.

I watched Josh out of the corner of my eye as Howard raised both his hands, while holding the napkin in one of them. 'Heck, I am not mad at you,' He coughed heavily into it. 'Nancy did a far worse thing.'

I didn't look at him. He didn't look at me. We felt each other's hurt, but had enough respect for our own not to say anything.

He sighed heavily. 'She's a crazy horse.'

He sounded incredibly sad, but forgiving. I couldn't be that generous. But I admired him for it.

'I don't know what to say. I love the bitch.'

He could be in a Western, or an old Ford Coppola movie.

I laughed.

His red face was lifted by my laughter.

'She's now asked me to run that foundation of hers. Jesus. That's my problem. But I'm more worried about you kids.'

I stopped smiling.

'You're not the old worn thing I am. You are a young hot chick, you can fly away. I get that.'

I let him talk. I didn't want to say anything.

'You can go for another life. You can run, but you can't hide.' He continued. 'I am hardly proud of my son for what he did. God no. If Nancy hadn't got a bee in her bonnet about him . . . '

The mention of Nancy in context of Jessie angered me. 'My husband, your son, fucked your wife . . . Howard. There is no conversation to be had.'

'She's a manipulative person. I can say that because she is my wife.'

I gestured to the waitress.

Howard spoke, his voice cracking. 'Listen OK, so she did many terrible things. Perhaps the worst was she made up all that horse shit about Social Services.' He looked down.

'I already worked that out,' I said brusquely.

And I saw his deep shame, as if I was a casual observer from the other side of the diner.

'She was on the board of the school so they trusted her to call Social Services on their behalf. But she never did. There was no case, no file, nothing. She made it up.' He shrugged. 'The school believed her, because of who she is.'

What was there to say? I maintained my strong silence.

He hurried on. 'She wanted Jessie and Josh. She has ever

since . . . sorry to mention it, but you know she covered your treatment. She felt, wrongly of course, Josh was her child.'

She couldn't get to me any more. Not any more.

He lifted his hands, as if to do a large high five. 'Listen . . . ' He stood up suddenly keen to get away from me. 'I'm gonna help you both to get out quickly, honey. Whatever it takes.'

I half expected him to hand me a wedge of cash. Instead he gave me a limp, large palm. I put it ever so gently on my shoulder. I swung my arms around his neck and hugged him. I felt him lean in on me. But he knew I couldn't, wouldn't support him.

I was already circling over Heathrow . . .

In true Howard style, he had arranged a suite of rooms for us on the Queen Mary 2. Our container of possessions would travel down below. When the removal men came to start packing this morning, Josh assumed we were all moving to England. I didn't correct him. That was easier to deal with back in England.

I had a gut feeling that Jessie would call. When the landline rang, I breathed in heavily before moving to answer it.

I heard Josh get there first. 'Hello Daddy. Where are you?'

There was only a short gap before Josh was speaking again. 'OK. I pass you to . . . ' He always paused, though he was going to give the phone to me, 'Mummy.'

I didn't move.

'Mummmmmmmmmyyyyyyyy. It's Daddy on the phone.'

I moved from the kitchen through into the sitting room, where Josh had dumped the phone on the floor. I could hardly breathe. I had no idea what voice was going to come out.

'Hello.'

'Anna.'

It was all he said. I was expecting pre-rehearsed apologies, long-winded explanations and signals of love. In the end, a stream of consciousness. I sat on the wooden sitting room floor and crossed my legs. I wondered whether the gulf between us was too huge even to survive this brief conversation. We should part without seeing each other. It was the only way.

'We need to talk about Josh.'

My stomach lurched and I instinctively looked at Josh splayed on the floor.

'I thought it would be better over a drink, don't you?'

I stalled, 'The packers have arrived . . . '

He hurried, 'Yes, yes of course.'

We lapsed into an elongated silence. Only my mind was whirring. I had an idea.

'What about the bar opposite our old apartment?'

It was our favourite bar, a glamorous, sexy Thai fusion place, modern and noisy. Perfect for what I had in mind.

'Yes definitely, OK.' He sounded thankful, grateful; it had been so easy.

I smiled to myself. 'OK. Let's meet at the bar in Rain at midday?'

I had reluctantly left Josh with a sitter from the resident's kids club. I strode into Rain at the end of our old block, fifteen minutes early. I wanted the advantage. I would be the one already sitting on a bar stool, in control. I was wearing black leggings, dark mustard knee high boots and a girlie black embroidered blouse. The impression of innocence was the one lure I still had.

I ordered a glass of wine. The restaurant had a bar, the shape of a measuring spoon with a long handle. Square seating in taupes and chocolates were arranged around it. There was no one else at the bar area. It was low lighting, dark wooden furniture and its Thai fusion menu was more suited to dinner than lunch.

I didn't turn towards the door to look out for him. I chatted to the barman. I listened to how he was raised in Greenwich; when he moved to New York; how he was training to be a mezzo alto at the Julliard school. I nodded enthusiastically at each turn and twist to the story to show I was listening, to make sure he didn't wander off. A waiter called him to the opposite end of the bar. I forced myself not to turn round. Not to look at my watch. Not to gulp my wine. I eyed the menu and decided to order some chilli beef to get the waiter back in front of me and on to the story of his first year in Julliard. A hand touched my shoulder. It could not be construed as anything other than a minute tap.

I didn't want to turn round. I had every intention of making this the best performance of my life.

I flicked my head up at him. 'Hi, Jessie.'

I have spent the last few hours thinking about what I wanted, what I was going to do. I had not thought about how he would be. I expected the same healthy good looks and sparkly intelligence. But Jessie had a green tinge to his skin that was dotted with spots. His eyes had no energy.

'You have a drink?' He asked nervously, though my glass was in front of me.

'I certainly do.' I gave him a confident smile.

Jessie nervously took me in and then quickly turned his gaze, with rather obvious expectancy, towards the waiter. Only he hadn't noticed Jessie. Finally he did.

'Your friend's here.' The barman echoed the cheery intimacy that I had encouraged.

I didn't correct him. 'He is.' I matched him in his enthusiasm.

He continued, 'You want a Sancerre too?'

'Yes, yes please,' Jessie sounded thrown.

'Are you a painter too?'

Jessie shook his head. I swung my legs round the stool to nudge his. The barman gave Jessie a glass of wine and continued chatting for a few minutes, before finally even he realised he was no longer wanted and moved away.

'So,' I gave Jessie another little, but strong, smile. 'You wanted to talk?'

'Yes, yes sorry. I'm slightly lost.' He surveyed the round footrest circling the legs of the stool. 'You seem . . . you look great. God, I have so much to say. I don't know . . . '

I waited. Unfortunately, I saw Nancy's pert nipples raw and bleeding.

'All I can possibly say is how sorry I am to have hurt you so much. You won't accept it. I wouldn't, of course.'

It was rather tedious. Of course, he did profess too much. Of course, he wanted a full confession of his sins. It wouldn't be any fun if he didn't kiss and tell eventually.

'It's difficult to explain: I suppose there is always the ultimate pleasure in pain.'

Nancy's line, no doubt. An intellectual analysis of S&M.

Jessie was silent for a moment. 'I am not going to defend myself. My behaviour is . . . indefensible, even to me, but especially to you.'

Words, words, words – tripping over me.

We sat facing the bar, wrestling with this stalemate of undeniable facts. So I gave what I hoped was a hurt, closed type of smile, which he took, as I expected, as encouragement.

'All I can do is explain to you how it happened. The real facts, if that helps you at all?'

I was silent. No desire to hear any 'real facts'. But I realised I probably had no choice.

'I lost my bearings, my balance I suppose. It's all you have – your emotional sense of gravity. I lost mine. That's not an excuse, just the way I see it now. Now it's all over. Which it is, by the way.' He sounded calm but flat.

I stared at the bar. All those bottles lined the walls. There were so many drinks, so many combinations of cocktails and shots all aiming to create the perfect titillation in a glass, hoping that numbing reality was a way to some sort of euphoria and the ultimate in desire.

'Nancy called me straight after the Opera. She acted like she needed me.'

I heard Jessie's voice clear, yet far away.

'I called in sick. I went to meet her at . . . that hotel . . . '

He blushed, which reminded me uncomfortably of Mary. It wasn't fair or right he was telling me all this. But it made everything so much easier. There was a part of me that craved the detail anyway.

'It was very physical. An aggressive thing. I can't tell you.'

'Well, it seemed a pretty good game to me. More's the pity I was never invited to join in.'

He was shocked, which made me laugh deep inside. Jessie gulped his wine and carefully put the glass back on the bar, 'You know I wanted a life outside my CV, outside the mainstream.'

I heard Nancy, but I calmly said. 'Yes I do understand. It just seems like an added perversity to pick your stepmother rather than a prostitute.'

'I didn't pick . . . ' he started saying.

'Oh yes, of course. She picked you.'

'Another one?'

I heard the upbeat barman.

'Yes. Yes please.'

'And you?'

I shook my head.

He fetched the bottle and poured in another full glass.

'Listen, Jessie, my battle has been with her not you,' I gave him what I hoped was a sincere smile. And I stood up first, with my feet on the footrest as if stretching myself up tall. Then I stepped off to the side of the stool.

He panicked, as I knew he would. 'Listen, about Josh . . . I can't give him up. You know I can't. I was hoping, I know it might take some time . . . that we would, you know . . . ' He touched the edge of my floating blouse.

I raise my eyes up to him, in a flirty, needy kind of way. 'I hope so.'

His immediate smile suggested it worked.

I vaguely made eye contact to say goodbye. Jessie lunged for me, brushing against my arms with his hands.

'Bye then,' I said, without looking at him.

'Don't. Don't go, please. Please don't leave me like this. Please.' He half-lurched, conscious of not grabbing me, but desperate to do exactly that.

I turned back and he kissed me. I kept Josh in mind as Jessie's hands circled my neck and his fingers drifted down below my collarbone. He finally stopped.

I excused myself and wound my way through the tables and down the narrow stairs to the restrooms. I got out my phone to call Howard. The conversation was brief.

Back in the restaurant, I took Jessie's hand and led him on to the street to find a cab. I knew exactly what I was going to do.

* * *

Jessie, Josh and I moved slowly up the covered terminal gangplank. It was one of those permanent but soulless structures with smeared fake glass panelling pretending to be windows. We walked on either side of Josh holding his hands.

'Swing all the way round!' he ordered.

We obligingly careered him up, sending him round in a full arc through the air, legs, clothes and tummy all twirling, one big wheel of childhood. He screamed with joy and excitement. As we gently put him down, I encouraged him to run ahead. We both watched him charge, slightly bow-legged and clumsy, with his little backpack bouncing against his back.

'I can't believe you are taking him away from me,' Jessie sighed.

235

And yet again, I didn't answer. I touched the lining of my inner pocket to feel the document Jessie had signed giving permission for Josh to move to England without him. I had kept it with our passports in the fridge until the last minute.

Nancy had fixed the situation. If Jessie let me take Josh, then she got the remaining copies of the film. And a written guarantee that I would never talk publicly about it again. Otherwise, I would haunt the chat shows; every network would know my name. It was as simple as that. And it worked.

I had slept with Jessie as my extra guarantee. I needed to appear genuinely keen on a reconciliation to give Howard time to work on Nancy without Jessie's interference. Perhaps I could have given that impression without going all the way, as the saying goes. But I chose to do it because I could. It was my decision. I was in control. That's all I want to say.

This morning, I told Josh that Jessie wasn't moving with us to England. Surprisingly, he accepted it as if he had already known. I insisted Jessie would come over every three weeks. This was our agreement, our written deal. Nancy would fund the trips, a nice twist I thought. I wondered whether Jessie would come, or whether, very soon, he would make his excuses.

The black town car slowly drove up to the front of the terminal. I saw it because I had been half-expecting it. It was noticeably shinier and newer than the other cars already lined up on the front.

'Bye then,' I said, quickly turning away from him.

He didn't say anything. It was his turn for silence. He called to Josh, who eventually wheeled back down the gangplank and gave him a last big hug. It hurt to see them together like that.

Then the car stopped, right below the gangplank. The driver jumped out of his seat to open up the trunk, he bent right in and pulled out a collapsible wheelchair. After assembling it, he wheeled it to the right passenger door. By this time, Howard had popped out of the other passenger door. He was his usual ebullient self. Recharged like a toy with new batteries. I smiled, admiring his resilience.

The driver lifted Nancy out as easily as if she was a fragile child. He placed her gently in the wheelchair. She was all in black: black boots, black fishnet tights and black jersey dress with a huge thick pearl choker round her neck. She had a plaster cast on one leg. Howard told me that she had also slipped a couple of disks.

I still couldn't help worrying about the documents for Josh, but they didn't ask to see them with our tickets. We were finally safe on board.

Josh suddenly started crying. 'I don't want to leave America. I hate England.'

I soothed him with comforting thoughts. Grandparents, the farm near my parents house, the tree house my father built. Of course, they were all signatures of my childhood, not his.

'It's always raining; I hate being wet,' he moaned.

I smiled. 'It rains heavily in New York. You have to wear waterproof trousers.'

He looked up earnestly. 'Then you can jump in the huge puddles.'

'They have great puddles in England.'

'But no pizza restaurants,' his face crumpled. Genuine tears poured down.

'Not near grandma and grandpa's house,' I diverted him, 'but on the boat, they have fifteen restaurants.'

He started getting his favourite things out of his backpack. They didn't include Nancy's dreaded Nintendo DS. Josh didn't even mention it as he packed his bag yesterday. The list of things he insisted on taking with him for the journey on the ship was so small. His little white bear, Roo, a metre of elastic, his magnet, his yellow Mini car and his secret journal. He fingered them now for comfort.

Inexplicably, his action made me think of Sharon.

To distract myself, I admired the view. The captain had already turned the ship round to face the Verrazano Bridge, readying it for its return to England. We could see the Statue of Liberty, Governor's Island and the New York skyline and the less glamorous Red Hook waterfront.

By the time we were standing on the lower deck, Howard had wheeled Nancy to the side of the road from where she would have a clear view of the ship departing. Seeing the whole of her no longer frightened me.

She was a tiny, old woman in a wheelchair, insubstantial and insignificant now. I could so easily have dreamed up everything. How could that cavernous body have caused so much carnage? Could it really be true? As I gazed down on her, I imagined wheeling her off the quay into the water. The thought of her lightness, her brittleness was a pleasure now.

'How many swimming pools did you say there are?' Josh asked.

I turned gratefully to Josh. 'Five,' I said, with enthusiasm, 'and a planetarium. That'll be fun won't it?'

I saw Jessie slowly walk towards Nancy and Howard. I liked to believe there was heavy reluctance in that walk. But I didn't know. I didn't know Jessie any more.

'Do you think the QM 2 is bigger than the Titanic,' Josh continued, having instantly recovered from his tears as he always did. 'Or, is the Titanic bigger than the QM 2?'

I squeezed Josh's hand to reassure myself he was there, right beside me. I would never, ever lose him again. And I breathed in the sharp winter air. Then I gave them one last backward glance.

They stood in a line, though they were all clearly in a different place. Howard looked happy and strong. I even thought he might be happier.

Jessie had his hands over his face. Nancy had clearly convinced him she would win a last minute reprieve, which explained why he had appeared to give up Josh relatively easily. As he moved his hands, he seemed tired, worn, even broken. Of course he deserved to be broken. But I couldn't entirely dismiss our hinterland. I didn't really want to leave him like this. That was the truth, however irrational. As he started to cry, publicly on the quay, beside Nancy and Howard, I prayed Josh wouldn't notice. And it hurt me. Somewhere, deep and indescribable. He was lost to me so long ago. But now that he was lost to himself, I felt sorry for him.

And Nancy. What about Nancy? She would probably sideline Jessie. After all, he had become tedious. He would be an emotional drain rather than an ego boost. She would be swiftly on to a new project. And she would compartmentalise this particular period of her life.

'Pizza?' I turned to Josh with a wide smile.

'Yes please!'

Acknowledgements

A huge thank you to my awesome agent Caroline Michel for her unwavering belief. Her charm and perseverance alone carried *Exiled* through to publication. To Tim Binding for being such a perceptive editor, generous mentor and friend. To my publisher Naim Attallah for being the first to say: 'I do'; David Elliott and Amber Sainsbury at Quartet Books for enthusiastically working hard to make it happen.

I am deeply indebted to Hilary Reyl for being so much more than my literary twin, this is as much her book as mine. And to Sarah Woodberry for her meticulous edit. To Charlotte Emmerson for her faith, friendship and for reading so many drafts on rehearsal floors.

Thank you to Camilla Cavendish, Charis Gresser, Kate Holroyd Smith, Judith Howard, Anthony Howell, Patricia Jilla, Becca Metcalfe, Nina Omaar, Denise and Mark Poulton and Sara Williams for being my great constants, and always asking after the health of my book. And Cyrus Jilla for his thoughtful and generous support.

But most importantly, to Guto Harri for being everything, then and now.